POWER FROM THE MOUNTAINS

JOHN EASTWOOD, HENRY HUNTINGTON AND THE GENIUS FACTOR

Barbara Wolcott

CENTRAL COAST PRESS

San Luis Obispo, California

CENTRAL COAST PRESS
P.O. Box 3654
San Luis Obispo, California

Cover photograph by Gene Moore. Barbara Wolcott is the author of the books *David, Goliath and the Beach-Cleaning Machine* about the massive Avila Beach cleanup.

Thank you to Charlie Basham and Southern California Edison,
Curator Dan Lewis and The Huntington Library,
and my families—birth, extended and professional.
Your kindness and support are a part of each and every page.

CONTENTS

IN THE BEGINNING...

What started out to be a recreational trip to Shaver Lake instead became a turning point. Along with camping with my fisherman husband, we discovered a jewel in the High Sierra that spun me around and pointed out the path to write about science and how it impacts people. Big Creek captured me and never let go.

From that point on my focus in writing remained with science and engineering. However, the larger picture of Big Creek still nagged to be told. The research was mind-boggling and it was clear that the huge project was accomplished in one of the most creative times in American history. The only way it could be fully appreciated was to put it into the framework of two of the most influential writers in historical nonfiction—James Michener and Leon Uris. Thus a story is woven through the historical facts to take the reader back to a time of unmatched vision and daring. It's the story of the two men who made it happen.

The battle between financial megastar Henry Huntington and creative engineer John Eastwood has one foot in the past and the other planted squarely in the halls of Enron Corporation. Their storied conflict was born and bred in the time of rising corporate power, honed by the Robber Barons of the eastern US and their western counterparts, the California Big Four. It took place during the Golden Age of Engineering, an incredible one hundred years between 1850 and 1950 when every modern convenience and technological invention used today was dreamed up, fabricated and put into production. It was all possible because of one of those inventions began in part when Ben Franklin flew a kite in a thunder storm.

Eastwood was a man of titanic ability and vision who made his mark in a deeply forested part of the Sierra Nevada Mountains called *Big Creek*. It was not enough that he was the driving force behind his dream. He had to convince Huntington and other money interests that what he proposed was feasible. The results of his tenacity were the largest electrical generation system and longest distance for transmission of power at the time—from the Sierra to Los Angeles.

Eastwood had to match wits with Huntington, a man who demanded control of everything he owned. In much the same manner that Enron executives robbed their investors by manipulation of stock, a hundred years ago Huntington pulled his own kind of behind the scenes investment maneuvering. Eastwood was out of the entire multi-million dollar project he designed not only without a penny to show for his extraordinary vision, creativity and skill, but perhaps more importantly, without recognition of his genius.

The Big Creek Project is not well known even within today's professional engineering ranks because it was planned and began construction around the time of the American involvement in the Panama Canal. Big Creek may take a public back seat to the tropics, yellow fever and media interest in the mystique of faraway places, but it is the equal in daring, design and massive construction accomplished with what is deemed primitive machinery today.

Thousands of workers overcame construction challenges of soaring rock slopes, heavy snows, penetrating cold and digging through solid granite. It remains the last great project done completely with private funds, a seminal project still producing massive amounts of clean, sustainable power.

Power From the Mountains relives the emergence of public electricity done within the political upheaval in Los Angeles that led to William Mullholland's tainted water project triumph and ultimate disgrace with the St. Francis Dam disaster. It is the struggle for power to illuminate a state, power to control the commodity and secure positions in the marketplace. The mainspring lies at the headwaters of the San Joaquin River when the paths of engineer John Eastwood and Henry Huntington crossed at Big Creek.

It took very little time for John Eastwood's Big Creek Project to become essential. On November 8, 1913, thousands of Los Angeles commuters were stranded when public transportation halted abruptly due to a major power outage. Businesses and the Red Car trolleys stopped in their tracks waiting for the electricity to come back online. At city generation plants, engineers determined repairs would require days leaving business paralyzed for the duration until someone suggested that the new plant in the Sierra might take up the slack.

The still-untested system at Big Creek began to send power for the first time, slowly building pressure until a full load was coming an unprecedented nearly three hundred miles from the source to users. The Sierra Nevada and John Eastwood's engineering had come to the rescue of Los Angeles, but few knew he was responsible for their deliverance.

The Big Creek Project is much more than a hydroelectric system of immense proportions that still powers California. Beyond the dams, miles of connecting tunnels drilled through solid granite and a tiny railroad with eighty-degree mountain ascents that rival present-day roller coaster rides, it is water politics and the collective work of thousands who made the vision a reality. Beyond Eastwood and Henry Huntington who put it into motion and then moved on, it is a multi-generation epic.

Once begun, it became the mission of men and women working in deep Sierra snows that cover the landscape for more than half of each year, and women keeping house in tents laughingly called "rag houses." The wives of men erecting power poles from the Sierra all along the central valley to Los Angeles had the most difficult time. Their lives were keenly isolated and friendless because they were shunned by local women along the way as gypsies, never living in one place for more than a few months at a time.

The Big Creek Project made a strong family out of thousands of men, women and children involved in the work, partly out of pride for a job well done, but mainly because it required trust in one another to cut roads, dig foundations for dams, pour concrete in weather extremes with machinery and hand tools that appear to be antique toys to construction crews today. While they worked, crews had to watch for grizzly bears and mountain lions.

Workers made close ties with one another and enjoyed a unique attitude that turned nearly every hardship into something to remember with humor. One visitor treated to a meal in a rag house was stunned to find the rough-cut table set with Haviland china. When snows cut off workers at the Florence Dam site about eight thousand feet in elevation, an Alaskan sled dog team made daily runs to keep the camp in medicines, occasional oranges from Los Angeles and most importantly for morale, mail.

It is no accident that electricity is commonly called *power*. Webster defines the word in ways that describe the gamut of emotions New Yorkers felt they did *not* have when cascading outages put the lights out in 1965, 1977 and 2003: influence, strength, ability, potency, force.

The use of power moved from Ben Franklin's kite to Thomas Edison's lab and then entered the world market all in one century. In one hundred years the technology leapfrogged from the frontier of Kit Carson into landing on the moon and it was done by standing on the shoulders of men like John Eastwood.

In 46 BCE, Cicero said that to be ignorant of what occurred before you were born is to remain always a child. Ralph Waldo Emerson underscored that with, "There is no history; there is only biography."

Gold brought thousands of people west, but did not keep them there. The harvest of hydroelectricity put California on the map at the perfect moment in history, and it took extraordinary men to do it.

Poet Sam Foss said it best:

Bring me men to match my mountains…
Men with empires in their purpose
And new eras in their brains.

This is *Big Creek*.

"Human wants are continually shaped and reshaped by civilization, its technical and social standards and Progress."

Karl Brandt

PRELUDE TO REMEMBRANCE

Cleveland, Ohio – Thursday, 14 August 2003 – 4:10 PM Eastern Daylight Time

    It happened in a heartbeat. The faux candles on tables in the restaurant flickered then died and the television went blank. Utter silence blanketed the room. Through the glass wall overlooking the airport, diners realized the extent of the outage. Six stories below, all the planes on the tarmac at Hopkins Field would be sitting there long after their scheduled departure, waiting for the massive computer generated system to come fully back on line.

    Emotions ran the gamut from nervous laughter to anger and fear. Bartender Kelly Torino could see that what must have come into everyone's mind was the obvious: Another 9-11 attack. He banged on the bar. "Let's keep it cool folks. I've got real candles if this lasts past dark and a real British torch." He reached under the counter and pulled out the flashlight along with a box of candles, then found a lighter in his pants pocket. "Just to help pass the time, drinks are on the house." A ripple of laughter broke the tension.

    The lone customer at the bar smiled. "Sounds like you've been through this before."

Torino laughed. "Yeah, and I got the kid to prove it. July '77. She starts college next month."

"November '65?"

"No. I was visiting grandparents and missed it. The one I did get to live through was enough. Can't live without electricity."

The man laughed. "Not much to do when the lights go out, at least until you get hungry. No refrigerator, no way to cook and if it weren't for backup generators, no water and sewage. Not fun climbing stairs in a high rise either."

The bartender sobered. "It was dangerous, too. Had a neighbor whose house burned down when he forgot about a candle. We were lucky because we camp and hike. Had enough equipment to at least be comfortable and we felt like pioneers at first. When it was off for more than a day the fun was gone. You know…we've never been without power for so long and we wanted it back."

Two customers from the tables walked up to the bar with their empty glasses and motioned for a refill. Torino filled new ones for them, then dried the last of the glasses on the drainboard. The two men lingered, sensing something more intriguing than small talk damning utility companies and griping about when they were going to get another flight home.

The man on the stool swirled his drink silently, and when he spoke again, it was almost a whisper. Torino strained to hear him.

"It didn't take long for us to go from having no electricity to being completely and utterly dependent on it." Again he was silent, seemingly lost in thought. Torino hung the last of the stemmed glasses and freshened the man's drink. "I've heard a lot of stories over this bar but never one about electricity. You got one?"

In the summer light the man's eyes were beacons, a clear cornflower blue with glints of hazel like a scattering of distant birds on a cloudless sky. He nodded almost imperceptibly.

"I do and it makes me proud to be an engineer. Had a family connection and heard about what happened in the western US from the time I was a kid, but the story's the same any place there's a visionary looking for opportunity."

The two customers set their glasses on the bar and took stools on either side of the man. "I checked my laptop and there's no electricity from here to New England and into Canada," said the one on the man's left. "We're not going anywhere tonight so let's hear about it."

The engineer smiled, took a long drink and began. "It won't be hard to *imagine life a hundred years ago, because it's like right now with gas lamps, and instead of waiting for a flight, you'd be taking a horse and buggy to work and then putting every business letter, computation and account to paper by hand. We may be light years away from those days in terms of our living standard but some things never change… like a man with a plan and a dream…"*

John Eastwood in 1909
 Michigan State University Archives and Historical Collections

"To have his path made clear for him is the aspiration of every human being in our beclouded and tempestuous existence."

Joseph Conrad

Chapter 1

THE CALL OF THE WILD –1890

John Eastwood sat shotgun on the wagon, clinging to the edge of the wooden seat with one hand and the metal side rail with the other as the team of ten mules and two horses struggled up the steep mountain road. He had watched for six days, placing imaginary bets on which animal would drop the next load of manure and whether or not he would be hit again as it scattered. Freight line owner Matthew Merryman was safe from the same fate as he rode astride the lead horse.

Small clumps of wildflowers pushed aside ice-crusted snow in places, dotting the muddy trail with tiny spots of color. After the low rolling hills of the Northwoods country where he had grown up, the rarefied air at five thousand feet energized him. The sound of the wind in the pines spoke to him like poetry, and every time he happened on an elk, fox or rabbit he felt he was meeting family. Despite the rigors of the trip he was elated to be back in the mountains.

Eastwood had worked as construction engineer for the Northern Pacific Railroad Company, designing the track and stations from Duluth, Minnesota through the Rocky Mountains to the Pacific Coast. The three years spent on the project were mostly in the mountains and he grew to love the feel and smell of the air.

He was firmly committed to engineering, a fire that was kindled at the 1876 Centennial Exposition in Philadelphia. He had seen the telephone demonstrated by Alexander Bell, John Deere's steel plow, McCormick's reaper and hundreds of other machines capable of doing the work of many men. Although able to see only a fraction of the 8,000 machines on display, he could easily imagine the difference steam power was making in the lives of everyone. When the Liberty Bell was rung as part of the festivities, he was moved deeply as though it were a clarion call to step up and join the ranks of those who invent and build.

He was twelve years old when the first Golden Spike was driven in Utah to commemorate the first American transcontinental railroad. Fourteen years later Eastwood watched as another golden spike was driven at Gold Creek in the Montana Territory to commemorate the completion of a railroad destined to become the cross-country Northern Pacific.

At the time he didn't know exactly what kind of engineering he wanted to do, but he was certain it was not to be with another railroad. He moved on to Fresno soon after the dedication ceremony because of a flyer posted in the last railroad station he helped build:

Come to the land of sunshine, fruits and flowers! No snow! No blizzards! No Cyclones! No tempests! No thunder! But health, wealth and happiness for all.

In Fresno, he expected to have the best of both worlds, meaning sunshine and warmth all year long with the mountains a relatively short distance away. His success in town as a contract engineer was moderate and mixed. At first he did land divisions based on his experience doing survey work for the railroads. However, he found many wealthy landowners miserly and unwilling to pay for his services without protracted negotiation, something he found exceedingly distasteful. That led to his time in the political arena and after helping the settlement of Fresno to become a municipality, he was hired as its first city engineer. Unfortunately, there was no salary and Eastwood was back doing survey work for uncompromising clients of the city seeking permits. His only remuneration, fees he was able to wrest from clients.

News of a project in the Sierra Nevada came at a time when he wanted very much to make another change. The job in question was huge—to survey for a gravity-run wooden water flume over fifty miles long to carry logs and cut lumber from Shaver Lake to the Valley. While he felt his ideas were forward thinking, he still wondered about the economic value of a flume that would be very costly. Any working engineer could design a project without looking at the costs, and he had done some of that himself in college. In the reality of business, the plan chosen was the one with more than reasonable expectations of making money for the investor.

He made arrangements to meet with the saw mill manager. It was not his first trip into the wildlands of the Sierra. The year before, Eastwood had undertaken to draft a rough plan for a small railroad to carry lumber from the harvest area to the Valley for milling. The project was doomed because one area called the Tollhouse where the grade rose 2,000 feet in less than four miles with some ascents as steep as thirty percent. Buggies traveling that part of the road often unloaded passengers to help lighten the load for struggling horses and mules and sometimes the travelers were pressed into service to help push. Women and children were not exempt.

The freight wagon he rode with some trepidation now labored up that same steep toll road. This final leg of the week-long trip he would have to act as brakeman, jumping off when the team slowed to shove a log behind the wheels of the wagon. Once they got above the toll road area, it was an easy trail to the mill.

From the first day on the road from Fresno, he questioned his sanity in accepting the ride on the freight wagon. Hiring a horse from the livery stable was expensive, and a week of work with teamster Merryman seemed to be a good exchange for a thrifty man. Eastwood could not leave his new wife without their lone horse and buggy for what could turn out to be a summer long absence if he were offered the job and accepted.

After slogging on rutted, muddy trails, it was almost a pleasure to ride on the toll road. Merryman had to pay a princely sum to use it— $12.50 for the wagon, the animals and the extra heavy load. If Eastwood expected to have an easier job this day, he was abruptly disappointed when they came to a part of the road paved with logs. His reverie vanished when Merryman turned toward him and shouted, "Push!"

Eastwood leapt off the slow moving wagon and ran to the rear. He braced against the end of the vehicle and pushed, but his high-laced work boots slipped on the wet logs. He looked up to see if Merryman was aware of his predicament but the teamster was bent over close to his horse's ear. Eastwood turned to dig his heels into the areas between logs and got some traction. He took three strenuous steps before the wagon suddenly picked up speed and he was left flat on a road still icy beneath the wet surface.

The wagon continued to the level area at the top of the slope before it stopped and the teamster ran back to find his passenger.

"Merryman!" Eastwood shouted. "What the hell did you do to that horse?!"

"I called her by name."

"You called both those horses by name every day since we left Fresno, and they never got a second wind like that."

"If I call 'em by their real names they do," Merryman replied as he turned back to the team and wagon.

With a burst of energy born of frustration, Eastwood sprinted up the slope and stopped in front of the owner. "*What* did you say to that horse?" he demanded again.

Merryman removed his hat and finger-combed his hair. "I trained her to answer to Buff, but my wife had a hand in raisin' both them horses. She spoilt 'em no end, and if I use the name she gave 'em they'll do anything I ask." He moved to step around his passenger, but Eastwood moved to block him again.

"All right! I called her Buff-Bellied Hummingbird. My wife said that as colts them two horses flitted around like birds so Blue is Blue-Grey Gnatcatcher…only when *she* says it to 'em, it sounds like singing."

Hours later as the freight wagon rolled up to the entrance of the Smith & Moore Timber Company warehouse, Eastwood still chuckled to himself about Buff and Blue. He was tired and dirty but didn't mind that he smelled like one of the team he had helped make the arduous trip from the Valley. They arrived in the familiar early April dark when light vanishes quickly once the sun slips behind tall peaks.

Lamps outside the mill buildings were bright enough for Eastwood to realize how pleased he was to have taken his wife Ella's advice. She had slipped a small, wax paper-wrapped cake of her homemade soap into his jacket pocket as she kissed him goodbye, suggesting that he might as well offer a clean hand when he met the new client. He watched a man in a cowboy hat approach the wagon in long, purposeful strides, and sent a silent kiss to his wife. He had used the soap to wash up in the last icy stream they crossed before arriving.

* * * * * * * * * * *

In the morning before dawn, Eastwood was awakened by something he had heard the first day of his journey. It was the clang of the saw blades being removed from the freight wagon. He knew that Merryman would reload with logs for the trip back down to the Valley, but if Eastwood got the job he would be staying the summer. The trip back down the mountains was every bit as hard as going up and he'd be wrestling logs again, this time tied to the back of the wagon to slow it on the same steep inclines. A good mule cost several hundred dollars, and Merryman would never risk losing one if the wooden block brakes failed and the loaded wagon plowed into the team.

On the way up, they had been fortunate not to have met up with other freight wagons, since as many as sixty of them made the trip each week. Some teamsters would want to pass slower wagons and the roadside was strewn with the wreckage of their bravado. Some locations were named for the worst of the disasters: Accident Hill, Last Chance and Jacob's Hill, named for a man killed there.

Eastwood slipped out of the cot and into his boots. Ice had formed on the laces and he struggled to move them through the eyelets. He had done some rough figures in his head and could not fathom how a flume so long and costly would be of any benefit to the company, but before there was time to entertain any more doubts, the door to the bunkhouse flew open and a mill worker strode quickly toward him.

"Mr. Buntline will meet you in the cookhouse, sir. He said to tell you that he will talk while you eat." The man turned on his heel and left without waiting for an answer.

Eastwood slipped quickly into his coat and was out the door. He had no time to wonder about transacting business at the breakfast table even though it was the habit of company moguls back east. In working forests and grimy mills, eating was time-out which meant the need for the flume assumed new significance.

In the eating area, Eastwood was surprised to find long tables spread with cloths, china and real eating utensils. Men and women in white coats and aprons brought food to each table, moving quickly to replace empty dishes. Off in one corner manager Ned Buntline sat alone. Eastwood sensed tension in the men as all conversation halted with his arrival. While each of them nodded in greeting as he passed by, he could feel all eyes following him. He shook hands with Buntline and, before he could sit down the table was loaded with food and the servers gone.

"Mr. Eastwood, I trust you slept well," said Buntline.

"Indeed, I did, sir. Mr. Merryman runs a tight ship and I was the only crew." The manager leaned forward on his arms, pushing the bowl of potatoes toward the engineer.

"Please eat while I give you some of the reasoning behind our flume idea." He reached for the bowl of butter and pushed it next to the mound of fresh bread.

"You know how hard it is to get up the mountain, but I have to tell you that it's also very costly. Merryman pays a pretty penny at the toll-house, and he's not cheap for us to begin with. We use him because he's faithful and has a better record for getting the goods through."

"A better *record?*" sputtered Eastwood. "You mean your other team-sters help themselves to your supplies?"

"No. A better record of not getting held up by outlaws. We have so many, we had to quit bringing up wages from the Valley to pay our workers. Instead, we give them vouchers to take down there and cash at banks. The trip is so long they waste a week getting down there and back again, so they've been selling the vouchers to others for 50 cents on the dollar. That means they're getting half the pay they deserve, but we have no better way of paying them right now. Don't forget we can work up here only April to November if we're lucky, and these men deserve a full pay for their work."

Buntline sipped his coffee. "That's only the half of it. If we ship the logs and lumber by wagon, it doubles the cost to get it to the Valley where lumber cut in the north comes in on trains. The going rate is $12 a thousand board feet, but we have to sell ours for $30 a thousand, and no one wants to pay that when they can get it for less even if ours is higher quality."

Eastwood nodded as he swallowed a bite. "I drafted a design for a railroad last year and it went well until we got to the toll road area. There's no way we could get tracks laid there. Are you sure you want to continue with this?"

"It's the only way. We've got enormous lumber stands here but can't get it to paying customers without shipping it different. That's why we want to look into a flume…a 54 mile one. We have the lumber, the water and a lot of the workers needed to put it up. We just need a route that will send it down by gravity the whole way. Another outfit tried to do the same thing a few years ago, but it leaked so bad it couldn't even float the lumber down to continue construction further down. Our company bought their rights of way and we want to start on it immediately."

Eastwood shook his head. "What makes you think I can overcome the failings of that first flume?"

"We're running out of money and places to borrow. That means we're also running out of time to do it. Everyone says it's a fool's mission, but I don't think so. Just because it's never been done before, doesn't mean it can't be done at all. You've worked in mountains before and you know what can and can't work here. All I'm asking for is a good look to see if it's possible."

"Who else is designing this flume?"

Buntline shook his head. "No one. They all say it's a waste of their time to even try. One engineer offered to draw up the plans but not boss the construction. We need someone who believes in it enough to follow through. You're our last hope. If you don't take the job we're out of business."

One part of Eastwood begged to leap at the chance while another hesitated. A new bride waited for him in the Valley, but the mountains held the promise of a grand future for them both. One large job could erase the need of ten smaller ones, meaning ten fewer battles with reluctant clients when it came to paying for services rendered. As he wavered within, the morning sun crested the last peak and slowly inched its way into the cookhouse spreading like a warm spring thaw. It felt like a sign.

Chewing the last of his meal, Eastwood sat back and smiled. "No one believed a railroad could make it through the Sierra Nevada until Theodore Judah convinced Collis Huntington it could be done, and *should* be done." He sat back and smiled. "They called him Crazy Judah for that. You suppose they'll be calling me Crazy Eastwood for this?"

Buntline stood up so quickly the table shook and coffee cups spilled onto the tablecloths. "When can you begin, Mr. Eastwood?" he asked, his hand extended. A roar of approval rose from the rest of the cookhouse and Eastwood turned a brilliant red.

"It appears I already have, Mr. Buntline."

Behold the turtle. He makes progress only when he sticks his head out."

James Bryant Conant

Chapter 2

PARTNERS IN PROGRESS — 1890

The sun shone thinly through a buttermilk sky, casting few shadows around Eastwood and Jory Morgan, the man assigned to work with him on the survey. They took quick bites of bread and cheese while packing two burros with equipment and supplies. It was important to make the most of daylight, because there was a smell of rain in the breeze. If temperatures dropped below freezing, there would be snow.

Eastwood glanced at the western sky where clouds thickened, hoping he had enough clothing to stay warm at night. The blanket he brought from the Valley was fine for the trip up the mountain, but he had some doubts it was enough for the abrupt change in weather. The elation of the project overshadowed any concerns, and he shrugged them off, eager to be underway. He handed the last loop of lashing to Morgan, and then walked toward his new client standing in the doorway of the warehouse.

"Mr. Buntline, I need a cloth in bright colors," he said motioning with his hands for size. "Brush under some of the trees is thick, and I'll have a hard time seeing the linesman any distance. My white flag might be hard to see in some parts where snow's left."

"I know where I can lay my hands on something, so just keep

packing while I get it. Daylight's a-wasting and we don't stand on formality here. Just call me B-line like everyone else."

"Thank you, and it's John…" Eastwood said to himself as the manager was already out of earshot. A fleeting smile crossed Morgan's face. He was tall and thin like Eastwood with the same kind of bushy mustache. Beyond that they were opposites. Where the engineer was cerebral and behaved at times like an absent-minded academic, Morgan was earthy with thick hands deeply calloused from working mines and mills. Despite the heaviness of his overcoat, it was clear that the Cornish immigrant was well muscled and accustomed to hard work.

Buntline returned with two pieces of quilting in hand, each done in a brilliant log cabin pattern—one clearly unfinished. "Here," he said. "My wife sends her best wishes with these and hopes they bring you good luck as well."

Eastwood hesitated. "They'll be pretty dirty when we return," he warned.

Buntline shook his head. "She gave them willingly, John. Don't refuse her kindness. She knows how important this is to the mill and every man who works here."

Eastwood folded the cloths carefully, and then put them in the last pocket of the burro pack that had any room left.

Buntline extended his hand. "If anything goes wrong or you need something, send Morgan and then stay put."

Eastwood shook his hand and said, "Merryman has a note to give my wife and if we need anything, we won't be far from the road. I can send a message with the stage or a freight wagon coming this way." With a tip of his hat, he was on the way toward the road with Morgan following behind pulling on the leads from the burros.

Eastwood set a strong pace. Not only was he elated about the unusual job but the opportunity also gave him time to be in the mountains. Nowhere else had a greater draw for him and of all the mountains he enjoyed, none had a more persuasive call than the Sierra Nevada.

Lodgepole pines were so tall that the wind at the top sang a different song than when it hit lower branches. White dogwood flowers contrasted sharply with the deep green all around and the shoots of blood-red Snow Plant poked out from the snowless aprons under small pines. Animal footprints dotted the melting snow. Elk, fox, bear, and rabbit—he recognized them all. However, trees captivated him. Knowing them so well, he could identify them by their bark—blindfolded.

He connected with trees and saw them as lyric mountain dress, but it didn't prevent him from seeing them as a resource of astounding abundance for the settlement of the Frontier. There was no conflict in his polarized view of trees. He had a deep and abiding love of the mountains and the only other human he knew who cherished them more was John Muir.

They met in Martinez where Muir and his wife were raising their two girls on a small farm. Eastwood was pleased to learn the writer had attended the University of Minnesota like himself, although at a different time. It was difficult to resist Muir's call to join him in starting up the Sierra Club. The main reluctance for the engineer was that he could not understand Muir's driving desire to preserve the deep woods from logging when there was a crying need for lumber.

It was easy to applaud the idea of conservation, but for Eastwood, it had to live with the reality of making a living. Somehow there had to be a middle ground beyond Muir's total commitment to preservation. Where was room for growth, or advancement or settlement? Did Muir not want the comforts that wealth could bring?

"I'm richer than the richest man in the country," Muir replied to the questions, "because I have all the money I want, and he doesn't."

It was surprising commentary for Eastwood to hear coming from a man reputed to know the Sierra so well he could spot an area where gold would be found. More than one miner struck paydirt after Muir pointed out places to dig.

Strangely, Muir's statement was comforting to Eastwood even though he was pulled in two directions. He loved the wilderness and every part of it down to the smallest flower or bug. However, he also had a driving ambition to design and build something great. The search came from within and pushed his vision well beyond anything dreamed by others. The only thing holding him back was learning where the path to greatness would lead.

The railroad he helped to build was not the first to come through the mountains and in less than twenty-five years, rail travel in the Frontier had become commonplace. Whatever future project would thrust him on the world stage was not clear. It was written on the wind, and discovery would come on the heels of giant steps into the Sierra.

* * * * * * * * * * *

The first week of the survey was quiet, without exceptional stress or quandary about how to proceed with the flume line. For the most part they were in familiar territory with slow descents from the mill. The trail joined the old abandoned flume from the Dinkey Creek lumber operations and following the remains of that project was no challenge. Eastwood took copious notes and was able to keep abreast of his computations each evening by the fire. As they neared the toll road area, everything began to change. Groves of trees thinned and the descent steepened.

For much of that morning, Eastwood was occupied with the thorny problem of taking the flume down the toll road area. He had a choice of moving it to the north and adding two miles to the length or putting it on deep trestles connected to the granite face of the mountain. Some of the supports would have to be nearly a hundred feet high. At lunch they stopped at a small sunny spot beside the road. While they ate, he pondered the alternatives.

"You got somethin' eatin' at you?" asked Morgan.

Eastwood nodded and looked again at the granite looming above them. "The same thing that sunk the railroad plan last year," he said pointing up. "There's no way around this part. If I keep the route here, it'll take a lot of lumber just to get it set there that high to keep the water flowing properly."

Morgan shifted around to follow his eyes. "You took us two miles around this peak, going north to check out that other way. You figure that'll take less lumber?"

The simplicity in the question startled Eastwood. Morgan was right. Keep to the path and do it where the flume will work best. "You think workmen would be willing to hang off that mountainside?" he asked.

"Hah!" scoffed Morgan. "You ain't seen sawyers work these woods. Nothin' they can't do, 'specially when a body says they can't.'"

Eastwood laughed. "Okay, let's see you get up that cliff and set the pole for me to sight from here. I expect you'll have to hang by rope from one of those trees up there."

Morgan swallowed the last of his lunch, and brushed the crumbs onto a rock. "Got a pet chipmunk back at the mill, and he might have relatives here," he said. "If I don't make it back, you'll have to take care of him. Nobody else's crazy like the two of us!"

* * * * * * * * * * *

The waters of Mill Creek were frigid. The melting snow pack cre-

A portion of the sixty mile long Shaver Lake lumber flume designed by John Eastwood. Abandoned in 1916, one part of the flume still exists and visible more than a hundred years after construction.

United States Forest Service Photo

ated a waterway traveling so fast and deep, large rocks tumbled within its down-mountain rush. The thunder of them hitting into one another along with the onslaught of water made conversation impossible. John Eastwood wished there was another way to get over the water, but there was no choice. They had already crossed it several times along the planned route of the flume, but the water in this area dropped precipitously. The power of the flow was astonishing.

Resolutely he signaled Morgan to throw the first line. The burly mill man took the end of the rope attached to a large metal hook and swung it around his head several times to build momentum. When he let it go, the hook sailed across the river toward a tall pine tree on the opposite bank, wrapping around the great trunk three times before imbedding itself into the bark. Then he tied the other end of the rope to a tree beside him making a strong knot with a pullout loop.

Eastwood stepped uneasily into the torrent, clinging tightly to the line. Water pushed against his legs as he stepped along the bottom, leaving him barely able to put one foot in front of the other. He continued into the river, keeping one hand fast on the rope with the other reaching ahead to move across.

Unseen in the roaring torrent, one of the rocks tumbling downstream knocked his legs out from under sending him beneath the water. His one-handed grip on the rope tightened as he struggled to get back to air, but his body was caught in the current as the wet rope stretched. He groped wildly above trying to reach the rope with his other hand, and finding it at last was able to pull himself erect. For a moment, he gasped for air watching as his hat continued downstream, then carefully made his way to the far shore.

Eastwood waved to Morgan to show he was all right, then made the rest of the way across. He sat on a large sun-warmed rock trying to catch his breath. Morgan waited until he saw Eastwood motion to send the survey equipment and supplies over. Another hooked line went sailing across to a second tree. Eastwood unwrapped it and pulled across enough line to double back to the other side. He threw back the end of the rope to Morgan who then attached it to a burro's harness. One by one each burro was led to the other side. By the time he made the trip himself and pulled on the knot to free the rope, Eastwood had a fire going.

The near tragedy struck him hard. The power of the river left him with a deep respect and reverence for the wilderness, certain it would define who he was. His name would be written on the rocks, and live in the water as part of the history of the Sierra. Somehow he knew it would also be his destruction.

"The universe is full of magical things patiently waiting for our wits to grow sharper."
Ralph Waldo Emerson

Chapter 3

THE SIX HOUR WATER RIDE – 1894

Electric lights on the streets of Fresno were only a few weeks old and already they made a huge difference in the lives of residents. While some streets were still dimly lit by gas lamps, the down-town stores were bathed in light from fewer than a dozen lamps. With the new invention, stores remained open beyond daylight hours, lending a new vibrancy to the area. Some people shopped and others ambled along, content to window shop instead of hurrying home before dark. As his wife Ella moved through the house lighting oil lamps, Eastwood compared the light within to that outdoors, wondering how long it would take for electricity to move into homes.

He had read that Thomas Edison patented an incandescent light bulb which he claimed would work inside, but until electricity could get from the generator to homes further than three miles, Eastwood knew there was little hope Ella would be turning on lights with a switch instead of a match. He also knew that the powerful arc lights were little more than a novelty since they were prone to fire. Even if they were able to be installed indoors, the light would be blinding.

One irritating fact of life for Fresno street lights was that they were often unlit because producing electricity with a coal-fired generator was more expensive than originally expected. When the supply of coal was used up, the electric lights were out until the next shipment of fuel arrived. The city was developing in an uneven march forward. Businesses dealing in new technology sometimes started up and then failed. In the wake of multiple economic downturns, Eastwood knew more than one manufacturer had to absorb the loss of a failed system and revert to gas-fired steam generators. However, retailers quickly became accustomed to the longer hours for sales and when the street lights proved to be unreliable, convinced the city to install gas lamps on some streets as a backup. Customers coming after dark proved to be a boon to sales.

Eastwood no longer worked in obscurity. The Smith & Moore flume at Shaver Lake was built in one year and made him a celebrity. Profit from the new flume spread in a wide circle, including Merryman Freight line. The business was now Merryman Trucking Company, and the freight owner was actively involved in carrying supplies to the work crews on the flume. One night around the fire, Eastwood asked him why he changed the name of the company.

"It was my wife what done it. She's got a habit of helping anyone who ever fell on hard times—neighbor or stranger," he replied. "She comes to me with a bundle and says, 'how about truck this over to Mrs. So and So, or down to Mr. Such and Such.' She's a big heart for givin' and me for the deliverin'. She even named my new mule Truck. Word got out so now customers ask me to *truck* this up to Shaver or *truck* this over to Visalia. I jist followed along."

The winter prior to the construction, the mill did not shut down. Instead, workers cut lumber from an enormous stash of logs. Hand cut and skidded to the millpond area to be cut and stored for partial drying, the lumber was carefully stacked with shims between each level to keep the lengths from freezing together.

When Eastwood had returned in April, word was already out that the mill wanted workers. Small shelters dotted all the level ground around the mill with men clustered around fires awaiting his arrival. There were mill returnees, out of work cowboys, farmers, miners and a scattering of adolescents not old enough to grow a beard—all of them eager to be hired. Interviews were short and to the point. What have you done? This is no picnic and you gotta keep up with the crew, so where's your bedroll? Show your hands—meaning, no calluses, no job. The hard work would separate the men from the boys in short order and while the food provided was abundant, the pay was not.

Beginning with a maze of chutes from the mill, the flume became one long vee-shaped, gravity-fed waterway. A lake already formed behind a small dam built to feed a steady stream of water deep and wide enough to carry lumber. In areas of the route vulnerable to jams, there was also a narrow walkway alongside for tenders. Twelve small cabins were built at strategic locations along the flume to house these fearless men who often had to work on a narrow plank more than fifty feet above the rocky ground. Without them a lumber jam would force a cascade over the side and undermine the flume foundation.

Work was halted each time cowboys appeared, waved their hats, and then went back down the mountain. It was the signal that a herd of cattle was on the way up the mountain to pasture for the summer. The animals were edgy by the time they reached the upper elevations and it took little to spook them into a stampede, including the time a man accidentally dropped a tin cup. The cowboys spent the next two days rounding up animals before they could continue the trek.

At the end of each week Ned Buntline sent a man to the construction site to pay the workers. It was a matter of courtesy since there was no place to spend or send it to family. While they were in the wildlands, each one asked that the money be kept in a company account until the job was over.

On one such Saturday Eastwood was surprised to find Ned Buntline himself coming to make the weekly presentation. With construction expected to join with the opposite end coming from the Valley in a week, Buntline had a long ride from the lumber mill. It did not bode well for Eastwood and he greeted the boss with trepidation.

"You're a long way from home, Buntline. You get lost between the bunkhouse and the mill?"

"Maybe next time I'll do just that," he grumbled. "This time I'm just the bearer of bad news."

"Can't imagine that with the job well ahead of schedule, you'd have anything bad to say about it."

"Eastwood, it's not the flume. It's water. We're spending $200,000 and using nine million board feet of lumber and hoped to offset some of that by selling water to Valley farmers. Now the Miller Lux Company is threatening to sue because they say we violated their water rights along the way."

"Everybody knows they're quick on the draw. I hear Miller has an attorney working full time. I thought we had it covered in the agreement with the company."

"So did I. It appears that the law is not written in stone as long as they can rewrite a contract by 'interpreting' it."

"Well, B-line, you came to the wrong person for that kind of advice."

Buntline waved the disclaimer off and sat on a log. Eastwood sat next to him, waiting for a response with a small sense of foreboding. After the work he did on the railroad route last year came to nothing, he wondered if his bad luck was continuing, especially this close to completion. He'd be paid, but without a successful project under his belt, it was his reputation that would suffer.

"I took another look at your estimates and without selling the water, we can still make a comfortable profit." Buntline looked directly at Eastwood. "How sure are you of your estimates? Is there any wriggle room here that could mean we fail in this venture?"

Eastwood shook his head. "No. There's no doubt about my figures if sales stay the same as last year. Even if new settlers coming from the east eases off, there're new businesses coming in. They'll need lumber and you'll probably have to cut more for raisin boxes. There're acres of new vines planted in the last two years, not to mention apricots. They take shipping boxes *and* drying frames."

"So you're saying that if we drop selling water from the flume entirely, we can still make it."

"No doubt at all. Matter of fact you might do better without it."

Buntline nodded, then shook hands and left to speak with the workers. Eastwood's misgivings vanished. For several weeks he had been looking for a way to test his idea that the water might be tainted by contact with the milled lumber's resin. His education did not include an abundance of chemistry, but his keen eye missed nothing. If logs sat in water there was no problem, but if lumber did the same, even birds avoided the contaminated water. Science was governed by laws arising from nature and if they broken consequences had to be considered. In this case the loss of income was better than bad business with farmers. Miller and Lux Company had saved Eastwood the distasteful job of bringing the news to the company himself.

The flume was an engineering wonder. People cheered to see lumber float into the mill making it from Shaver Lake in six and a half hours. The same distance still took people several days to traverse and the idea of such rapid transit was not lost on the intrepid. Increased activity in the mountains reduced the incidence of robbery on the road and regular pay days resumed. Some of the mill workers with money in their pockets would ride the water down to the Valley in a flume "boat" which made saloon and brothel owners very happy. Even the owner of the mill once used a flume boat to catch the stage he missed at Shaver Lake. In six minutes he was waiting for the coach at the next stop.

The time Eastwood spent supervising the construction of the flume fortified his connection with the Sierra. He would have loved to live year-round in the Shaver Lake area but knew that his wife would have been lonely and life much more rigorous than in Fresno. Ella had many friends who helped to fill the void of her not having had a child. He could not take that connection with other women from her, so he compromised and found a piece of land on the Kings River, a comfortable distance from their first home in town. Their house was built on a small knoll a short distance from the river. Eastwood's encounter with the waters of the Sierra didn't leave him fearing another brush with his mortality. He was too busy with the business of invention and innovation.

He was very pleased to find his estimates of lumber needed for each section of the project was accurate when all was in place. However, he was not yet finished with the Shaver Lake project. Just as construction was completed, he received a second personal message from the mountains. He had been dropped into the icy Mill Creek and shaken like a rag doll the first time, and this new message was from the water again.

Torrential rains filled the basin behind the fifty-foot high earthen dam, then spilled over the top, quickly eroding the foundation. The existing dam failed completely and Eastwood was hired to design a replacement, his first dam of any consequence. It would change his life forever. Five hundred feet high, the new dam impounded a sizeable lake and ensured the flume would continue to send lumber to the Valley in spite of occasional drought. The new dam helped to solidify his connection with the Sierra and from this success a new plan began to take shape in Eastwood's mind. He would harness the power of water and build a hydroelectric plant somewhere below Shaver Lake.

By using the movement of water instead of burning coal, gas or wood to power the generators, initial construction costs were higher but the investment was recoverable within a few short years. Eastwood felt the idea was the perfect match for the abundance of water in the Sierra. He would meet the Sierra water on its own terms, tapping into that power to create electricity to light homes with Edison light bulbs. Ella would never again have to soil her hands cleaning lamps and trimming wicks.

Henry E. Huntington, circa 1873
  Henry E. Huntington Library and Art Gallery

"Don't be afraid to take a big step if one is indicated. You can't cross a chasm in two small jumps."
David Lloyd George

Chapter 4

POWER CHESS GAME IN SAN FRANCISCO

Two hundred miles from Fresno in San Francisco, an event quite removed by both distance and prestige unfolded at a meeting of the Central Pacific Railroad Company. It was destined to have major implications for John Eastwood as well as the rise of electrical power in the Frontier. While the genesis of electrical power was in its infancy, the connection for its meteoric rise in experimentation and use was directly tied to the railroads. The relative comfort of riding in a railcar was far more attractive to settlers than a wagon train and its extraordinary rigors. People began to emigrate west in large numbers. Leland Stanford was no longer president of the railroad company that was a part of the first transcontinental transportation line in the country: Henry Huntington had witnessed his uncle Collis wrest control of the board of directors in a vote that was close, but clear. Ever the diplomat, Stanford appeared to be graciously resigned to his defeat but HH was certain the former governor of California was seething beneath his outward calm.

In the years since he had come to work for his uncle, HH recognized that the tension between Stanford and his partner Collis was inevitable. Their backgrounds were vastly dissimilar with the former coming from wealth and Collis having reached his position by bare fisted competition in the marketplace. While Stanford polished his negotiating skills in the courtroom and the halls of government, Collis worked his hardware store with a keen eye toward cornering any market he could and making the most of it.

Both were merchants who were successful in providing forty-niners with equipment and materials necessary to work the gold fields. In six years, the Sacramento hardware store Collis ran with his partner Mark Hopkins became the largest mercantile establishment in the west.

Everything changed when engineer Theodore Judah came to Collis and Hopkins to see if they would be willing to bankroll a transcontinental railroad. Initially unwilling to even consider the project, Collis was convinced of its value by the volumes of market research Judah had done. He could report the number of wagons that passed a particular point on the expected route of the railroad, the number of passengers in coaches, and the estimated tons of freight going both ways.

"There are other financial benefits to consider such as lumber sales," Judah pointed out to the partners. "If 300,000 acres of the land along the right of way each contained a mere ten trees per acre, from which can be cut six logs twelve feet long per tree, and averaging 24 inches square, the result would be 3,400 board feet measure per tree. Delivered at Sacramento for sale at $15 per thousand, the partners could reap $150 million."

The partners were very impressed.

Judah was not the first to propose a railway of such immense importance, but he was the first to design it specifically. His infectious excitement and enthusiasm about the construction of a transportation miracle earned him the nickname Crazy Judah. HH knew if the visionary were able to convince his uncle, Judah could convince anyone. It was not surprising that Judah eventually traveled to Washington DC to push for government subsidy for the railroad. Collis became the driving force behind the first transcontinental railroad in the US, using his wit, wisdom and wiles to gather a partnership of men with the money, power and connections to see it through.

HH came to work for his uncle in San Francisco three years after the first Golden Spike was hammered into the final tie in Promontory Point, Utah. He could see that his uncle's partners had all the attributes and abilities necessary to pull strings in Washington, especially through the rapid changes in political climate that preceded the Civil War. Stanford and Judah were able to convince the US Congress and President Abraham Lincoln that the railroad was imperative. Support then came with a multi-million dollar subsidy through the Central Pacific Railroad Bill of 1862. It would be the first of many pricey private industry partnerships with the federal government that were deemed necessary for the common good.

Despite their differences, the men worked through unforeseen problems brought about by mammoth consequences of driving a road through the Sierra Nevada. Trains had to find passage through areas seven thousand feet high, necessitating bridges and tunnels, some drilled through solid granite where in winter, snow is sometimes thirty feet deep.

In the public's eye the partners were giants, but in private the stories of shady business practices worked against them. The contract with the US government stipulated that no subsidy would be forthcoming until forty miles of track were laid. The money ran out after twenty miles. The cost cutting that ensued included reduced wages and comforts for the workers, and the labor force necessary to complete the project evaporated. It was Hopkins who solved the dilemma by finding a new source of laborers and by the end of the construction, ninety percent of the railway construction workers in the west were Chinese.

They existed on rice, tea and dried vegetables and were the only ones willing to put up with half the pay previously given to white men, backbreaking work, and few comforts along the way. The death rate was astounding and it was no accident of culture that the phrase "Not a Chinaman's chance" was coined at this time. It was a stark reminder that their lives could be taken by an explosive charge gone awry, the resulting rain of rock underestimated, malnutrition combined with exhausting work in high elevations or dozens of other death traps in the camps.

It was Collis who negotiated with investors and tightened the controls on extraneous expenses. "Henry," said CH to his nephew, "it is absolutely imperative to control every possible facet of a business or construction project." HH knew of Crazy Judah from the stories of others but recognized his uncle's hand in how the engineer was pushed out of the final plans.

Judah had demanded more and more control over the construction even before it actually began. When the partners were unable to get him to compromise, they simply ignored him and proceeded as they wished. When he continued to protest, the partners bought out his interest in the project for $100,000 and some stock options. Judah was unwilling to let the matter rest, and set out for the east coast to convince the Vanderbilt investment group to buy out the California partners. One mosquito bite changed everything.

Judah traveled to the east coast by ship to the Isthmus of Panama, took a forty-seven mile train trip across to the opposite side and then another ship to a port of landing. On that fateful trip with his wife, Judah contracted Yellow Fever on the way across the Isthmus. The disease, spread by mosquitoes, racked him with a high fever and withering chills. Dr. Walter Reed's pioneering research about the malady was decades in the future, and for those unfortunates who developed such serious symptoms at Judah's time, no medicine could help. His damaged liver turned his skin a sickly yellow and although alive when the ship put into New York Harbor, he died a week later. The California Big Four partners would not lose control of the railroad. However, Stanford did lose control of the board of directors.

HH took every lesson to heart and stored them all for future reference. He learned that the first law of successful enterprise was to establish control by creating a market. Collis did it when he shipped in shovels, barbed wire, plows, coal, nails, springs and whiskey, then stored them until demand rose, at which time he could ask any price. There was no such thing as a price tag at the time and he sensed just how high he could go, never wanting for buyers. He also harvested an enormous crop of resentment for his tactics which did nothing to influence his future dealings. He earned a reputation as the west's Robber Baron. Along with Crocker, Stanford and Hopkins in the railroad business, the partnership became known as the California Big 4.

Collis applied his tried and true business tactics to the railroad, raising and dropping freight prices to suit his needs and the changing market without interference from other board members. Mark Hopkins had died several years before the fateful board meeting, and Collis's wife as well. The fourth partner, Charles Crocker, was inactive due to injuries suffered in a traffic accident in New York. The vote to oust Stanford appeared to gut the power of the board, giving Collis free reign to run the Pacific Railroad Company as his personal fiefdom. The members functioned as a rubber stamp for whatever the president wanted to do.

Business took on even more importance to Collis because he was paving the way for his nephew to take over the reins of the board when he himself was not around. The very idea brought a great deal of satisfaction to HH as the heir apparent to San Francisco's business minions. He took the role seriously and became proactive in managing his personal assets, especially for investing in railroad and trolley enterprises. The success of cable cars in the city prompted him to spread his financial influence beyond San Francisco. He bought the Los Angeles Railway, a failing conglomeration of older rail companies in the southern part of the state.

Not many people in business thought it was a good move. The City of Angels was considered to be a ruffian settlement by San Franciscan cosmopolitans who derisively called it the "Queen of the Cow Counties". The self-confidence of San Francisco was broadly evident the night the last spike was driven to join West to East with the first transcontinental railroad. A sign in the celebratory crowd crowed: "California annexes the US." HH had, however, honed his business sense at his uncle's side and was confident the Los Angeles enterprise was a mother lode waiting to be mined.

Business continued to thrive for both Huntingtons, and Collis married again, this time to Arabella Duval Worsham, his paramour for many years. His second wife was considerably different from the first and Collis's excessively thrifty ways soon began to wither under her tutelage. Their home moved from bare necessity to sheer luxury with Arabella's exquisite and expensive taste. The marriage would have major import for John Eastwood in less than a decade.

During the time the railroads took center stage and spun off into a multitude of city trolleys and streetcars, the development of electrical power as an industry and social catalyst was building a head of steam with an 1891 demonstration project built in Germany. The 112 mile, 30,000 volt, three-phase system erected between Frankfurt and Lauffen was a success but never used. The science found immediate acceptance and a year later the first commercially successful electric line seventy miles south in Heilbroun was serving happy customers.

Events began to build that would set the stage for Eastwood's entry in the field. That same year American engineer Almerian Decker designed a commercial electric power system in the Pomona area of southern California, east of Los Angeles. He used George Westinghouse's design for a 10,000-volt, single-phase system, fifteen miles long with an additional circuit of 28 miles in length to serve the San Bernardino area as well.

Eastwood and his peers were involved in debate about the merits of where the science was heading. In New York, Thomas Edison's Pearl Street generating station was ten years old. The system, using direct current (DC) power, was falling behind with dramatic improvements in alternating current (AC) designs.

"The AC system with transformers moves electricity further and faster," Eastwood said to his friend Matthew Merryman. "Westinghouse won a bid to put up lamps and power for the Columbian Exposition in Chicago. Imagine! He brought 200,000 lamps including replacements for it, and then built a working model of a polyphase system with transformers and switchboard."

"Eastwood," said Merryman. "I know *you* know what you're talkin' about but you're tellin' it to a man who drives horses and mules for a livin'."

"This from a man who built a business from his wife's kindness. Merryman, you're a lot smarter than you know. When the time comes, you won't need the whys and wherefores. All you'll have to do is use the electricity. If anybody can make a profit and lead the way, it's you!"

"I'll remember that the next time I shovel the manure out of the stables."

"You just write this down. On this day I predicted you will one day have electric lights in your livery stable and the horses will be out to pasture. Just remember that I told you about it when Westinghouse got the contract to design the first hydroelectric power plant at Niagara Falls."

The prediction was closer to reality than either man dreamed. In a few short years, the availability of electric lighting would hopscotch from a mere curiosity demonstrated by a traveling circus to business and household necessity. While fossil fuel burning generators were first used to create power, Eastwood's interest in hydroelectric generation and its economy was poised to push it to assume the mantle of king. There would be no cookie-cutter kind of repeat design as science pushed the limits of voltage and transmission distances. Along with the new technology, engineers became famous as their rapid advances in efficiency made nearly every new installation a vast improvement over the last.

In the Sierra Nevada, John Eastwood tramped the wilds from five to nine thousand feet high, tracing waterways that began as trickles in high elevations and raced to join others to form the San Joaquin River. His understanding of the potential power there was recorded in voluminous ledgers with flawless mathematics and solid science. His calculations and numbers were about to clash with the reality of the marketplace, politics and human nature.

"Genius develops in quiet places, character out in the full current of human life."

Johann von Goethe

Chapter 5

LIGHT FROM THE MOUNTAINS – 1893

After two years of long separations for the survey and construction of the flume, it was a comfort to be with Ella every day, but Eastwood was getting restless to return to the Sierra. His two loves would forever pull him first one way and then the other. He knew Ella wrote regularly in a diary and sometimes wondered how she could find much to put to paper about their lives together when he was gone so much.

Eastwood had traveled south to see engineer Almerian Decker's new hydroelectric project. Decker had emigrated west for his health and looked to the dry air to cure his tuberculosis. What he found instead was a passion to design and oversee the construction of a groundbreaking power production plant on Mill Creek, upstream from the Santa Ana River southeast of Los Angeles.

While he missed meeting Decker, Eastwood made an important personal contact in Redlands: President of the electric company, H.H. Sinclair. The two men became friends, sharing an avid interest in electrical power.

"Sorry you missed him," said Sinclair. "Decker dived into the project when he should have rested. He never saw the plant in action."

"There aren't many people who can move the science a giant step ahead," observed Eastwood.

"It wasn't enough to have the information. He had to work like a Trojan to convince George Westinghouse to build the system the way he wanted."

"Edison gets reporters excited when he walks across the street, but there are a lot of other people doing just as much work without anyone knowing about it. If I didn't read professional journals, I'd have no idea about it myself."

No successful engineer could ignore what was being done by others because their success bred that of others. Design of a system had to stand alone to attract the money to build it and professionals had to convince investors that their money was safe in their hands. Most of all it had to have the potential to make money and make it fast. Standing still on the railroad track of progress ensured one would be run over. For the moment Edison was stalled on those tracks.

His use of DC electricity limited the distance it could travel because electrons flow all in one direction, losing strength as it moves along. In AC technology, electricity is directed through huge oil-filled transformers where the electrons forward movement is reversed in split second intervals. Generated electricity now traveled well beyond its previous limitations because new transformers were capable of moving voltage pressure up and down much like water in a garden hose. The slingshot action pushed power to travel farther and farther well beyond the original two to three miles of Edison's Pearl Street plant.

"Decker calculated that it would take one thousand volts of pressure to move electricity one mile," continued Sinclair. "At the receiving end of the line, pressure had to be reduced by opposite direction transformers for residents. He pulled together the best of what's available, even using Orville Ensign's new "petticoat" ceramic insulators. Amazing how he got an added push to the power. Decker's science was so accurate it's likely going to be the standard for a long time."

The two men walked into the powerhouse and were enveloped by the hum of generators. Eastwood looked at the system and immediately memorized it, surprised to see the name General Electric on the equipment. He ran his fingers over the name and looked questioningly at Sinclair who motioned him back outside.

"Decker's design had never been used and Westinghouse didn't think it would work. He refused to manufacture the equipment for a three-phase transformer, AC system so Decker turned to General Electric Company."

Eastwood shook his head. "Don't know how some people can sleep at night but if Edison hadn't cheated Tesla out of the money he promised him to improve the dynamo we might not have the AC system now."

"Right. And then Westinghouse paid big money for Tesla's AC patents. Shows how competition can make or break a company because even though he had a goldmine in his possession, he never capitalized on it. It took Edison's General Electric Company to make sense of it and actually manufacture Decker's generators and transformers."

"You have to credit the fact that Edison's retired from the electricity business now and sticks to inventing equipment."

"True enough. It also helps that GE has a bunch of young engineers not afraid to take chances. Decker's design presented an opportunity it embraced to the point they have opened a west coast office in San Francisco."

"Well, that's a surprise considering that eastern interests figure the Frontier is only good for Indian Wars and railroad robbers like Butch Cassidy and the Sundance Kid. About the closest we can get money to make the trip is from Chicago where the bonding company is."

Sinclair chuckled. "You said it and even though GE was enthusiastic about the project, they had some limits. The 5,000-volt capacity Decker wanted was pared down to 2,500, and the company was reluctant to use the new high voltage transformers. In spite of it all our Redlands power project is here and we've got the country's first successful commercial polyphase system. With our transmission lines fifteen miles long, that's a world record for distance."

Eastwood looked toward the southern mountains. "Do you think I'm foolish to consider a hydroelectric system that will travel thirty miles?"

Sinclair did not answer immediately, seeming to follow Eastwood's vision toward the mountains.

"GE's got a telegraph in their office up north," he said at last. "We get quick answers to any questions and it's cut the time to get parts from Chicago down to about two weeks."

"...if the lines don't go down," added Eastwood. "We're still an outpost in Fresno and the money to build any kind of project has a much harder road to travel to get that far, even if we have the engineers to get it on paper."

"It's not any easier for us here in the southern part of the state. We can't find backers in San Francisco because they live in *The City* and we're the barefoot backwoods folk. Some say it right out that we should just ship oranges and forget building anything."

"At least you've got a port not far from here and Sacramento has the government. The rest of us are all lumped together as farmers. It's like the train goes one way and I swear, Sinclair, one of these days they're gonna wake up and find we have something they want very much and it won't come in a boxcar. Hydropower is the only way to make electricity pay and the only water in the state is in the mountains."

"You may be right, Eastwood. Even though Decker couldn't get GE to make the generator he wanted, they're building one now for Sacramento's project at Folsom. Not only did they meet his original plans, they're exceeding it with an 11,000-volt, three-phase system sending power twenty-two miles. I still don't know why those transformers work they way they do."

"You're not the only one!" Eastwood laughed. "I'm a civil engineer by training, but I'm very interested in hydro energy designs. With all that's happening lately, I think it'll be necessary for engineers to work just with electricity—you know…an electrical engineer like I'm a civil. That's even different from a mechanics man and they already have their own professional group back east. I know a transformer just winds the wire one way or the other, but I still don't know why that would cause the voltage to rise or fall."

"Doesn't matter, John. All you need to do is calculate the flow rate, pressure available in the water and design the overall plan. Decker had it easy here because the location was easy to reach for the dam and powerhouse. He just put it all together and you could do the same and more in the Sierra above Fresno. It'll take some serious planning at that elevation."

"Don't have the money, nor do I know anyone in San Francisco, let alone Chicago or New York."

"At least look into it, John," he urged. "As fast as engineering is moving, if you don't do it, someone else will."

Eastwood shook his head. "I'd like to believe it and wonder why I'm here since I'm tainted, Sinclair…ever since I got tied up with that irrigation company at home. Had no idea they were selling stock on land outside the district and more than that I didn't know it was in the law that they couldn't. Don't know much about the financial end of the business, but at least I didn't suffer anything more than losing my investment. On the other hand, I was the engineer for it and that means investors will think I had my fingers into something shady. The state's regulating water now, so how long do you figure it'll take them to do the same with electricity and gas?"

"Can't say, but I do know they're not going to keep people from moving out here because it's a really big state. The only way business can grow is if settlers keep coming. At least California politicians are here and know what's going on, but the ones in Washington have never set foot this side of the Mississippi. It won't take long for them to figure out that there's more than gold in our hills."

Eastwood pulled on his moustache while he pondered the possibilities. It was public knowledge that John Muir was openly courting federal regulation in the west and that his prediction of a totally desecrated forest was not wide of the mark. Giant trees had been felled sometimes for the sport of it. There was little profit in those immense logs because they were too large to transport and frequently broke into unusable pieces when the cut tree thundered to the ground. Loggers were taking only full-grown trees, but clear-cut enormous tracts just to get at them. Only a fool would pretend that government regulation was not far behind those who destroyed more than they harvested.

More and more Eastwood saw the necessity for man to live with the mountains in harmony. If he shrank from the responsibility of demonstrating the way, others with less than honorable motives were bound to fill the gap.

"I can do the work, Sinclair," he said, "but I have no idea where to look for financial backing."

"I do." Sinclair reached for his pen and dipped into the inkwell. He wrote quickly and then blotted it and handed the paper to Eastwood. "J.J. Seymour, president of Fresno Water Company, and tell him I sent you."

"To renew ties with the past need not always be day-dreaming; it may be tapping into old sources of strength for new tasks."

Simon Strunsky

Chapter 6

FIRST STEPS TO POWER – 1894

For a moment Eastwood hesitated, torn between protecting his horse and presenting himself well to J.J. Seymour. He opted in the horse's favor, then reined the buggy toward Merryman's livery stable knowing that despite his large umbrella, he would be soaked from the knees down by the time he walked the two blocks to the office of the Fresno Water Company.

As he approached the livery area the double doors swung open wide. Merryman could hardly be seen through the downpour but Eastwood's horse hesitated to enter. Merryman's arm appeared out of the gloom, impatiently motioning him to enter but the horse hesitated. With a sharp flick of the whip on its flank, it finally made the last few feet into the stable.

"Whoa!" yelled Merryman. "Ease off the whip! It's the truck that's spookin' him."

"I don't see your mule," replied Eastwood testily.

"Not the mule, it's the German carriage."

It took Eastwood several minutes to become accustomed to the daylight-dark of the storm, despite several lanterns hanging from an old buggy wheel in the ceiling.

"If that's a carriage, you'll have one devil of a time getting it hitched to a horse. Where's the singletree? There's no way to harness."

"Don't take no horse, and I thought engineers know all about these things."

Eastwood peered intently at the machine at the far corner of the room. "All I see is a nameplate…Daimler, something. What're you going to…wait…Daimler! That's a horseless carriage!"

"Comes the dawn," said Merryman removing the remaining cover from the rear of the machine.

Dropping the reins Eastwood clambered quickly down from the buggy. "What do you plan to do with it?"

Merryman shrugged. "Don' know fer sure. The missus has family livin' next door to Daimler's in the old country. She writes back and forth with 'em and heard about it. Then she talked me into getting one shipped out. Nuthin' but a toy. Says I can take her ta church in it and if I put a longer bed in back it's good for around town makin' deliveries. Hell, I can't even find a way to get it past horses without makin' 'em shy, so how am I gonna get to my customers?"

"Merryman, your wife has more good ideas than most of the rest of us put together. You'd do well to keep an open mind. I've got an appointment at the water company. Should be back in less than an hour." With one more glance at the Daimler machine, Eastwood picked up his umbrella from the buggy and left.

He was feeling uneasy about meeting Seymour for the first time. He could see from the chimneys above the office that wood stoves were going full tilt against the January cold. He expected to provide a goodly amount of steam as his clothing met the warmth inside.

Hoping to drain off somewhat while he waited for his appointment time, he was disappointed when the secretary ushered him directly into the inner office. Seymour sat at an enormous desk, shouting into a metal horn. He held another horn to his ear this one connected to the first with a long woven wire.

"No! Don't wait! I want that pipe protected now. Use the brains God gave you to figure out how, just don't let it break. The engineer is on the way."

Seymour placed the horn on the desk, extended his hand in greeting then motioned to a chair. Eastwood slid his hand along the side of his coat hoping to dry it a little but he could tell it was a soggy greeting on his part. He masked his discomfort as he sat down and pointed to the apparatus on the desk. "Is that a telephone?"

"Yes. The company engineer worked for Alexander Bell before coming west and he rigged it up to keep us connected with people along all our pipelines. With this much rain coming all at once, we could have some problems. The water's rising fast."

Eastwood relaxed. The telephone fit neatly into his presentation for the planned hydroelectric system he envisioned, but he waited for his opportunity. Seymour wasted no time on extended pleasantries.

"Sinclair wrote me about your idea and I have to say I'm not entirely convinced it's practical. A hydro power plant in the mountains seems like too large an investment for a few customers to turn on a couple lights."

"Well, Mr. Seymour, it's been less than a hundred years since the Italian Volta invented a battery to create electricity you can carry around and already the Germans have a carriage that runs with a motor instead of a horse."

"Yes, they do, and they're tinkering with an internal combustion engine to do the same thing. That could mean portable electricity's a fad that's already finished. I'm not anxious to get involved in the public dispute between Edison and Tesla over the merits of DC over AC. What I want is customers who need what I have to sell. They can't do without water."

"True enough. However, streets in London, Paris and New York are lined with electric lights. Don't you think people who live here want the same?"

"Possibly, but Tesla's invention to increase or decrease the voltage in electrical current has had less than ten years to prove itself and in that same time it's changed constantly. Every time you turn around, there's a new model. Where's the value in that?"

"The value is precisely in the changes. With the Niagara power plant using Tesla's latest transformer to push the power farther, we can use it here where people are more scattered. Even Edison appears to think this is the way to progress since he partnered with Houston to open the General Electric Company and they're not pushing the DC system any more."

The pounding of wind-blown rain on the windows was the only sound in the room while Seymour appeared to be deep in thought. Eastwood hoped the thoughts were coming toward his own way of thinking and averted his eyes to keep from revealing his eagerness for the answer he wanted.

The inside of this office was not much different from the parlor of the house where he had grown up. The oil lamps hung from the ceiling in a fashionable carved rack instead of simply placed on furniture. On the dark oak hutch behind Seymour's desk was a highly ornate ewer in a large saucer unlike the plain glossy white one in his parent's home. Eastwood judged the towel next to it was likely imported Irish linen and the soap milled in France. However, he knew water was heated on stoves just as it had been for him for a bath as a child. Beyond the gentrification of the usual items, life was close to the same as it had been for generations, but electricity had the power to change everything. Seymour jolted him out of his reverie.

"Even if generators run well enough for us to make electricity, who would buy it? This is a farming area and what good is it beyond lights? I don't see much room for a business to grow here." Eastwood eased back in the chair, comfortable at last with his chance to lay out his plan. For weeks he had reading scientific periodicals gleaning from them every logical reason to embrace the new technology. Seymour got to the point much faster than expected, but Eastwood was ready.

"Did you know there's an electric motor that lifted a thousand pounds? It was an experiment, but well documented. And steam turbines. Don't you think plugging into instant electricity is better than building a head of steam in a boiler? How much wood would it take to build the same amount of energy in a donkey engine at a saw mill compared to using the free power of water coming down from the Sierra? Businesses will find ways to use electricity very quickly and it won't take long for the women to find other ways to put it to work, like taking the hand crank out of the washing machine, or heating water to come right through the spigot. It's not going to make that much difference to a man, but you can bet it will to a woman. I believe electricity will make anybody who gets in at the beginning much more successful than one waiting to see it in action. It'll exchange a horse for the power of a dozen horses coming in through a wire."

Seymour sat back in his chair and Eastwood sensed a change in the man's interest.

"Can't imagine anything more reliable than a horse, but then it wasn't long ago they were dropping like flies. My wife lived through that equine sickness spell back east and she still gets tears in her eyes when she speaks of her father and brother pulling the wagon themselves. You know…no work, no pay. Thousands of animals died in such a short time and if it happened once, it might come back."

Eastwood felt he was making enough headway to introduce the reason he was there.

"I can do the entire design for the construction and machinery, but I have no way of raising the money."   Seymour did not blink and Eastwood continued. "There's one other problem. Every year Sacramento and Washington take over more of the forest lands. Unless we stake our claim in the Sierra now, there might not be a chance later."

Seymour shook his head. "The state tried to regulate logging with the Board of Forestry but then never voted money to keep it going. I think they have the right idea, but the federal people are different. First Lincoln made Yosemite Valley a national park then gave it to the state. Now there's talk the state's giving it back and it seems they act with whatever political wind blows at the time. If we had more businesses to protect in the Sierra, the state might not be so quick to let the forests go. Not sure what I need to do, but I'm sure I can handle it."

Eastwood could feel his project building energy of its own. He used his trump card. "I've registered some important water rights on the San Joaquin River and know the territory well. There's a spot not far from the road where the powerhouse could be built and I can provide all the expertise needed. Sinclair said he would back me up if we have any problems."

For the first time, Seymour smiled. "You do your work well, Eastwood. I can't promise I can get the money to build the project, but I have a brother-in-law who knows people with money in Chicago. How long will it take to draw up the plans and estimates?"

"I'll head back to the mountains in April to confirm everything. It might be October before I can be sure of all the specifications. I think you know the plans and projected costs for the Shaver Lake flume were very accurate."

"I do. Fresno's a small town so I say we keep this between the two of us for the present."

The two men shook hands and a very happy Eastwood left, finding it difficult to walk sedately.

"Those who lose dreaming are lost."

Australian Aboriginal Proverb

Chapter 7

A MAN TO MATCH THE MOUNTAINS

With the potential backing of Seymour and the encouragement of Sinclair, John Eastwood plunged eagerly into planning a new hydroelectric system. His usual caution and thrift gave way to hiring Morgan to help with the complete measurements and locations in the Sierra. When winter rains in the Valley gave way to clear April skies and warming temperatures, he set off with two laden mules and two horses to rendezvous with Morgan at Shaver Lake.

For five weeks they tramped the woods before Eastwood had enough information and could settle on an area forty miles long containing the waters from two tributaries of the North Fork San Joaquin River. The last morning in camp Eastwood packed his papers into a sealskin packet, then took a final look around the camp. Dogwoods below the towering Lodgepole pines were covered with white flowers against deep green leaves. A coyote call could be heard across the distance, bouncing off the hills and valleys and from below, the *oof oof oof* breath of a bear walking slowly and unsteadily as he shook off the remains of hibernation.

The forest was both inviting and somewhat intimidating with thick cover under densely branched trees. With the sun at bay, only dappled light broke through the canopy. Eastwood had begun his survey northwest of Shaver Lake, and now was about to end it near the same place. He was eager to get back to the office to finish his report, but he wanted to tarry just for the pure pleasure of it. Only the memory of his confrontation with Mill Creek kept him from throwing caution to the winds.

"Looks to me like you're not ready to head home down mountain," said Morgan.

Startled out of his concentration, Eastwood laughed at having his thoughts read so easily. "Got a load of business on my mind."

"You don't fool me, Eastwood. You got the look of a man rememberin'. Is it the crossin' where you lost your hat?"

Eastwood nodded but didn't speak. He pretended to watch a Flicker walk up and down the trunk of a sequoia before he found words. "I never forget it and now that I'm here again near where it happened, it somehow calls me. Can't help but wonder if I cheated death there for a purpose. I mean the water…the strong current…something about it makes me want to know more."

"Don't know much about what you're doin' but I know you want water for power. If you want more I can show you some you missed."

Eastwood had taken a broader route than needed simply because it was important to know as much as he could learn about the watershed emptying into the San Joaquin River. Although it was not necessary for the plans, he felt it added a great deal to his understanding of the mountains to learn how the waters were connected. Morgan was expected back at the mill this week but Eastwood had to ask.

"How far is it?"

"We can go and be back here by nightfall. Another day's trip and I'm back at the mill."

Eastwood grinned, "Sold!" he said, then turned to load a mule.

Morgan stopped him. "No need for that. We can go shank's mare with some food in our pockets. Let the animals rest today."

"What about my equipment?"

"Leave that to me." Morgan lifted the long leather case holding Eastwood's transit and then reached for the slide rule and ledgers. " Saw a place that'll do," he said motioning away from the camp…a good-sized holler log. Jist give the animals a long lead in that patch of grass at that glen yonder." He didn't wait for an answer.

* * * * * * * * * * *

The forest duff underfoot was deep and spongy. Centuries of leaves, needles and shredded bark left a thick carpet to muffle the sound of their steps. Above birds chattered like old biddies at teatime. Eastwood spotted scat on the trail and wondered aloud how far away the bear might be.

"Looks like grizzly to me," said Morgan. "I figure we'll meet it near the waters."

Eastwood stopped. "You mean we're heading right towards it?"

Morgan kept moving forward. "Mebbe. Likely fishing for salmon. They spawn about now and bears like 'em better'n people." Eastwood hurried to catch up, embarrassed to have been gulled into Morgan's humor.

Above the sounds of the forest a distant hum grew louder slowly until Eastwood was shouting to be heard over roaring waters unseen. He felt Morgan had to be mistaken. The deafening roar could only come from the San Joaquin River. When at last they broke through the trees, the scene was stunning! Eastwood stood in awe as waters rushed down from a precipitous drop above. "That's the biggest damn creek I have ever seen!" he exulted over the din.

He estimated the distance of the fall to be a thousand feet but could not see top nor bottom of it. Only the thunder told him it had power to create more electricity than even he had dreamed about producing.

Morgan pulled him back from the edge. "That's why I call it Big Creek, but it only happens like this in spring," he shouted.

Eastwood moved away, wanting a better look, but Morgan again forced him back, then pointed down mountain. At the edge of the water less than a three hundred yards away, a grizzly waited for salmon spawning up the near-vertical stream.

"One who fears failure limits his activities. Failure is only the opportunity to intelligently begin again."

Henry Ford

Chapter 8

ECONOMIC FREEFALL — 1896

True to his word, Seymour's brother-in-law Julius Howells convinced the Municipal Investment Company of Chicago to provide bond for the new venture. The project became the San Joaquin Electric Company with Seymour as president and Eastwood as chief engineer vice president.

The project had a rocky start that later would seem like an omen. Federal authorities came to Seymour's office and arrested him for starting the project before it had been approved. He was released from custody when he showed proof he had applied for the permit and acted in good faith when it was verified that he had verbal approval from the US Forest Service.

For $200,000 the company had a powerhouse with the latest equipment from General Electric Company, seven miles of flumes and ditches for water to travel to the small lake behind a twenty-foot high earthen embankment.

Along the way it also paid for a four mile dirt road from Auberry carved out of the wilderness using a small steam-driven shovel plus a team of mules to pull road scrapers popularly called "fresnos" after the town where they first appeared. A massive wooden trestle bridge was built over the San Joaquin River, strong enough to accommodate the delivery of large generators and other powerhouse equipment. The building material was harvested in the mountains, with rock coming from a quarry and wood from the mill. A crew from General Electric strung the transmission lines and installed the electrical equipment but all other work was done by cowboys, mill hands and drifters, many having worked with Eastwood on the Shaver Lake flume.

On April 14, 1896 at the Fresno Courthouse, Ella Eastwood pressed a button nervously, signaling her husband to open the valve. As the access opened, water dropped 1,400 feet heading into the powerhouse where it reached an unprecedented pressure of 609 pounds per square inch, to spin three Pelton wheels which moved corresponding generators. Transformers raised the electrical pressure from 700 to 11,000 volts sending electricity to the Valley. One hundred eighty-eight microseconds later, electric lamps in the courthouse sprang to life from electricity produced thirty-five miles away.

Spectators and reporters were astounded by the fact that power to light Fresno could come so fast from so far. Many surmised that electricity was like the water that produced it, flowing incredibly fast through a small wire. One person wondered if the water was still usable when they took the electricity out of it. Another observed that they were seeing a whole lot of candlepower.

When he arrived home two weeks later, Eastwood was elated at the success of the plant. He had not only conquered the Tollhouse grade, but also designed and bossed the construction of the world's first hydroelectric project of such magnitude, attracting worldwide attention. The *Journal of Electricity* in San Francisco featured the San Joaquin Electric Company (SJEC) in two major articles, and New York's *Electrical World* praised it lavishly, as did *Electrical Review* in London, England.

Power from the Sierra ran irrigation pumps, a flourmill and the Fresno Agricultural Works, replacing steam generators as Eastwood had predicted. It also ran part of the city's streetlights. That did not go over well with the Fresno Gas and Electric Company because it infringed on their previous monopoly with municipal outdoor lamps. Eastwood was too elated to give it much thought, but he would soon learn that to solicit business in established venues can be a costly error in judgment.

As it published more and more of the latest technology for professionals, the *Journal of Electricity* quickly became the hub for news of successful practitioners in the field, including Eastwood. The success of

SJEC spawned a boom interest for the production of electricity, spreading like wildfire in the west. German technology at the time was shortchanged by a strong new government bent toward military empire-building. In that country's creative engineering void American engineers took their work and advanced it in power plants that made money for investors, not conquest. With so much professional and financial interest coming from all directions, the journal successfully spearheaded the idea of a Pacific Coast Electrical Transmission Association (PCETA).

August 17th of 1897 found Eastwood presenting a paper at the first convention of PCETA in Santa Cruz, speaking to the particular issues that his company faced such as the development of transmission line poles. At the meeting Seymour was elected to the first board of directors, making the event memorable for both of them. When Eastwood arrived home following the meeting, some of the air left his balloon of excitement. There was a problem at the powerhouse.

An excess of sawdust coming from upstream was fouling the Pelton wheels. It was impossible to know exactly where it was coming from without tramping the thousands of miles of wilderness that encompassed the watershed into the plant. The amount of contamination in the water was far more than would have been expected from logging in the area, and it was a mystery how such great quantities caame into the powerhouse. However, before any decision could be made to investigate and remedy the situation, enough rain fell to wash the problem downstream. Ella was not as relieved as her husband.

"I've heard things in town, John, and they're not kindly. Some say Fresno Gas and Electric did it deliberately since you took business away from them."

"What's a few lights to them? They're so poorly run I don't know how they stay in business. They have a coal-fired generator and when it gets too expensive to run, they shut it down. No electricity, no lights. Don't you think paying customers deserve a constant supply?"

"That's not why I brought it up. You say the sawdust problem is gone because the rains returned but I spoke to Sweet Face..."

"Not again!" he interrupted. Eastwood knew his wife could make a friend out of any woman, but felt Ella put an inordinate amount of trust in the word of a Miwok woman. Even though she was part of a shaman family, the science in him was far too exacting to accept the pronouncements of an aborigine even though the tribe had well trained astrologers. He was scornful of a tribe that would not fight when chased out of the Sierra for the benefit of gold miners by the Mariposa Brigade. *If they are so well educated in their own ways, why didn't they defend themselves,* he thought, but Ella gave him no time for rebuttal.

"Yes, again, and this time you listen to me. Her family knows a lot more about weather than we do and she said there are few acorns this year. That means not much rain this winter. What will you do the next time the sawdust comes floating down and there's nothing to wash it away?"

"Ella, we have water storage behind the dam. Nothing's going to happen and there's no way Sweet Face can convince me that the acorns dropped by trees this year is an omen for the next." He left the house quickly, giving her no chance to reply because there was enough truth in what she said to give him pause.

Even though Howells was able to get the money to build, a major depression lingered throughout the country. Venture capital was hard to find and when they received confirmation of an amount less than they sought, the offer was accepted.

The fledgling company had to cut corners in the project. With General Electric extolling the virtues of their latest generators and no way to save money on the penstocks (heavy duty piping), the only option was to reduce the size of the dam. Instead of one fifty feet high, Eastwood had to settle for one at only twenty feet. That meant less than half the amount of water he had expected could be impounded. Sinclair suggested as an alternative they build up business, then add another dam further upstream when they could afford to do it themselves. Eastwood agreed and already had a place picked out at Crane Flat. He put any misgivings aside about competition causing trouble and hitched his horse to the buggy then headed for the company office.

Ella's electric lamps in the house had caused a minor stampede with other wives to have their homes wired. The same frugal rates the company charged for commercial customers were also the impetus for homes—thirty cents a month to light lamps in a sitting room, twenty-five for kitchens, dining rooms, and halls. Parlor, pantry and barn lamps cost fifteen cents a month with bedrooms, baths and cellars costing ten cents. Within a short time after the plant went on line, the number of customers increased enough to warrant upgrading the equipment at the powerhouse. The transmission of electricity was increased to 16,000 volts to permit it to reach the H.G. Lacey Company in Hanford thirty miles south of Fresno. On the surface, Eastwood's company appeared to be solidly based, but the rapid success coupled with a natural calamity and competitive dirty tricks combined to doom it to failure.

With the numbers of new hookups increasing every day, plans for the new dam assumed additional importance as the Miwok prediction became abundantly clear. By the spring of 1899 the entire state was in the grip of a major drought. Not only was there little rainfall, water into the holding area above the powerhouse abruptly dropped to a trickle. Eastwood knew that if it were the lack of rain, the stream would have had a gradual decline. He set out to search for the reason upstream from the powerhouse and had to travel no further than the Shaver Lake Mill for the answer.

"It's the Goode Ranch," said Buntline. "Cowboys who usually work there were here looking for jobs and they said the owners were taking water from the North Fork. Told me they didn't know why because there was more than enough for the cattle since they cut the herd way back, but they got the idea there was a kind of deal with somebody in the Valley. Can't imagine why."

"I know why," said Eastwood. "I'd give my last dollar betting it's Fresno Gas & Electric Company trying to drive us out of business. Can't make it on their own and they want us out of the picture. Nobody wants gas lights when they can have electric ones."

Buntline rubbed the back of his neck as if searching for words. He looked Eastwood directly in the eye. "I was at city hall three weeks ago. Had to find out about new rules for building a warehouse at the mill in Sanger. We've got to get those stacks of raisin box lumber under cover so we can..."

Eastwood stared intently at Buntline. "What happened at the city office?"

"I...ah...was at the counter...heard somebody talking from an office nearby...asking how long they were supposed to delay payments."

"Damn! I knew it! The city owes my company a lot of money but they keep saying the treasury's too low to make the payments. They pay the gas company even though we charge them less for better service."

"That may be the reason. I think you made an enemy in town and he has powerful connections. If it's any consolation, the voice I heard was defending you so there's still a friend at city hall."

"I know who it must be, but he's not one of the higher-ups. I saw him when we had a meeting with the mayor to discuss how to help the city through this money crisis. The gas company man was there and he wanted to contract for lights only on nights without a moon. Said it could save the city a lot of money. Of course it helps the gas company because they cut their expenses that way."

"But your electricity is free…"

Eastwood stopped him with a raised hand. "Only after paying our people to run it and we still have large bond payments, too. When that *free* water is diverted before it gets to us, we have nothing. Right now we can send our customers electricity only half the time. You must have the same concerns with the flume."

"Would have if you hadn't done such a good job. Sure glad you talked us into the larger dam or we'd be in the same boat."

The lesson was not lost on Eastwood. He returned to the Valley intending to give the new dam his total attention but by August the SJEC could not make its bond payment. The company went into receivership. Bondholders asked both Eastwood and Seymour to remain on the job despite the fact they lost all their investment in the company. The visionary who dreamed up the project, tramped the wilds to plan it and then found the backing to do it was reduced to caretaker status in the company he helped to found.

As the drought deepened for three more years, the bondholders in Chicago decided the dam had to be built if they were to see any of their investment again. They put the money together to do the project and even though they used his design, Eastwood was not asked to oversee the construction. The new dam destined to become Bass Lake was the responsibility of Seymour's relative Howells, an engineer with little experience.

It was no consolation to Eastwood that Howells nearly botched the new dam completely by not noticing an outlet pipe was defective. Internal water erosion nearly caused the half-finished gravity dam to collapse completely, and the bondholders had to be satisfied with a smaller structure, one thirty feet lower than planned.

With the company on the road to being somewhat solvent, the assets and water rights were immediately sold to William Kerckhoff and Allan Balch of Los Angeles.

The failure left a lasting impression on Eastwood. He had survived

1903 Eastwood survey party crossing Big Creek. John Eastwood on the
upstream rope.
Photo Courtesy of DC Jackson/damhistory.com and Charles Allan Whitney

the economic disaster of the stock manipulation by irrigation investors
only to fall victim to another financial fiasco that removed him from his
own project. His vision, hard work, personal investment and reputation were tied up in SJEC. That it was gone was a very bitter pill but he
accepted his lot and moved past it by concentrating on another grander
project in the mountains.

He would never shortchange the need for water storage again. The
Sierra had the water as well as places where it could be stored. It was a
simple equation: a larger dam equals more power. The dam was key and
he turned his attention to designing one able to hold vast quantities of
water, never forgetting the problem of financing. He planned for it to
work with exceptional economy of material for construction, inventing
a multiple arch dam made of thin-shelled reinforced concrete.

He took the idea of a traditional gravity dam constructed of a single
large scallop with the top of the arch upstream and instead designed one
with a series of scallops. The engineering of one arch needs to take into

consideration the enormous water pressing against it from upstream. The arch shape strengthens the dam as the weight of water presses against it, just as the arch in the design of bridge foundations is able to hold up under much more weight than those built of simple trestles.

With the multiple arch design, Eastwood could see that instead of having to build one enormously thick and strong wall to hold up the water as it pressed against a single arch, a series of arches with buttresses between each of them across the chasm would distribute the pressure along the entire structure. The result would be a dam as strong as a single massive arch with the added benefit that the material necessary to do the job would be reduced to nearly half that of the traditional construction.

His optimism returned, sending Eastwood back to the Sierra to find the perfect spot to build it.

"A person can grow only as much as his horizon allows."

John Powell

Chapter 9

TRIUMPH OF THE TROLLEY – 1900

Henry Huntington stood in the middle of the railroad tracks facing the setting sun. Uncle Collis had died leaving him a fifteen million dollar legacy, not to mention an extraordinary business sense. What the elder could not bequeath was his seat as chairman of the board of the Central Pacific Railroad Company. The glory days for HH in San Francisco were over without his mentor. Leland Stanford achieved revenge for having been ousted from that office by Collis.

Although HH enjoyed status equal to being Collis's heir apparent, he was no match for the collective sons of the remaining Big Four when they allied with Stanford. After the votes were counted, Stanford resumed his place at the head of the table and there was no succession for HH. If he couldn't have the chairmanship he would contribute nothing more. He broke with the rail company, selling his investment in it as well as all others he had in northern California. He was leaving for Los Angeles without his wife Mary Alice who chose to remain in the Bay Area. HH took his wits and one piece of fine art— Albert Bierstadt's "View of Donner Lake, California"—not to mention a very large amount of money.

He had commissioned Bierstadt's painting soon after arriving in

San Francisco to work for Collis. "I want a large oil of the panorama from the summit of Donner Pass looking toward Donner Lake high in the Sierra Nevada" he had told Bierstadt. "It will be a daily reminder that the first transcontinental railroad my uncle personally helped push through this country's tallest mountain range opened that hidden beauty for everyone."

Bierstadt found when he struggled to get to that lofty perch, it was also a tribute to the engineering ingenuity it took to run rails through territory that defied weather extremes at staggering elevations over 7,000 feet never previously conquered.

While he waited for his private car to get hooked onto the train to Los Angeles, HH thought about how he had burned his bridges in The City by the bay. The sun set on his years there and he was leaving without a look back, moving forward to make his mark in a new venue. The last rays of amber light hit the rails momentarily turning them into brilliant gold all the way to the vanishing point in the distance. It looked like a long, emphatic arrow directing HH to a new mother lode. In a flash the gold was gone but he felt the message was clear—his future lay in rails to the south. What he couldn't foresee was that it was also tied to electricity and John Eastwood.

* * * * * * * * * * *

HH established his residence in one of the rooms of the hotel suite on Bunker Hill. His life was immediately busy at the office he established on Broad Street, and any time he felt a need to get away from it, visited newfound friends, the George Pattons who lived in the hills outside the city. With millions in the bank and an eagerness to put it to work, HH directed his attention to the Pasadena and Los Angeles Railway Company. His investment in the five-year old company was about to vanish because it did not have enough cash to pay bondholders.

The lines of the railway ran from Los Angeles downtown to Pasadena, and HH felt there was a good market for the company if it were managed correctly. He bought out other investors and reincorporated it as Pacific Electric Railway Company, extending the line to Long Beach by mid 1902. The new company competed with Southern Pacific Railway, a vestige of his former San Francisco associates and it was eminently pleasing to plunge into the work of making his own company profitable at the expense of his former San Francisco cohorts.

He ordered all the old electric lines and cables be scrapped, replacing them with new rails and ties, as well as every car for the entire line. Then he extended railway lines to each nearby city he felt would provide riders. To ensure people would not confuse his cars with any other, he had them painted red for the interurban runs and yellow for those within Los Angeles.

The new line proved to be very popular and HH soon realized that to run it required nearly all available electricity in the city. He had invested in Kerckhoff and Balch's San Gabriel Electric Company in 1898, established to sell power to the city of Los Angeles from a small hydroelectric plant in San Gabriel Canyon near the city of Azusa. Remembering his uncle's admonition to keep control of all aspects of the business, he partnered with Kerckhoff and Balch again in 1902 reorganizing the small plant as Pacific Light & Power Company. The new venture manufactured electricity to run HH's rail and trolley lines.

Two years after the plant began to function, the city fathers, alarmed at the vast numbers of electric, telephone and telegraph lines overhead passed an ordinance requiring all be installed underground.

"The law is very specific," complained engineer Balch to his partner Kerckhoff. "It has to be done in tubes made of grooved two-inch by twelve-inch planks—Oregon pine, no less. It even goes on to say the planks must be routed out with half circles for the cables to lie in and the two wooden halves held together with spikes. Did you ever hear of such an outrageous expense?" It was one that nearly drove their San Gabriel Electric Company under.

Balch may have disliked the incipient regulation but Kerckhoff was more concerned about the competition.

"We can handle that, but now the city's talking about building their own utility. They must think we are all millionaires!" said Kerchhoff.

"We're in a strange business, my friend. Couple years ago electricity was a novelty and now the Times is saying electricity, along with piped water and sewage to every home is necessity, not luxury. Says they think the people's business should be run by the people, but that means elected politicians. Nobody stops to think it has to be profitable and with taxes a bottomless pit, they don't have to work the way we do."

The concerns in LA differed from Fresno. While Eastwood was being told his hydroelectric plant might be a fad in the Valley, HH was in the middle of an entirely different battle for his electricity and transportation assets. Not only was the technology not a passing fancy, it had already moved into a public outcry for more.

When the pace of business forced him to seek peace and quiet, HH turned to the Patton home in the area outside the bustling city where he retreated. He was attracted to the family with a rich military history and loved that their home had a clear view to the ocean above the Los Angeles basin for more than twenty miles. At night electric lamps sparkled in small clusters as far as the eye could see. It was a view fit for a king, or a business magnate.

When the San Marino Ranch next door became available in 1903, HH purchased it without hesitation. His new manor home would be on land where an occasional bear or mountain lion still roamed. HH spent more and more time at the small ranch house and when Collis's widow Arabella came to visit she found San Marino to her liking. The comparison between the two women in his life made HH blink. His estrangement from Mary Alice was reaching the point of no return and Arabella was becoming a very influential part of his life.

Widely traveled, Arabella spent a great deal of her time in Europe. She loved the life of aristocracy there and had begun to collect valuable objects of art. Her running commentaries about the history of the previous two centuries was exciting, especially when she spoke of ancient books. HH had been a book lover since he was a boy, eagerly absorbing his mother's avid interest in reading. As a girl herself, she had begged her own father to give her an advanced education but he refused. Undaunted, HH's mother read every book in his library from scientific texts to antiquities. HH acquired the same thirst and any time he was able, bought books to fill his own library. He had filled the walls of his house in San Francisco with them and he continued to buy them for the Los Angeles home—that in addition to the residence he maintained in New York. Huntington's life was changing dramatically as he moved closer to Arabella. He made the move to divorce Mary Alice.

The demands of planning and construction brought him into the company of his neighbors more and more often, and George Patton, Jr., destined to become his family's first Army General, became as close to him as HH had been with Collis. The families were so compatible the construction included a private access built between the two homes.

George Jr. left for Virginia Military Institute in 1903 after years of home schooling and a few terms at a local private academy. On a bright day in spring HH sat with his neighbors on the Patton terrace.

"VMI is a step on young George's way to West Point," observed his father.

"We'll all miss him but he's continuing a fine military commitment to the country. He told me he was following his Confederate Army colonel grandfather who also graduated from VMI and died in battle during the American Civil War."

George Patton Sr. sipped his coffee before answering. "I didn't follow the same military path," he said cautiously. "I chose law instead and served for a while as the Los Angeles District Attorney. Ran for the US Senate but didn't get elected. The campaigning was not something I'd like to repeat. In the end it became important to run the ranch instead. My wife inherited it and I've made a lot of improvements."

"George Jr. told me you're very proud of the family's military heritage. You read the *Illiad* and the *Odyssey* aloud to him when he was five. Also said you made sure he was adept at horsemanship, marksmanship and military history, and had a soldier's uniform custom made for him."

"We tried to give him room to make his own choice. The boy was showered with both comfort and rigor. We hope he chose well."

HH applauded the Patton family's reverence for army service and began to assume an undeniable military posture himself, using an unusual strategic planning to achieve his business goals. He honed to perfection a way of creating a market by extending his trolley lines to remote areas where he had already purchased large tracts of land. The availability of transportation made the property value soar as people snapped up lots and began to build. A decade earlier when HH had arrived in San Francisco to work for his uncle, the population of Los Angeles was 11,000. With the railroad and electric lights in town that number soared to over 100,000 by 1900. In twenty more years it would top a half million.

Technology continued to explode and by 1902, electricity came into the city from 127 miles away. Not only was the length of transmission lines extended, the voltage was increased. With greater power, mules on the Bunker Hill trolley line became unnecessary. Needed to pull the trolleys up steep hills to augment the weak pressure of electricity, the animals rode back down on a special platform built at the rear of each car.

HH continued to invest in oceanfront property and in an effort to lure people to buy lots in Redondo Beach he hired a young Hawaiian-Irishman to surf in view of the hotel there. The idea was unheard of on the mainland and people came from miles away to see George Freeth entertain guests twice a day by "walking on water." Freeth and his customized surfboard were a sensation at the hotel for eight years. He remained until his untimely death in the flu epidemic of 1919.

In spite of ever increasing power generation capacity by small companies, public use outstripped it each year. The cost to produce electricity by steam generator was four cents a kilowatt-hour. For hydropower it was one-tenth of a cent, driving HH to meet John Eastwood at Big Creek.

"Thoughts, rest your wings. Here is a hollow of silence, a nest of stillness, in which to hatch your dreams."

—

Spinoza

Chapter 10

STARTING OVER — 1900

Eastwood left the dust of defeat on the trail along the San Joaquin River in early April. He washed it from his soul in the icy snow melt but was careful not to challenge the swift moving waters. For weeks he tramped the hills, dales and mountain passes from China Bar, Little Jackass, and Hells Half Acre to The Thumb above 10,000 feet. Then he moved along the high ridges in a southerly direction mapping the entire watershed of the San Joaquin. He attempted to reach Mount Morgan hoping to stand there and salute his Cornish friend with the same name, but snows still lay deep in the upper meadows.

From the lofty heights he could see that most of the river slopes ran in a gradual northerly direction before arching west and heading southwest to the Valley. The great roundabout path was due to the intrusion of Kaiser Ridge. One huge portion of the watershed diverted to the backside of Kaiser Ridge and Mount Tom where water flowed east before running south to join the Kings River. The recent drought continued to bother him. While he was unable to figure a way to use that backside of the watershed, he made copious notes in case he found a way to make it possible.

For two months he scoured the mountains measuring without an assistant to set the marker pole. He had left Ella with more than enough money. However, his recent financial setback weighed heavily on his mind, leaving him to scurry across the expanse as his own chainman to set the pole then trek back to the transit to take measurements, then return to retrieve the pole. It was tedious but completely absorbing. The depression of the recent loss retreated and exhilaration took its place.

Eastwood returned by way of Big Creek, this time taking the high trail and making copious notes about the waterway from above. He found sites for water storage that would use the same water three times to make electricity on its way down mountain. He calculated the head height from which the water would fall to powerhouses each more astounding than the other—1500 feet, 1900 feet and 2100 feet. There was no way he could find the money to do the project, but he wrote all the information into his ledgers with hope for the future.

The main focus of the trip for him was to survey for a power plant at Mammoth Pool west of Kaiser Ridge around China Bar. He measured that head height at 1700 feet and located the planned powerhouse below the natural impoundment of water in Mammoth Pool.

With a traditional gravity dam to enlarge the natural pond, the enhanced water storage would easily allow the plant to function during another prolonged drought. Plans for his thin shell multiple arch dam took a back seat to economy because the common gravity dam could be accomplished by simply dynamiting the escarpment above the edge of the pool. The falling scree would drop into a perfect cleft in the land producing an instant barrier to the moving water.

The economic enticement for investors was that Eastwood planned to send power two hundred miles to San Francisco. Several of the Fresno area men who had lost money in the failure of the San Joaquin Electric Company still believed in him and were willing to back the new venture. One of them sent his son to rendezvous with him at China Bar to assist in the final measurements along with a photographer to help verify the locations of water rights.

When he returned to the Valley, Eastwood's plans jelled and included a 20-mile tunnel bored through solid granite. He wanted to ensure the plant would function year-round and not be stopped by deep winter ice blocking the water flow. The plan was thorough and it was massive. The investors did not challenge Eastwood's calculations, nor his vision. However, they would not provide the financial backing because they felt the plant would produce *too much* electricity without the market to purchase it.

Still confident it was a viable project, Eastwood enlisted the support of his friend H.H. Sinclair who came to Fresno to review the plans. Now vice president and general manager of power development for the Edison Electric Company in Los Angeles, he concurred with the investors.

"John. I think this time you have to let the investors lead the way. It is a doubtful project for the time."

It was enormously difficult for Eastwood to hear his friend say his project was not a good one. With no one willing to risk putting up money for it, he was resigned to defeat once again. He retained the water rights and stored the plans, then went back to designing small engineering projects in the region.

* * * * * * * * * *

In the summer of 1902 Eastwood attended the second convention of the Pacific Light and Power Transmission Association in San Francisco. Again he delivered a scholarly paper to the group on hydroelectric power and the possibility of building the Big Creek project. The idea of so much power produced so far away for use in San Francisco was met with suspicion and scorn. Some professionals said it was far too visionary for a region that required the most practical applications of engineering.

In addition, they pointed out that market demand for electricity and planned projects was growing so rapidly, technology threatened to outstrip the ability of private capital to meet it. The railroads had government subsidy, but it came at a time of great upheaval in the country during the Civil War which contributed to the political will in Congress to fund it and keep the western regions from joining the South in their rebellion. There was no such urgency at the turn of the century even though the economy was recovering. Despite the poor climate for interest at the biennial convention of the electrical transmission association, Big Creek stirred the imagination of R.S. Masson, an electrical engineer who had previously worked for HH's streetcar company in the city.

San Francisco was not experiencing the same exponential growth as Los Angeles, but the advent of electric lights and horseless carriages was making a major impact. Masson approached Eastwood asking if he had actual plans for hydropower ready to discuss.

After his most recent failures, he was not eager to fall into another trap, but cautiously outlined details about Big Creek construction and capacity. Masson's eager response was startling after all the turndowns, but Eastwood remained suspicious.

"I know two men who have access to a big investor," said Masson. "I know the investor myself, although not well...more by reputation."

Eastwood tried not to be too eagerly responsive, but his heart stirred at the possibility. "I live in Fresno. There's no one in my area with the wherewithal to put up the money. Where is this investor?"

"Not far from Fresno. In fact two of his associates are here at the convention. Is there a ten percent finder's fee if you meet and make a deal?"

Stifling a smile, Eastwood nodded, thinking to himself, *ten percent of nothing is nothing.* "Yes, but it can't be in cash and the project will take time to build. What would you base your share on? I doubt there is a salary involved and I can't spare any money to invest myself."

"We decide that when the time comes, and I'm quite sure it will. After all, a man's word is still his bond."

* * * * * * * * * * *

Even though he realized that the men to whom he was introduced were already a sad part of his own life, Eastwood did not hesitate to speak with them. Kerckhoff and Balch may have purchased his company but that first big dream lived on, reorganized as the San Joaquin Power Company. These two men were not the ones who had pressured him out of his own company and they certainly had nothing to do with the reasons the company failed. The potential investors agreed with Eastwood about hydroelectric power in the Sierra: the need for Big Creek was a foregone conclusion.

Eastwood did not wait for the end of the convention, but took the next train to Sacramento and then a stagecoach home. With the two men taking the idea of Big Creek to Henry Huntington, Eastwood was racing to reorganize his files, complete the proposal and be ready when the call came to consummate the deal. The gentleman's agreement required that he complete all the specifications for water storage, locations of powerhouses, routes of penstock, tunnels, tramlines and access roads as well as electrical equipment. In return he was to receive ten percent of the company's stock plus $12 a day for office work and $15 per day for field study in the mountains. Masson settled for ten percent of Eastwood's stock and would wait for it to mature before asking for payment.

The contract to build the Big Creek Project in the Sierra was signed a month after the convention but only the signature of Balch appeared on the document. In essence the agreement assigned Eastwood as an agent for the development of the project and all money to be raised was the responsibility of "Balch, et al," meaning Kerckhoff and HH. Ninety percent of the stock would remain in those hands. Masson's commission was written into the agreement as an obligation for ten percent of Eastwood's shares.

The agreement did not commit to building the project but rather to the partnership investigating the possibility of it. To Eastwood it was the end of the rainbow and he immersed himself in the work immediately. Within two months after traveling more than three thousand miles on horse and by stagecoach to do the job, he had completed all the necessary investigation and measurements. This time he had to include application for permits from the newly established US National Forest Service since most of the area in the project was now public land.

Elated, he wrote Balch that the "reconnaissances, surveys and water appropriations have broadened the scope of the scheme to such an extent that it now includes the whole of the commercially available waters of the San Joaquin River, all of which can be condensed in one system in the Big Creek Basin."

Incredibly, after having the much smaller project at Mammoth Pool rejected by investors as too grand, Eastwood now had one in mind that would dwarf even that. Unknown to him it would take five months after signing the contract for Kerckoff and Balch to find the right time late in the year and enough courage to present the idea to HH. Their business relationship as partners in the Pacific Light & Power Company in the San Gabriel Mountains was only a few months old. The company was established specifically to provide electricity to HH's trolley system and at the rate the lines were being extended, Kerckhoff knew it would not take long for the young company's output to be surpassed by demand. By December it was clear that if trolley use continued to grow as it had for the previous year, available electricity would not be enough to keep it running.

Kerckhoff relied on his perception that HH was adamant about controlling every possible facet of his businesses. Electricity, at the time, was as wild as oil exploration would soon become. Business and attendant dealings were upgraded and ad libbed on a daily basis. In the Los Angeles region the saga of the Walter S. Wright Electric Company set a new standard for the time because of the creativity and tenacity with which he got his company up and running.

Walter Wright got together with electrical engineers to enter the market for streetlights in the newly dredged deep-water port of San Pedro west of Los Angeles. However, the city failed to secure a grant necessary for financial support from Washington to do the job. Wright and his engineers turned to Los Angeles where in four years since electric lights were introduced, the population had grown from just over 11,000 to well over 100,000.

Wright put up a power generation plant on the outskirts of the city with one eighty horsepower steam engine running one boiler and one generator but no customers. When he discovered the city had a vacated franchise already available, he jumped at the chance to enter the market. The major drawback was that the franchise had only two weeks left to run and in that amount of time Wright would have to put up three and a half miles of transmission and distribution lines.

With a total of eight employees including himself, he pressed every man into service. They ran lines on existing poles of other companies, along the roofs of buildings and in some cases draped them over saw-horses. The work was completed with five minutes to spare. The technology of the times was squeezed into the fabric of life. Maintenance men walked the lines for repair by simply pushing a wheelbarrow full of tools and equipment. A thick web of wires strung from multiple poles spread through the city covering every street, crossroad and alley with electric lines, fire alarm lines, railroad signals, telephone lines, arc lights and trolley power lines—all of them using the same right of way. Dozens of small companies vied for customers on the same streets, none of them with standard connections or technology. The most valued asset of each company was a list of customers.

By the time the twentieth century was two years old, the Los Angeles Edison Electric Company was a $10 million business and electricity was deemed a necessity by the public. HH could see that it was not going the way of steam and portable power. Electricity was here to stay. He joined Kerckhoff and Balch to investigate the construction of Big Creek.

"Strength does not come from physical capacity. It comes from an indomitable will."

Gandhi

Chapter 11

WATER AND ELECTRICITY POLITICS – 1902

J. Seymour sat stiffly in a high back chair at one corner of the Eastwood parlor. Ella poured two cups of coffee, setting them on the table between him and her husband. Both men smiled thanks but said nothing until she left the room and closed the door. Then Seymour exploded.

"John, when you told me about Kerckhoff and Balch, you never mentioned Henry Huntington! Have you taken leave of your senses?"

Eastwood sipped from his cup before answering. "He's willing to take a chance with Big Creek and I doubt he would brook failure," he answered.

"Damn it, don't you know the man's reputation?"

"If you mean his success in Los Angeles with trolleys and developing outlying areas of the city, then yes, I do know about him."

"Don't be naïve. He's been taught at the knee of a master—Collis Huntington. I heard about it from those who know him and they tell me he was a ruthless crocodile. Henry learned everything he knows about money from him. He even paints his town trolleys the same yellow his uncle used on every one of his railroad stations. You're a lamb going to slaughter!"

Eastwood pondered his friend's outburst. In the silence a large clock on the opposite side of the room ticked like a time bomb. He was not interested in making a fortune from Big Creek. His only expectation was a comfortable return for his work and recognition for his personal contribution to engineering. Huntington could make all the money he wanted, it mattered little.

"You're my friend and I appreciate your counsel, but there's no way anyone else is going to bankroll so large a project. When I designed Mammoth Pool everyone said it was too big and this one is far and away larger. You said at the time there wasn't a market for so much electricity and this time it'll go to San Francisco *and* Los Angeles. Can't imagine there's not enough of a market there."

"John, electric use has doubled every year since it's been available. Can't you just work the project into sections and plan to build it as the market in the Valley grows? It's a much safer way to go and…"

"No. I'm thoroughly committed to this as it stands especially since I found a way to tap into the Kings River watershed of the North Fork behind Kaiser Ridge."

Seymour straightened in his chair. "That's impossible. There's no way you can get that water to China Bar."

Eastwood smiled. It was a moment to savor and he let it ride for a few seconds before revealing his secret. "It's a tunnel. About 13.5 miles long through Kaiser Ridge."

Seymour appeared to be slow to absorb the idea, but Eastwood could see the gradual realization on his face of what it meant. "That mountain is solid granite."

"Right, and I plan a tube fifteen feet by fifteen feet right through it."

"With men hand drilling holes for dynamite and carrying out all the scree…"

Now oblivious to anything but his own enthusiasm, Eastwood was euphoric. "Yes! That's exactly how it will happen."

Seymour leaned forward in his chair. "Do you have any idea the amount of risk you're taking? Think this through before you sign anything because you've got a fine reputation in this area. If you fail with Huntington, word will spread like wildfire."

The idea of another failure was sobering but Eastwood had not ignored it and came to the same decision—sign with Huntington. He reached into the inside pocket of his jacket, pulled out a folded paper and began to speak slowly. "There are no guarantees of any kind for new

ideas. When the transcontinental railroad opened up, no one could foresee that the end of the war between the North and the South would send
thousands of men roaming the countryside looking for work. There was
no way anyone could have predicted all the train robberies with the likes
of Quantrell's raiders, the James brothers and the Hole in the Wall Gang.
It took the telegraph, Pinkerton's and Wells Fargo to put an end to that.

"I don't claim to know everything that could come from Big Creek
but I keep this to remind me." He opened a small clipping. "I cut it out
of a magazine last year and it's a quote from Wilbur Wright who's trying
to build a flying machine with his brother back east:

*"If you are looking for perfect safety, you will do well to sit on a
fence and watch the birds, but if you really wish to learn to fly, you must
mount a machine and become acquainted with its tricks by actual trial."*

"John, do you really think two tinkerers who make bicycles can
make something weighing hundreds of pounds actually *fly*...even with a
gasoline engine?"

"Can't say as I do, but my mind's open. I promised myself Ella
wouldn't have to trim wicks and fill oil lamps five years ago, but I never
expected to see that vow come to pass so quickly."

Seymour took a last sip of his coffee and stood up. "I don't doubt
the times are changing but I think you're moving much too fast. Last
time I was in Leadville there was a sign in a saloon saying, *Don't shoot the
pianist, he's doing his damnedest.* That's still a measure of life in these
parts and there's nothing to lose if you wait to see what happens." He
jammed on his hat and headed for the door. "I'll see myself out."

* * * * * * * * * * *

On a trolley ride to the ocean, a young boy watched eagerly for the
Pacific to appear. A large billboard loomed on one side of the car an-
nouncing their arrival at Huntington Beach. "Mama!" the boy cried.
"You said the trolley belongs to Mr. Huntington. Does he own the beach,
too?"

The mother smiled indulgently, "Yes, dear." The boy pondered her
answer, then asked another question.

"You said at home he owned the trolley cars. Does he own the
hotel where we will stay tonight?" Again the mother said, "Yes, dear.".

One more question needed answering. "Mama, does Mr. Huntington own the ocean, too?"

* * * * * * * * * * *

On a pleasure outing Arabella arranged for a sunny day in May, HH watched as plumage from ostriches was harvested for the hat market. "Can't imagine how anyone could make money doing this," he grumped.

Arabella laughed and gently poked him with her parasol. "You would if you ever went shopping for a ladies hat, but I didn't bring you here just to watch the birds get undressed. Walk over this way and tell me what you think of the first plan I had drawn up for your gardens at San Marino."

HH struggled to find a way to tell her roses were not one of his favorite flowers. They seemed to be a woman's kind of garden, soft and prissy. Cactus was more of a man's garden—that and huge palm trees. "Why roses?" he finally asked.

"I knew you'd say that," she laughed with another playful poke of the parasol. "It's not just roses, it's history…knights, armor, castles, grand halls and the beginnings of great schools. There was even a War of the Roses, but I don't…"

It was his turn to chuckle. "You better put that umbrella up. You've gone daft with the sun."

"Look there," she commanded. "Tell me what you see." Ahead the Lincoln Park Ostrich Ranch house appeared before them, surrounded with formal gardens. "I purposely had you take the carriage on the back road so I could surprise you. When I see roses and smell their perfume I think of the medieval times when they bloomed in castle courtyards and witnessed the spurt in the growth of civilization. There's a story in each one of them…where they were cultivated, where they were cross-bred and how they came to travel the entire world. These flowers are history in a bud or a full-blown flower. Now tell me what you see."

"It appears I see there is a lot to learn from you and I can see a rose garden by my terrace when the house is built. Now how about that cactus garden?"

"Only if you tell me you see African history and its thorny road to progress."

* * * * * * * * * * *

HH was interested in the additional power Big Creek could provide in order to meet the needs of his rapidly expanding trolley network, but he was not sold on the idea of actually entering the electricity market itself. His interests drew him in other directions, particularly real estate. Some of his dealings were done by partnering with others for developments in the San Fernando Valley, Hollywood and the outskirts of

Los Angeles. Often it was with three local men: Isaias Hellman, founder of Farmers and Merchants Bank—the first in Los Angeles—and two early pioneers in the Los Angeles Times & Mirror newspapers, Harrison Gray Otis and Harry Chandler.

Despite his successes, all was not rosy for HH, although he did not recognize it at the time. Noting the astronomical success of private electric companies, plus the mayhem it sometimes induced with a multitude of duplication of service, city hall in Los Angeles began to move to initiate municipal utilities beginning with water and electricity.

As the population of Los Angeles grew exponentially, need for additional sources of water and power was a hot topic of conversation. For several years the city attempted to enter the market by building an electric plant, but the funds voted were not nearly enough to do it. Alternatively, the city looked to build a distribution system and buy power from H.H. Sinclair's Redlands Electric Light & Power Company, some twenty miles away.

The city constructed a steam generation plant but demand quickly outstripped its capability to produce. The Edison Company was contracted to serve the city but demand again was not met by available power.

In 1902, the city purchased a private water company and named it the Bureau of Water Supply. William Mullholland, an Irish immigrant with no formal training, was hired as chief engineer and manager of the new department. The competition between private and municipal resources picked up speed.

Mullholland immediately began to look northeast to the Owens Valley for both water and electricity. Companies like Edison were alarmed since they had to completely retrofit each of the smaller companies they had been purchasing in order to meet customer demand. That investment in upgrading prevented private companies from meeting any competition to their customer base once the city entered the market.

Other cities entered the race to produce power by putting pressure on private companies to extend street lamps to lightly populated areas of the city. If companies complied with the city's requirement, that capital expense reduced their capacity to compete. If they did not, the contract was voided. It was a free-for-all business atmosphere for HH at the time, and even though he sewed up the rights in a contract for Big Creek, he was slow to commit to getting it accomplished quickly.

"Change is the law of life. And those who look only to the past or the present are certain to miss the future."

John Fitzgerald Kennedy

Chapter 12

POLITICAL IMPACT FROM THE SOUTH – 1904

Eastwood's plan for Big Creek's initial stage was for three power-houses to be built in descending elevations below an enormous dam. Not only would he store more water than ever before, it would be used three times to produce electricity before heading to the Valley for use in farming, an economy of resources that had not been designed by anyone previously. His plans included traditional grav-ity dams but he was unsatisfied with that design at so high an elevation.

Economics pushed him to look at a different way to build a struc-ture sufficient to hold vast amounts of water and yet able to resist the elements that tend to be severe in winter. He was well aware that win-ter storms occur in *any* month of the year. He had to plan for the amount of material to be removed to reach solid rock for a foundation, and then accurately calculate the needed rock fill and concrete facing.

Eastwood knew granite was available near the site in good supply but he could not ignore the weathering proclivity that it shared with concrete. While seemingly impervious to the elements, granite forms tiny cracks when temperatures drop. As warm air begins to melt the snow in the Sierra, water trickles into the cracks and then freezes again at night. The pressure on the surface of the rock produces a *spalling* where thin slabs of granite flake off the mother stone. In addition, roots of young trees and shrubs spread over rocks seeking the moisture in those cracks, then remain there and grow, spreading the cracks and eventually causing chunks of granite to fall off. The result is the same—the rocks disintegrate as would concrete under the same weathering. While it is a cycle in the forest to benefit the biosystem, it could be the death knell for a man-made structure.

Eastwood returned to the mountains during the time he waited for action from his partners. On one such trip, he found that the peak overlooking the location where he hoped to place Powerhouse #1 was unnamed. In honor of his new benefactor, he named it Kerckhoff Dome. Eager to see the project become a reality, he drove himself hard—well past prudence—remaining late in the year to assess the backside of Kaiser Ridge. His enthusiasm could have cost his life if winter snows had been on time.

As if rewarded for his foolishness, he finally settled on a location above the Big Creek area where he first saw the powerful waterway. Over and over again he checked his figures, sometimes leaving his notes to lie unread for days before returning to them. He tried to cultivate a fresh approach to the plan each time he looked at it to ensure he missed nothing. If the new design were to make the impact he expected, everything had to be perfectly planned. It was imperative that nothing be left to chance.

For a year nothing was done to begin construction and Eastwood turned to small projects as he waited for the go-ahead on Big Creek. At the same time HH consolidated his position in the electricity market by buying out all the local investors in Eastwood's failed Mammoth Power Company. He reasoned that if it were to be a part of Big Creek it was necessary for him to control it. Ominously for Eastwood, whereas most of the investors had lived in the Fresno/Hanford area, they now resided in Los Angeles. Of all the partners remaining, only Eastwood lived away from the big city. While he retained a small financial interest in the non-functioning business, he knew that HH now controlled the water rights as well as the San Joaquin Power Company—those rights he had worked so hard to win. HH had pocketed the keys to Big Creek and both of Eastwood's previous projects. J.J. Seymour's words about the power of businessmen began to nag him.

Before he could worry himself too much, Eastwood turned to a variety of small projects in the Valley area, designing minor irrigation dams and bridges. He kept his mind busy and only in the moments before sleep overtook him did he return to his Big Creek concerns. His remedy was to put in longer hours, some days to the point of exhaustion. Body and mind flagged but his dedication to Big Creek never wavered and when word came from the US Forest Service that his permits were approved, Eastwood thought his worries were over.

However, his joy faded to caution when the newspaper reported the agency would be transferred to the US Department of Agriculture. While the transfer of responsibility was not a problem, Gifford Pinchot, who headed the agency, created one for the Big Creek project.

In what was viewed as a blatant attempt to curry support of President Teddy Roosevelt, Pinchot used his power over the forestlands to extract higher fees for licensing hydroelectric projects and the rights of way for the transmission of electricity. The most fearsome threat for Eastwood was that Pinchot would not agree to long-term contracts, reserving the right to summarily end agreements. That meant permits could be revoked at will. Pinchot's will.

Eastwood was not the only one to feel caution. The news cast a pall on the recruitment of investor money and since HH could not run the project by himself, it was shelved for the time being. Elated the project was not dropped entirely, Eastwood persuaded himself it would yet become a reality. He turned again to engineering business as usual until the unstable political climate calmed.

* * * * * * * * * * *

At home in his new base of operations, HH had his hands full. The active progressive movement had spawned a number of union organizations and his Los Angeles Railway was struck by a labor walkout.

"Any employee of mine who joins the union is out of a job!" he growled to Chandler. "I'll just hire new ones and cut schedules...show them bastards!"

The result was that cars were crammed full of riders trying to get to work or back home again. HH also cut crews to one on each car, leaving the driver to collect fares. The trolley service that had promoted eager buyers of outlying properties was now the target of public outrage.

Without realizing it, people everywhere had become utterly dependent on the trolley car system. They complained bitterly about the service or lack of it, but ultimately it was a question of use it or not. If the latter, it meant going back to horse and buggy, getting up earlier for a sixteen hour day of work and then another slow drive home. Few liveries remained in business and they were no longer located within convenient distances to homes throughout the city.

To complicate matters, the emergence of horseless carriages threatened at times to completely block streets. At busy commuter hours the only dependable way to get anywhere remained on the trolleys—stuffed with riders or not. A necessity had turned into a monster to which the public was now beholden.

In a small office on the outskirts of the city, HH's two partners in Big Creek were trying to make some sense of the rapid economic changes in the region. In a few years LA had skyrocked from a sleepy farm town to a city spawning a host of support groups all clamoring for a chance to make decisions in running it.

"You're an engineer," said Kerckhoff. "How do you make\sense of something like this? It's crazy because everything is new."

Balch shook his head. "It's like any problem. You've got to separate it out into smaller bites."

"But people know that HH controls the trolleys and if they don't like the way he runs it, it's back to a horse or shank's mare for them."

"That's not our problem. What worries me is if the city decides to go into the electric business we're out in the cold. Once they start to sell power, they can undercut us any day of the week because they don't have to show a profit. If HH doesn't settle the strike soon, it'll feed a public push for control by the people. At least a poorly functioning official can be voted out."

Kerckhoff was unconvinced. "HH predicted Los Angeles would never succeed in competition with the private companies because they can't take the ups and downs of a business but look what's happening all around us. Riverside and Anaheim are already running their own water and electricity systems. I hear from Pasadena there's a ballot issue coming up for them to do the same there."

"You're right about Riverside and Anaheim, but Pasadena's already negotiating with Edison to do theirs."

"You think they'll get the contract?"

"Dunno. I hear the city wants them to run lines into the outskirts of town."

"Not many paying customers there."

"Yeah. So guess who's going to pay for putting in those poles, lines and transformers, not to mention getting the right of way."

"So what do we do about Big Creek?"

"What *can* we do? City people don't have any experience. Hell, Mulholland was digging ditches just a few years ago while we were sending electricity to Fresno from the Sierra. Until we have a good reason to start construction, we sit it out, just like HH said we do. He's pulling all the strings."

* * * * * * * * * * *

With public pressure pushing it to have electric streetlights everywhere, Los Angeles elected to enter the market with a small electric plant specifically for that purpose. Their cost to produce electricity could not compete with the private Edison Company but the city reduced rates to compensate, running the plant at a deficit. The race to have the lowest rates reached the point that the city had to pass additional bonds to make up the difference.

When their Kern River hydroelectric project came online, the Edison Company was able to reduce the costs to their regular customers in other areas. City officials accused the company of manipulating the market by undercutting what they charged customers, and the company once vilified for high rates was now condemned for having lowered them. The city's position was to remain constant even to the point that it had to increase taxes to make up the difference for their small electric plant. At one point they attempted to increase revenues by extending their lines outside the city limits for new customers, something denied to private companies by state regulation since cities were exempt from the law.

The struggle continued to escalate but eventually was settled by an agreement between Los Angeles City and Edison. However, tensions remained like an elephant in the parlor and set the tone for adversarial relations between the private and municipal sectors for generations to come. The result was that public service was secondary to political infighting and led to one of the greatest debacles in state history.

By 1902 Los Angeles was nearly out of water. It passed a $2 million bond issue to find new sources and looked to private industry for a solution. The city purchased an existing company where one of the employees was William Mulholland, a self-trained man who signed on as chief engineer for the newly established Board of Water Commissioners.

With the political atmosphere poisoned by acrimonious competition and the Miller Lux Company having tied up nearly all water rights on the west side of the Sierra Nevada, Mulholland turned to the eastern side to find water and power for Los Angeles. Eastwood did not realize at the same time he was working on the western slopes, the city engineer scouted the eastern side of the same mountains. They came within fifty miles of one another. The greatest difference between them was that one wanted to merely harness the water on its natural course, while the other intended to raid the eastern part of the state of its most precious resource.

Mulholland's project in the Owens Valley was primarily for water, but he added a hydroelectric plant in order to have electricity for pumping water over the Tehachapi Mountains when gravity flow was not possible. The project was marked by secrecy from the start. While publicly declaring it was only for water, Mulholland had other designs. The part of the plan dealing with the production of electricity was buried in the technical data so as not to incur the wrath of existing private companies in the field. However, engineers at Edison and the two other small electric companies serving the city were able to understand the specifications in the proposal and the news added fuel to the already raging fires of controversy.

Even more telling, private industry professionals could easily discern that while the report said nothing about power plant locations, the entire route was clearly determined by suitable places to put them. The city had a major problem with credibility and it was widely reported in newspapers. Everyone had an opinion but everyone also had a stake in whether or not the project succeeded. The power issue had little effect on the public but water was the driving force for residents to support Los Angeles officials in the project.

The city put a new bond issue on the ballot, this time for $23 million to build the Owens River Aqueduct two hundred fifty miles away—without any mention of power production. The *Los Angeles Times* stoked the conflagration with editorials painting the private companies as villains out to take advantage of the public. The *Times* and other newspapers praised the wisdom of the city producing electricity while remaining silent to the fact that Mulholland lied to farmers about the ultimate destination of the water when soliciting their rights and then swearing them to secrecy about it. No mention was made that Fred Eaton, Los Angeles City Engineer, and Mulholland represented themselves as ranchers looking to establish a large ranch in the area.

In addition, the men met privately with the US Department of the Interior's Reclamation Service which was investigating the possibility of putting in an irrigation project in the same area. They convinced the supervising engineer for the federal agency to tell his supervisors that the project was not viable. It was put on hold.

Mulholland and Eaton continued their efforts and tied up the majority of water rights before residents realized they were about to turn the area into a desert, not a ranch. Newspapers in Los Angeles also ignored the protest in the Eastern Sierra which claimed the city raped that part of the state.

The bond passed with the largest margin in the city's history, riding the momentum of the popular Public Ownership Party and union labor's call for gas and water socialism. In the wake of their stupendous success at the polls, Los Angeles officials admitted to the planned hydroelectric system on the aqueduct and announced it was a public necessity. For the majority of the route water would move simply by gravity from the mountains to Los Angeles close at sea level. It was deemed a waste of energy not to tap into it for power with a hydroelectric facility, especially when it would be used to pump the flow over mountains without having to buy electricity from the private sector. The public was pleased but private electrical companies were alarmed at the turn of events.

With Los Angeles going to the electorate for more money to compete against them, private industry was faced with the reality it was living on borrowed time. If the pace continued with more and more bonds passed allowing the city to keep utility rates low, most residents would not easily connect their rise in taxes as a part of the monthly cost of power.

Banking interests and local corporations assumed that the city would only produce electricity with private companies taking over the transmission and distribution. However, when Mayor Alexander announced another bond issue would go the voters to raise an additional $6.5 million to complete the power distribution network and lines from the plant on the aqueduct, it deepened the gulf between the city and private business. The political arena was pushing the city to chaos.

Conflict erupted among the trade unions because it was felt that as long as they were not represented on the Los Angeles City Council, they could not influence government. The unions represented a powerful force for the previous passage of bonds when they came out in favor of them. Much of the success at the polls was due to their political activism. Now feeling left out of the process when their push for union candidates was not supported by the city council, they threatened to withhold their endorsement of the coming bond issue. The bond issue was getting heavy public pressure from the three private companies—HH's Pacific Light and Power, Southern California Edison, and Los Angeles Gas and Electric—which served the city. The behind the scenes alliances worked and the bond passed with more than the required two-thirds majority. The council got the message from the unions in time and carpenter Fred Wheeler won a seat.

The city was confident enough following that success to ask voters for another $3.5 million bond for the construction of a second hydro-electric system on the aqueduct. It appeared they felt the electorate was not in the mood to just vote for the money again without getting some-thing unique in return. This time they promised the moon to get the San Francis dam and hydroelectric system built at the head of the San Fernando Valley, claiming it to be the answer to municipal money needs forever. Mayor George Alexander and the Public Service Commission said, "We may never require another bond issue for this one may lay a foundation that will pay for itself for the rest of our future improve-ments." The bond passed with a ninety percent vote.

In Fresno John Eastwood read the news with trepidation. What had begun as a visionary project was now in jeopardy. The transmission line to San Francisco had been deleted by HH because of his antago-nism toward that city, and now the one to Los Angeles was in question. The tangling alliances were taking a terrible toll.

"Study the past if you would divine the future."

Confucius

Chapter 13

A FORK IN THE ROAD TO THE SIERRA – 1909

With George Patton, Jr. no longer living next door, HH's striking military manner softened. Those who knew him attributed the change to Arabella Huntington and the construction of the manor house at San Marino Ranch. His business associates thought HH took on the stature of English aristocracy in the wake of his purchase of antique paintings, sculpture, china, tapestries and ancient books as well as the history that came with the items for the new home.

The ranch moved from citrus production to showcase garden when HH hired botanist William Hertrich to plan and build lily ponds and formal parklands featuring palms, desert flora, historic roses and a magnificent Japanese garden. Arabella's influence was everywhere from the soaring halls and salons indoors to the paths through history by way of flora surrounding the mansion. Built in the French Classical style, the San Marino residence was easily the most lavish in all of southern California.

It mattered little to Arabella that people said she was haughty. She was one of the world's richest women and those who sought to discredit her by searching into her past were doomed to disappointment. Arabella completely erased her past. There was no evidence she ever existed before becoming a Huntington—no birth certificate, no baptismal record and no previous marriage license could be found although she brought a son to her marriage with Collis.

It was whispered that during the American Civil War while living in Richmond, Virginia she was consort to a gambler. No one knew or was willing to speak of how she became a financial advisor to Collis and even a lobbyist for a period of time. A survivor, Arabella soon became his mistress and after many years in that liaison, his wife. She never looked back and while she zealously protected her own past, she was avidly interested in the history of others.

Newly widowed after Collis died, Arabella loved living in Paris but she began to spend more time in the Los Angeles area. She oversaw the construction and planting of the rose garden at San Marino, a showcase tracing a thousand years of history through the flowers. The oldest strains of roses were descendants from the medieval and Renaissance years. They took center stage in what she named the Shakespeare Section. She guided HH's purchase of antiquities for the new mansion and helped him select books for purchase including an extremely rare copy of the *Gutenberg Bible* and Ellesmere manuscript of *The Canterbury Tales*. Eventually, as the aristocracy of Europe went into decline and fortunes disappeared, HH purchased entire libraries. The nobility sold off assets to the highest bidder and much of it ended up at San Marino Ranch. Inside the new house heroic French and British art covered the walls including Thomas Gainsborough's 1770 *The Blue Boy*, and Thomas Lawrence's *Pinkie* from 1794.

While he changed outwardly, HH remained the well-tutored heir to Collis and his business dealings reflected that. Stories he heard as a young man about the business of the transcontinental railroad were very much a part of his business acumen. He took his uncle's experiences with the transcontinental railroad to heart. Of the four partners to break new ground in national transportation, HH felt strongly that his uncle was the constant guiding force for progress, having taken the idea to the others and then assumed the role of ramrod to see it through.

It wasn't enough for Collis that the company received $25 million in government bonds and 4.5 million acres of land to build the western end of the route through the Sierra to Utah. Behind the scenes he pressured cities for support to complete the historic transcontinental railroad. Sacramento gave $400,000, and the state came up with $2.1

million. Los Angeles gave $200,000 for stock of a local railroad, plus $377,000 in cash.

Collis made more money from soliciting sponsors in small towns than he did from the railroad. If the town fathers declined to "invest" in seeing the rails come to town, the route took a wide swing away from the offending settlements and businesses suffered as a result. That meant any location that did not get on board was left to wither while those that did thrived as designated railroad stops.

HH looked on Collis's business dealings as a way to make up for other inequities. When word got out about the actual start of construction, the cost of rails went from $55 a ton to $115. A small locomotive if available was $14,000 instead of $10,000. The payment from the federal government was given in greenbacks, an unreliable currency worth around 57 cents on the dollar. To make up the difference CH and his partners devised their own builder entity , the Contract and Finance Company, through which all funding was channeled for additional profit.

The contract with the government had built-in deadlines and to meet them, work continued throughout the winter. In 1866, forty-four blizzards battered the highest area around Summit Tunnel through Donner Pass, and although work continued some days the progress was measured in inches rather than feet, yards or miles. Despite incredible odds against completing the work on time, the crews found creative ways around problems. A chemist was hired to manufacture nitroglycerin at the work areas where it was used when black powder was impossible to buy because of Civil War demands. When the schedule became unavoidably delayed as they neared the end, workers set a new record and laid ten miles of track in one day. At the ceremony in Promontory Point, Utah, the men were delighted to see that both Leland Stanford of the Central Pacific and Thomas Durant of the Union Pacific missed hitting the Golden Spike with their first attempts.

With a family history of such magnitude, it was no surprise that HH was driven for the same kind of control over his business interests as his uncle.   While John Eastwood bided his time in Fresno looking for the go-ahead on Big Creek, HH was busy in Los Angeles buying and selling property with his financial partners in the area, not yet convinced that the huge electrical project in the Sierra was ripe for the market.

Eastwood took advantage of the waiting game to fine tune his multiple arch dam design. While he had mentioned it in the new agreement signed with Huntington, Kerckhoff and Balch in 1906 for construction of Big Creek, HH was not interested in breaking new ground with a colossal construction that was unproven. He was convinced that the engineer was beginning to look like Crazy Judah, refusing to accept that the man with the money and connections was the person in charge—not the dreamer. Not having dealt with anyone of HH's stature in the financial world, Eastwood found it easy to attribute the man's non-committal reaction to the multiple arch dam as tacit agreement and recognition of engineering genius.

Still Eastwood waited for the word to begin the final preparations for construction. In 1907 he found a home for his first planned dam in the mountains not far from Big Creek. It would test his plan for the larger project.

Two other attempts had been made to design a dam for the Hume-Bennett Lumber Company without success before Eastwood tried. His proposal outlining a new type of construction that cost 40% less than that of a traditional gravity type dam of massive construction nearly met the same fate. The company sent the unusual plans to a Michigan engineer for a second opinion. The professional assessment came back not in favor of the plan.

"They said it was dangerous," Eastwood groused to Seymour. "Imagine! No mountains in that state and he had the temerity to call my dam too high and too expensive. I gave him the figures and my plan was half the cost of the usual gravity-fed structure."

"I'm not an engineer, but I've always trusted your skills," said Seymour. "The only thing we've ever disagreed about was your tying up with Huntington."

"I can't imagine why a company wouldn't jump at the chance to have me get it done in less time and save three million at the same time."

Seymour tented his fingers against his lips before replying. "You and I broke ground with the San Joaquin hydroelectric plant and it wasn't the dam that failed. It was that we didn't build one big enough. Tell the people at the Hume-Bennett Company they can come talk with me about it. At least we know how to build in the mountains."

* * * * * * * * * * *

William Kerckhoff was uneasy when HH took the PL&P Company effectively out of reach for the original investors by incorporating it.

"I'm happy we got new investors for Big Creek," he told Balch, "but with the partnership gone, all we have now is a group of people we don't even know. HH is in a stronger position as president of the board but he got there at our expense. You and I are no longer in charge of our own business."

"I'm still the chief engineer for Big Creek and that's what I know best in that part of the company. You've been able to get us through some rough spots before, but keep a keen eye on matters. I don't want to end up on the short end of the stick like Eastwood."

When HH bypassed Eastwood to expand in favor of a New York firm, it was mainly to appease his widening circle of investors on the East Coast. The seat of power for the partnership—and now the corporation—had moved from Fresno to Los Angeles and now was spreading to New York and Boston. The implications of that change did not escape notice. After HH maneuvered Eastwood into limbo and effected a total takeover of Big Creek, Kerckhoff was very uncomfortable with the frosty manner in which the engineer was treated after the agreement was signed.

When everyone else had taken leave of the meeting where position and power in the company abruptly changed, Kerckhoff and Balch remained to push for Big Creek to be built.

"We can't do much in the mountains until April but we can start the Valley end of the railroad," said Balch.

"Nothing moves until I say it moves," snapped HH. "Pinchot's Forest Service is with the Department of the Interior now and he's pushing his weight around. He wants a new fee schedule based on how much electricity is produced plus more for each acre of land covered by water behind the dam. There's no way I'm going to pay to see he stays in office."

"But the contract says we start this year," protested Kerckhoff.

"We start when I say we start and there's something more important right now. Eastwood wants his stock to pay dividends. It's common stock for God's sake! He wouldn't budge until I finally said yes, but not until preferred stock is paid. Now he wants an untested dam up there and to tell me how to run the company. The man's another damned Crazy Judah! He's got to go."

Where he had been only uneasy, Kerckhoff now became alarmed. If HH would dismiss the futurist who brought the world's greatest hydro-electric project to him with all the details, plans and costs, what chance was there he and Balch would be around to enjoy any of the profits from it?

* * * * * * * * * *

By the time Seymour's recommendation convinced the Hume-Bennett Company to accept the Eastwood plan for the multiple arch dam, winter weather closed early delaying any construction until the spring thaw. Despite a slow start in April, the Hume dam was complete by fall of 1907. However, Eastwood kept the bypass water open, allowing the river to continue to flow. He waited to fill the lake until the following spring runoff. Even though he was certain the dam was perfect, he still wanted to be sure the fresh concrete had enough time to cure thoroughly in the thin mountain air.

The success of the new dam impounding what was now called Hume Lake made headlines in the press and trade publications. *Engineering News* reported that Eastwood had been getting so many calls about the construction, he was having trouble responding to queries and working at the same time. With no word from HH and his partners about Big Creek, Eastwood plunged into building another multiple arch dam, this time in the Big Bear Valley east of Los Angeles.

Big Bear already had a small dam for agriculture interests. It met the same fate as Eastwood's San Joaquin Electric Company, meaning it was dry for three years during the same drought that bankrupted the hydroelectric plant. The economic aspect of Hume Dam caught the interest of investors in the south. Eastwood was so pleased with the accuracy of his planning and execution of it in the Sierra, he guaranteed the new dam's investors that his cost estimates would be firm, meaning no overruns.

In the contract he signed, he agreed that he would accept a fixed sum of $6,000 for his fee and the total cost of the construction would be $80,000, which was a far cry from the previous estimate of $140,000 for a rock fill dam with concrete reinforcement. If any overage occurred, Eastwood said it would be taken out of his share. It was a substantial risk which he accepted willingly, so confident was he of his inspired design for the multiple arch dam.

Such enthusiasm was infectious and when the actual construction began, investors decided to raise the height of the dam an additional seven and a half feet. The resulting cost increased to an estimated $137,000, but once again Eastwood's engineering was so exact, the final bill came well under the amount and his fee was not reduced a penny.

Much of the reason for the economy on the job was the way Eastwood used on-site materials. Stone was quarried nearby and sand gathered from tributaries entering the small existing water storage area. Word about needing workers spread quickly sending a steady stream of operators with their flat-bottomed scows struggling up the steep mountain roads to apply for contracts to dredge sand.

All lumber was milled six miles from the dam and fuel for the boilers was gathered from downed trees. Where Eastwood built a trestle at the Hume Dam to carry material for deposit in the dam, this time he used a wire cableway with the same precision. Woven half-inch wire cables were used to haul logs to the mill. When that work was complete, the wire became reinforcement for concrete. For the first time skilled carpenters were a part of the construction crew for a dam, necessary because of the precise measurements Eastwood demanded for the concrete forms for the arches. In one hundred and fourteen long work days, the dam was complete.

People came to watch the construction. The multiple arch dam basked in the sunshine of success at Big Bear Lake and Kerckhoff and Balch moved to protect themselves from HH by turning to Eastwood's original hydroelectric plant. Having bought it at bankruptcy, the partners now expanded the San Joaquin Power and Light Company in the mountains above Fresno with a much larger powerhouse. In addition, the dam height at Crane Flat south of Yosemite was nearly doubled to 150 feet. That water impoundment was named Bass Lake.

Eastwood was disappointed to learn he was not their engineer of choice. That he was not asked to bid on it was unsettling, given his intimate connection with the original construction. That the contract was given to the J.G. White & Company of *New York* was more than disquieting.

"No bird soars too high, if he soars with his own wings."

William Blake

Chapter 14

UPHEAVAL AND OPPORTUNITY – 1910

W ell overdue by early 1910, Big Creek finally "went into labor." The birthing process would change everything. It began in Washington DC when President Taft fired Gifford Pinchot of the US Forest Service. The Service had been transferred from the Department of the Interior to the Department of Agriculture five years earlier but Pinchot was not able to effect his plan for conservation of public lands without incurring the wrath of the private sector. Henry Graves succeeded Pinchot and HH was able to negotiate a fifty-year permit that was not at risk for summary rejection by bureaucratic whim.

Still HH dragged his feet on the construction, preferring instead to gather rare books at an astounding rate. He broke the previous one-day record for purchases at Sotheby's in London, adding entire libraries from English Renaissance repositories in New York, London, California and Europe to his own. His million-dollar purchase of over two thousand volumes of the E. Dwight Church collection of rare British and American materials included the manuscript autobiography of Benjamin Franklin.

In Los Angeles, HH's transportation lines were reaching maximum power use again. Flickering lights as well as slowing trolleys forced him to face the need to find more electricity. Instead of turning to Eastwood and the Sierra, he sold his interurban lines to Southern Pacific Railroad to reduce the requirement for overall power for the rest of his trolley lines. Big Creek languished in limbo until Kerckhoff laid out a set of circumstances HH could not afford to ignore.

"Mr. Huntington, if we don't act soon some of the water rights could be vacated," he began. HH said nothing and Kerckhoff sensed a lack of any interest in the problem. Still, he pushed on. "We don't need to do everything immediately. However, I feel strongly that we must establish a strong presence up there and proceed in good faith. If we do not act quickly we stand a good chance of losing everything to competition."

HH looked directly at him. "Meaning what?"

"Meaning that since electricity use has doubled every year for the last ten, it won't be long before you'll be looking for another way to keep the trolleys running. The Edison Company is constructing a new plant in the Kern River area. They will have three more large generators, not to mention the new backup steam site they have at Rattlesnake Island."

"I don't call that steam plant progress. It's in a tideland and needs a huge crew to work it. Water cooling tunnels have to be cleaned out and I see them cart off railroad carloads of sand and muck every day—all of it done by hand," HH scoffed. "Last winter it was cold enough that pipes lying on the ground wouldn't let fuel oil get into the powerhouse. They had to build fires along the line to get the oil moving."

"And how long do you think it'll take for Edison to get enough electricity coming from the Kern River hydro system to replace it? It's not a question of *if*, but *when*. Right now you're in the same position your uncle Collis was with the railroad. Do you get on board in the engine now or ride in someone else's caboose trying to catch up? Mulholland's Owens Valley project is underway with one hydroelectric plant and word is out that he's found another site for the second. What will happen to your trolley profits if you have to purchase power from the city?"

HH stood up abruptly and turned to stare out the window of his office. Kerckhoff waited for the answer he wanted to hear. It came with surprising swiftness.

"We will proceed…but only with initial construction. I won't risk it entirely on my own and it'll take time to raise enough from other investors." He turned and glared across his immense desk. "One more thing. Eastwood has become a distinct liability and I want to proceed without him. Are the plans complete?"

Kerckhoff nodded. "The man's very thorough and we've got second and third professional opinions about his figures and plans."

"Have the prospectus ready for the next board meeting in two weeks and call it the first phase with two powerhouses. Balch will be our engineer. Tell him to contact the J.G. White & Company of New York and London to look at the project. That'll get eastern money out here."

HH returned to his window, and Kerckhoff knew he had been dismissed. He wondered how long he could expect to be a part of the Huntington empire if Eastwood, who brought him a world class project for enormous profit, was about to be cut off for having the temerity to suggest Big Creek use an untested dam design and asking that his stock pay dividends. Big business in Los Angeles was rapidly becoming a big headache for anyone not a part of the top echelon.

* * * * * * * * * * *

Once he made up his mind, HH moved quickly. He reorganized the Pacific Light and Power Company from a simple partnership into a *corporation*, leaving Big Creek to remain a separate investment entity. John Eastwood was required to sign over all his interests in the Big Creek Project, including all plans, designs and water claims, filings, maps and permits in his name in return for $600,000 in stock, ten percent of which was pledged to R.S. Masson as a finder's fee for bring the principals together. HH now controlled everything that Eastwood had ever built or planned to build in the Sierra Nevada for the production of electrical power.

At sixty years of age, HH was no longer interested in conquering commercial Everests. His businesses had set records for nearly everything he started. With the pleasure of his antiquity collections taking center stage in his life, he was prepared to make one last splash in the Sierra with Big Creek. After that he would retire to San Marino and live a life of leisure surrounded by the fruits of his labors.

Kerckhoff's warning of Edison Company's success in the boom market for electricity was accurate, but his warning about Mulholland's entry into the power market lacked emphasis. The city engineer had abundant political clout to succeed in providing the same service that private industry had so far been able to do, and that alone added enough pressure to begin work at Big Creek.

Technology quickly became part of everyone's life in the country but it was especially evident with all forms of transportation. Railroads were proliferating like rabbits in spring, criss-crossing every state in the Union. Wilbur and Orville Wright had actually taken flight in their awkward bird at Kitty Hawk. Only a few years following that historic event, the US Army was experimenting with the use of an airplane to move mail between large cities.

However, it was the introduction of Henry Ford's Model T that had the greatest impact for HH. LA streets were crowded with all forms of transportation—from automobiles, bicycles, diesel trucks to horse-drawn vehicles—all competed for the same road space. The introduction of trolleys had usurped the monopoly of horse-drawn vehicles. Industries that supported the care and shelter of animals for transportation went into a quick decline. Now HH faced the same fate as automobiles and bicycles reduced ridership on his lines. To complicate his business, the rise in political power at city hall made running a company much more complex than it had been a decade earlier.

While Mulholland had many of the same rough and ready qualities as himself, it was disturbing for HH to watch the city engineer bulldoze his way through one crisis after another. Warned that water was running out, Mulholland originally scoffed at the idea. When it became clear that was indeed happening, he took water from the Los Angeles River until it, too was bled dry. It was at that point he and his boss, William Eaton, perpetrated their fraud in the Owens Valley and began to build the massive aqueduct to bring water two hundred fifty miles to the city.

Unlike private enterprise, the project did not have to show a profit and when bids came in to do the job at fifty to one hundred percent higher than estimates, Mulholland accepted them and began construction. Much of the route was an engineering nightmare without any shelter or provision for worker comfort, or even water in the vast desert expanses. Worse, there was no overall contractor to keep construction running smoothly, nor could necessary material be purchased in local communities. Everything from piping and concrete to food for men and horses had to be trucked to the site from railroad sidings many miles from the actual route of the aqueduct.

In addition to the badly underestimated costs of the project itself,

Mulholland had to build five hundred miles of roads in both desert and mountains. Before any work could begin, he had to create a small town where the army of workers hired to do the job could be fed and housed. Forty-nine more times he met the same challenge of erecting towns along the long route for the five thousand men who worked on the project.

The greatest engineering obstacle to completion was the San Fernando Mountain Range. To maintain the gravity flow, a five-mile long tunnel was dug through solid granite. Workers on that part of the project were paid a bonus to get the job done faster and they completed it ten months ahead of the scheduled five years. Owens Valley water began to slake the thirst of Angelenos in 1910, but the spigot was opened only a short time before Mulholland was told it was not enough. Again, money flowed like the water he worked to move, a luxury HH was neither willing nor able to match.

The need for water was so great that complaints of Mulholland's heavy-handed methods and wasteful use of the public's money fell on deaf ears. Even the growing controversy about adding hydroelectric systems in the aqueduct that would unfairly compete with private electric companies did not dim his public acclaim.

HH seriously considered Mulholland and the competition in the city before he would commit to the construction of Big Creek. When he finally said yes to Kerckhoff it was with the belief the incredible luck Mulholland had would soon be worn thin by his repeated, grievous errors of ignorance and arrogance. The Los Angeles water engineer was riding a wave of fame but even HH could not have imagined that it would soon crest and drop Mulholland from the height of commendation into an incredible abyss.

"A minute's success pays the failure of years."

Robert Browning

Chapter 15

BIG BEAR SUCCESS — 1910-12

For much of the rest of 1910, HH was only moderately successful in getting more investors interested in Big Creek. Late in the year and by now impatient to get the project done, he moved to interest eastern financial circles by severing his connection with the J.G. White Company in New York in favor of the Stone and Webster Construction Company of Boston. Charles Stone's partner Edwin Webster had a close connection to money in the area. His father was a partner in the Kidder, Peabody and Company banking firm, and represented a clearer path to the halls of high finance in the east for HH.

The choice of this construction firm was not necessarily a wise one based on technological expertise since the principals had no experience in western mountains at all—let alone the highest ones in the country—for the world's largest hydroelectric facility and the longest transmission of power. The search for new money paid off and brought in enough investors by the end of 1911. One of the most important people the change attracted was E.W. Rollins.

The son of E.H. Rollins, a major banking figure in New England who had served as governor of New Hampshire, the younger Rollins was a pioneer in the electrical industry and a respected member of the Colorado Scientific Society. His involvement in Big Creek had a large impact on others who chose to invest in the project since he was a graduate of MIT and understood the new technology.

When HH made the financial switch to move Big Creek onto the national investment scene, he again told Kerckhoff and Balch in no uncertain terms to get rid of Eastwood. Late in November, they sent a letter to the engineer saying they wanted to discontinue his connection with the Big Creek project. They asked for all his maps, plans and technical data in return for 5,400 shares of stock in the newly reformed Pacific Light & Power Corporation. The PL&P had grown to ten generating stations in Southern California plus Eastwood's first hydroelectric plant on the San Joaquin River. Stock at the time was valued at one hundred dollars per share. However, the payment to Eastwood was reduced by six hundred shares to Masson for his finder's fee.

While he had never expected to become a millionaire from his dream project, Eastwood was nonetheless taken aback by the financial manipulations of big business. Despite the reality that relations between him and the owners of the project had cooled considerably, he still expected to be part of the construction. When it became abundantly clear he would not be the engineer of record, he immersed himself in the plans and design for the Big Bear Valley Dam. It was another opportunity to fine-tune the multiple arch dam. He looked forward to presenting his case to Stone and Webster to use the design when Big Creek was ready to break ground.

There had been a goodly amount of publicity about his Hume Lake Dam, including an article in the *Journal of Electricity Power and Gas*. In the same issue that described his latest triumph, Eastwood had purchased a small advertisement where he called himself a designer of dams with a specialty in his Multiple Arch Type. He claimed this was a fine choice for any height or site. For the first time he was connected with the phrase "the ultimate dam," a popular description of his invention for future installations. He was so enamored with the design, he compared its permanence to that of the Sierra Nevada itself, saying that it was impossible to find a better design for the most reasonable cost of construction and well within the parameters of safety.

Response to journal articles came from far and wide, including one from C.E. Grunsky. A widely known San Francisco engineer, Grunsky was part of the Isthmus Canal Commission formed by President William McKinley to look into the feasibility of constructing the Panama

Canal. The massive project to connect the Pacific and Atlantic Oceans was well under way at the time and Grunsky's cautious endorsement of the new dam design gave Eastwood a substantial professional boost up the ladder of recognition. It also made the rejection of Huntington, Kerckhoff and Balch less painful and he headed south to manage the construction of the Big Bear Dam.

By contrast to his experience with the Big Creek plans, people in southern California welcomed Eastwood. Their history of agriculture boom and bust had brought farming to a crossroads. Either they had to invest more heavily in the future by securing a regular supply of water, or face the reality that drought was a regular visitor to the area. There was ample evidence from the previous ninety years that the use of stored water was the only way to make a living from farming in that region.

The settlement of San Bernardino, sixty-five miles east of Los Angeles, had a history of irrigation use since 1820 when Mexican farmers dug a *zanja* (ditch) from the Santa Ana River to water crops. After the US-Mexican War ended in 1848, Mormons settled in the area and continued the practice, broadly expanding the system. By the time the state of California was five years old, they returned to Utah to support the church-sanctioned settlement and the push for statehood there. When the California State Engineer's office surveyed the area for a potential reservoir prior to 1900, it found the area along Bear Creek to be what was described as one of the best locations in the southern part of the state for one to be built.

However, the office had neither funds nor interest in getting the dam built, leaving it for the people themselves to build a small storage for water in that location. At the 6,700-foot level of the San Bernardino Mountains above the new town of Redlands, farmers formed a business partnership to put together the money to raise a dam. Everyone welcomed the water, and the expectation of more business from the impoundment of water moved the owners of the dam to expand their operations too fast and too far. When the prolonged drought at the turn of the century hit the area, the irrigation business in general and the dam partnership in particular fell into dire straits.

For years the farmer partners struggled in the water business before lapsing into bankruptcy, then spent more years trying to extricate itself from the legal morass. By the time the group was ready to build a well-engineered project, Eastwood's Hume Lake Dam was in the newspaper headlines. A larger dam for less money than they expected to pay was more than attractive. It was necessary if the company was going to stay in business. Eastwood felt the contract was a perfect match for his design. He was eager to get to work on it, but his heart and soul remained in residence at Big Creek.

So confident was he that the dam would be built according to his specifications, Eastwood wrote up a contract for the job accepting a flat fee of $6,000 no matter how long he was on the job. In addition, he said the dam would cost no more than $80,000 including his fee and if it did, he would accept a ten percent cut in his fee for any amount over the stated total cost.

Again Eastwood used available materials since transportation to the site was over fifty miles from the railroad. Instead of a trestle to bring materials to the dam, he opted for a cable stretched across the entire canyon where the dam would be located. Materials were sent out by way of the cable to workers below. When it came time to fill the forms, concrete poured from a continuous line of two-cubic foot bottom-dump buckets sent along the cable above.

Some of the same boat owners arrived with their scows at the site when they heard the man who put them to work in the Sierra at Hume Lake was now doing the same thing in the San Bernardinos. Spectators watched as the Eastwood dam arose just as they did at Hume Lake. This time they included the Bison Moving Picture Company filming *Lucky Bob* against a background of men working on the dam. When the company partners paying for the structure began to realize what a bargain they were getting, they asked that seven and a half feet be added to the height of the dam. The original estimate increased to $137,000 but Eastwood insisted his fee remain the same.

As winter approached in 1911, construction was complete and the dam awaited the spring runoff to fill. At the same time, less than a hundred miles west in Los Angeles, HH was marshalling his company resources to begin the last great engineering achievement done entirely with private funds. Big Creek would be the equal to the Panama Canal achievement in size, engineering ingenuity and construction, but would forever be overshadowed by the conquest of Yellow Fever and the romance of a jungle trek from the Atlantic to the Pacific Ocean in Central America.

* * * * * * * * * *

During the winter he waited for the Big Bear Dam to cure before it filled, Eastwood expected to have idle time on his hands. All his leisure vanished with a knock at the door to his office in Fresno. It was H.H. Sinclair. The two had not spoken since their meeting in Redlands, but seeing one another again, the friendship immediately rekindled.

"What a sight for sore eyes!" exclaimed Eastwood. He reached for Sinclair's hand and eagerly embraced him. "I've really missed your attorney approach to business."

"And I've missed your unbridled enthusiasm, John. You have no idea how deadening it is to work with stiff-upper-lip bores."

"Come sit," Eastwood motioned toward the stove. "I guarantee you won't lack for warmth here. Heard you hired on at Great Western Power Company up north."

Sinclair's face sobered. "That's why I'm here. They wanted me to clean up a mess the company got into at the Big Meadows site."

"They got the right person for that. You know every part of a project from plan to production. If anyone can help put that company to rights, it's you."

"I appreciate your endorsement, but right now I'm in the thick of it with a jackass by the name of Freeman. GWP has a plan for a large hydroelectric system in the Feather River area, but they wanted to get some money coming in before they dived into constructing the greater part of the project. They put up a small plant downstream to send electricity to Oakland. Trouble is that the plant is not well planned and often not able to send power. That was when they came to me for help."

From a thermos on the desk, Eastwood poured two cups of coffee and put one in front of Sinclair. "Black, right?"

"Right." Sinclair reached for the cup with what Eastwood thought was a slightly trembling hand. Both sipped from their cups before Sinclair used both hands to return his to the desk. "Got the small plant straightened out after consulting with engineers outside the company. John Freeman had done the work at the start and made a mess of it."

"Freeman from MIT?"

"That's the one. He also worked the Owens Valley Project but I don't think his sterling reputation is at all deserved. The man's nothing but trouble and any time he doesn't get his way, he contacts the board and sweet-talks them into accepting his ideas and plans, forgetting he has already loused up the one that gave them the trouble."

"I've heard he's a bit hard-headed."

"That's a kindly way of putting it. When we disagreed over the new construction, Freeman went to the board with a lot of gibberish. When they questioned his proposal, he insisted they didn't understand what he does as a professional. He ended up with their permission to hire Mulholland from LA and Arthur Davis of the US Reclamation Service to join him in doing a new study of the big dam and a diversion structure as well."

"Why Davis?"

"Not sure. The idea of government regulation is that great unknown right now. I expect any time they can get a foot in the door they'll take it. Freeman's just using the Service for his own purposes."

Eastwood laughed. "You came to the wrong man to help with an arrogant engineer! My reputation is solidly based on my ability to antagonize everyone I deal with."

Sinclair ignored the self-condescension. "I need to know if you'd design a Multiple Arch Dam for the site. I still think it's the best way to put one up and in this case the savings is imperative. Freeman's interference has upped the costs of any construction nearly out of reach."

Uncertain what he thought he heard, Eastwood questioned him. "Do you mean you want me to bid on the project...put an Eastwood dam at Big Meadows?"

"Yes. I heard you were dumped from constructing the Big Creek Project by HH's Pacific Light and Power and hoped you'd have time to come to my rescue." Sinclair smiled. "Didn't surprise me they went for an eastern company. That's where the big investors live."

"Word travels like lightning."

"We're a bit inbred here...the same bunch who started pushing for electricity ten or fifteen years ago. Your old investor Julius Howells started on this project until the company hired James Schuyler to check out Howell's plans. That attracted Freeman and my problem now is that he's invested in Big Meadows and the board loves him regardless that what he says makes no sense."

"You asking me to challenge his plans?"

"No. I'm stuck with him but I'd like you to take a look at the site and give me a plan for it using the Multiple Arch design."

"No need to ponder that one. I'm your man."

"It's not all rosy. I'll need you to be more accessible than Fresno.

Can you move further north at least temporarily?"

Eastwood smiled to himself. He and Ella had already discussed moving north because of the heartache with Big Creek. His dark moods had not escaped the notice of his wife no matter how well he thought he concealed them and she was the first to propose the idea of leaving Fresno. Interest in the Ultimate Dam was now coming from other western states and having a more readily recognized address in the San Francisco area would serve him well. "Done," he said simply. "Ella and I have already been looking at doing just that, but we'll keep the Kings River ranch."

The two men said their goodbyes. Eastwood stood with his hand on the door latch watching his friend make his way onto the street. In the bright November sun what Eastwood first thought was his imagination was now undeniable. As Sinclair hailed a Hansom cab it was clear he had lost weight and his gait was unsteady. Eastwood hoped it was because he was extremely tired rather than not well.

"Action is the proper fruit of knowledge."

Thomas Fuller

Chapter 16

RAILROAD TO BIG CREEK – 1912

Dan McGrew stood in the doorway to Matthew Merryman's trucking business. A cold March wind blew past him stirring the top layer of the dirt floor, and while animals were no longer inside the former livery, the smell of horse sweat and manure was unmistakable. With a brilliant sun glinting off the puddles left from a heavy rain outside, it took a moment for his eyes to become accustomed to the interior lit by several small incandescent lamps.

In the back corner John Eastwood and Merryman stood next to a chain-driven Mack Truck. Behind McGrew another gust of wind pulled the latch from his grasp and the door closed suddenly, pushing him into the large room. Merryman walked toward him. "What can I do for you, Mister?" he asked wiping both hands on his shirt and then extending one to McGrew.

"I'm Dan McGrew with Stone and Webster, the company doing the Big Creek project in the mountains. I'm looking for a way to get a lot of materials up there for about ten months."

"First off, McGrew, there ain't no ten months in a row you c'n get anything up them mountains, and second, I'm the biggest trucking company in these parts which means I can't tie up all my shipping for that long just for one customer no matter how much you pay."

Eastwood spoke from behind Merryman. "I knew you were coming, just not when. I'm Eastwood and I think I can help."

McGrew took a stumbling step backward and then flushed in embarrassment. "Mr. Eastwood, I think you should know that I have been told quite emphatically that I must have no dealings with you. If Mr. Huntington knew we exchanged two words, I'd be out of a job. I'm...ah...very sorry."

With a resigned smile, Eastwood turned to his long-time friend. "Merryman, you really should listen to your customer and try to help. Why don't you tell him about dealing with the Mack Company directly? It will likely cost much less to buy the trucks than hire every other freight company in the Valley."

Merryman nodded eagerly, then turned back to McGrew. "If you really need that much trucking I can give you the name of the salesman for the Mack Company. He's stationed in San Francisco and you can talk with him on the telephone down at the telegraph office."

McGrew picked up on the gentlemen's agreement immediately. "I'd like to do that, Merryman, and if you know of anyone with a good design for a dam, you might tell that person to speak with E.H. Rollins in Denver. The man is heavily invested in Big Creek and he's an engineer from MIT."

Eastwood stifled a smile and turned back to studying the new truck. He enjoyed his visits to Fresno now that he lived in Oakland but never expected the depth of heaviness being on the outside looking in at the construction of Big Creek. Although he himself was one of the reasons technology moved so swiftly, it still amazed him how news appeared to travel in the blink of an eye.

                    * * * * * * * * * * *

Three weeks later in Denver, Colorado, E.H. Rollins delighted Eastwood when he said he was open to using the Multiple Arch Dam design in Big Creek. He agreed to contact the Stone and Webster people in Boston to suggest they take a good look at the Eastwood dam. In his professional opinion the anticipated $2 million savings and excellent engineering was well worth it.

Raised in very comfortable circumstances in New England, Rollins had the natural curiosity of a born engineer. He built a vacation home in Denver, equipping it with the latest in technology. Windmills on the property pumped water to a large tank in the upstairs of the house, putting gravity-fed water into each bathroom as well as the kitchen. The house was often pointed out by passersby as one of the finest in Denver. Neighbors argued about whether the Giant Redwood paneling in the library was a greater asset than the complete indoor plumbing. By the time the house was ready to occupy, Rollins had fallen in love with the mountains and moved there permanently.

Impressed with the thoroughness of Eastwood's plans and enthusiastic about the idea, Rollins also planned to bring up the subject at the next board meeting, leaving Eastwood to feel a new personal investment in Big Creek.

* * * * * * * * * *

A mere eight days after Stone and Webster signed the contract to build Big Creek, the company began to construct a small railroad necessary to bring the hundreds of thousands of tons of materials, food, and equipment into the Sierra to build the massive project and support thousands of workers and their families. Originally, company management felt it could do the job with trucks and wagons, but with a $20 charge per ton, the railroad quickly became a more cost effective alternative.

The first road scrapers went into action at the Valley end of the line on February 5th, connecting the new line to the abandoned section of Southern Pacific tracks at the old Friant Depot eighteen miles northeast of Fresno.

Just as it had been with hiring for the construction of the flume twenty years previously, interviews were short and to the point. "What have you done? This is no picnic and you gotta keep up with the crew, so where's your bedroll? Show your hands—no callouses, no job." There was one difference—hard rock drillers and carpenters earned a little more.

The work took hundreds of men using wheelbarrows, hand saws, shovels and Fresno scrapers pulled behind mules. With the Sierra locked in winter snows, work on the lowlands progressed quickly for the first five miles where the rise was between one and two percent grade over foothills. As crews neared the tiny town of Auberry, the grade increased as did the degree of curves in the deep wilderness.

Progress slowed to a crawl in some places where the tracks had to be doubled back before moving up the mountain further. Trestles had to be built, in some areas where slopes increased to over five percent. In other areas, work crews moved so fast they pushed the surveyors just

ahead of them where they were usually days apart. Construction continued without a Sunday break. At night they worked under lights pow-
ered by a line from Eastwood's first hydroelectric plant, now a part of
the Pacific Light & Power Corporation. Laborers, teamsters and drillers worked at least ten hours a day seven days a week for twenty-seven
cents an hour. The turnover rate was high and most did not work longer
than a few weeks at a time.

The single track had ten passing stations and ultimately forty-three
Drillers and carpenters earned more because of their skills. Sawyers cleared the way of trees for the railway, then sliced them into lumber for buildings and bridge trestles. Other crews cut logs for cross-ties
under the rails, using well over 2,500 of them for each mile. Work to
blast through the granite was difficult and dangerous. In the first ten
miles of roadway, well over six thousand cubic yards of crushed granite
was laid under the tracks. Although cattle were open-ranged in the
mountains, the right of way for the railroad was ceded by ranchers only
if the company built cattle fences in some areas.

The single track had ten passing stations and ultimately forty-three
trestles were built—one nearly 600 feet long. Some trestles had to be
bolted into the granite mountain slope. Small crews remained behind
to build eleven station houses along the way as well as a redwood tank
to hold close to ten thousand of gallons of water at each location. At
Auberry, the men erected a major maintenance complex with a blacksmith shop, storeroom/office and machine shop. When construction
reached Cascada, the planned site of Powerhouse #1, the track changed
dramatically.

Eastwood had selected the location for the best possible use in creating power from Big Creek. However, that required the railroad be run
up an eighty percent grade, meaning nearly straight up. The solution
was to lay a cable system from Cascada to the top of the grade some
2,100 feet directly above the town to pull each car up the final distance.
The steepness required that all cars have "hogbacks," a type of fence at
the back of each car to keep freight from slipping off the rear end as it
was drawn up the steep slope. It also meant that no material could be
longer than the cars carrying it. Freight cars rode up to the top one at a
time to deliver materials to construction crews at Huntington Lake Dam
where work had already begun.

For the entire time of construction, steam engines pulled materials, food, supplies and equipment to the end of the line every day.

Despite the daunting blocks to construction, the last spike was driven on July 10th, an astounding record of 157 days for what was described as the "crookedest railroad ever built in the world." Despite the rigorous construction in thick wilderness and steep terrain, not one life was lost, something engineers likened to an industry miracle.

Two days after completion, the little railroad began carrying passengers. With well over two hundred steep grade rises and nearly eleven hundred curves, the train treated passengers to a slow but exciting ride. At one point the engineer might entertain riders by stepping off the moving engine and its load of cars, then walking across the neck of land where tracks made a particularly sharp turn. He would then reboard as the engine came toward him and resume the controls.

* * * * * * * * * *

With the meeting in Denver so encouraging, Eastwood returned home to Oakland with a light heart, never dreaming that the good news in Colorado would result in the ultimate humiliation and wrenching separation from Big Creek. HH was furious about the visit to Rollins and he was fully prepared to do what he could not get Kerckhoff to do— get rid of Eastwood permanently. The issue of who was in control was paramount.

On July 5th the meeting went without controversy until Rollins brought up the question of the multiple arch dam and how much it would save the company.

"You know I'm an engineer," he said. "I've given the plans a thorough going-over and have gotten the same kind of reaction from two other fellow engineers from MIT. We all agree this has never been done before but it is based on sound theory."

"Twenty-two years ago the Johnstown flood from a failed dam claimed the lives of 2,200 people in Pennsylvania," groused HH. "Perhaps you would do better to ask the survivors if they would trust new technology."

"That dam was overbuilt for the site and not according to engineering standards," protested Rollins. "This one is…"

"Walnut Grove, Arizona in 1890 and Ash Fork in 1898…those were new dams as well."

"New is not necessarily better…"

"1907, Hauser Lake, Montana and Austin, Pennsylvania last year. That one cost seventy-seven lives. I say we stay with tried and true. Let someone else take chances."

Around the large table Rollins could see the discomfort in the other board members. No one spoke up to support him and all of them suddenly found their papers needed sorting. Rollins did not know HH personally, but he did know how to read people. There was no doubt the board president was not going to relent in the slightest. With all the decorum he could muster, he demurred.

"Perhaps we can take up the subject at another time as Big Creek grows." The impact was not lost on anyone. The dams at the head of Powerhouse #1 were already under construction and while there was still time to change the design above the necessary riverbed foundation, Rollins could feel extraordinary heat in HH's reaction toward the idea of the Multiple Arch Dam and would soon learn it was directed at Eastwood.

The meeting continued with little discussion and no opposition to anything HH proposed. The last item was not listed on his agenda and he dropped it casually as if it were of little consequence. "Since we are facing a deficit in capital necessary to see Big Creek to completion, I'm proposing a five dollar per share assessment on all capital stock. All in favor say aye."

Without hesitation every member agreed but across the table Rollins saw Kerckhoff blanch. HH gaveled the meeting over and Rollins make quick goodbyes to each man, saving Kerckhoff for last. He took him by the elbow, ushering him out of the room and down the hall, all the while making small talk about engineering.

When they were well out of earshot, he stopped and confronted him. "What happened in there?" he demanded. "I saw your reaction to the stock assessment and you were shocked. What's wrong with it? Is it illegal here in California?"

Kerckhoff shook his head. "No. Not illegal, just vindictive. He just got rid of John Eastwood. Permanently. If he did it to the man who gave him the original plan and all the water rights to Big Creek, I think he'd do the same to my partner and me."

"Explain that. Eastwood is one of the largest stock holders in the company and only you and HH own more. I'm an investor in Big Creek but was invited to sit on the board because I think HH wanted to curry favor from me. If it's not illegal, what's wrong with it?"

"Walk with me to my automobile and please look like we are

having a light-hearted conversation. If HH sees us from that corner window, we can always say we talked about business."

At the curb Kerckhoff unrolled a thick set of plans for Big Creek. "Look at these while I talk and you can point or appear animated about the project while I tell you that vote just destroyed all the stock Eastwood has in the company. He will have to come up with nearly $30,000 in cash to make the assessment. That's impossible for him. He has nearly six thousand shares that were artificially inflated in value to $100 when he signed off on Big Creek. They're worth about $8 right now."

"So even if he borrowed the money, he'd be essentially buying his own stock just to remain a part of the company."

"If he doesn't come up with the money, the stock will be sold on the courthouse steps to pay the assessment. Since the market is down right now, no one will bid on them. They will revert to the company with zero value to be sold to new investors who will buy them in the future. He'll be handing over all his rights in the company that he hasn't already signed over to HH in previous contracts."

Rollins' hand crushed the edge of the plans he was holding. "Look alive here. HH is at the doorway."

Kerckhoff rolled up the plans and raised his voice slightly. "...and with the railroad just about to lay the last of the track, we are ahead of schedule. By next week you'll be able to ride directly to the location of Powerhouse #1."

Rollins tipped his hat to HH. "Will you be going, HH?"

"No. Arabella has plans. We're leaving for New York to hear someone sing at the Metropolitan."

"Aida?"

"No...name's Caruso. Enrico Caruso...I think."

"Hold fast to dreams
For if dreams die,
Life is a broken-winged bird
That cannot fly."

Langston Hughes

Chapter 17

THE REDINGER BRIDGE TO BIG CREEK — 1912

Both the cableway and Eastwood's planned wagon road were busy beginning in April of 1912. Stone & Webster began construction simultaneously at the site of Powerhouse 1 and the dam more than 2,000 feet above it. At the same time the railroad moved towards them both. A steady stream of equipment was brought to the sites on wagons with teams of as many as twenty mules and horses which were needed to pull materials up the mountain. Some trainloads were so laden with cement the engines could haul only three cars at a time.

At the future Huntington Lake, three dams were rising in a great arc to impound an enormous amount of water across the area above the powerhouse. Crews laid thirteen additional miles of track for nine locomotives within the site to harvest, then move logs and granite within the area to the actual site. Carpenters built storage sheds, water tanks, machine shops and fuel stations.

Even though Eastwood was not present, his creative know-how seemed to influence crews to find ingenious ways to solve knotty problems such as devising a method to signal the cable house. Two electric lines were strung along the steep tracks. When it came time to notify the cable master the crew wanted to move a car, a worker would reach out with an insulated metal rod touching both to cause a short that rang a bell. Two rings meant they wanted to come uphill and five meant they wanted to come down.

* * * * * * * * * *

By the time David Redinger came to work on the project the area was a beehive of activity. At 3 AM on August 13th, he stepped off the train into the cold mountain air carrying his bedding the way all men traveling to remote areas did, rolled into a *bindle*. He became one of the construction family immediately.

"Hey you! Construction stiff! Hit the hay over there," he heard from a man who pointed to an unfinished office building and then was gone.

Redinger did as he was told, making a bed in a large pile of wood shavings in one corner. The cold light on the eastern edge of the mountains told him sunrise was not far off, and he could hear the cooks begin to make noises in the kitchen of the mess hall. He closed his eyes expecting not to be able to sleep in a place that did not feel, smell or sound like anything he had ever experienced. The thin air moved voices farther and faster and during the time cooks were not banging pots, the forest was more than just quiet. Redinger felt it was a strong presence of towering majesty and magnetic power. He was completely at home.

Three hours later he was wakened by meal call rung on a large iron triangle. For a moment he thought he was back at a mine in Colorado where his uncle had gotten him a job right out of high school. Part of his work was to be a handyman and general git-boy to accompany engineers underground. Too shy to ask what it meant, he soon learned it was "git me the small pick" or "git me the test kit," or "git some grub."

Science and mathematics fascinated him. He observed engineers take the laws of physics and apply them to a project of immense proportion. The result was eminently satisfying. After five years working as a laborer, he left to get a degree in engineering at Kansas State University.

His first job as a professional was in Alaska as a US Government investigator surveying the Bering River coalfields. When that job contract was finished, Redinger and the rest of the crew returned to the US General Land Office in Seattle to put the final touches on their report. H.P. Banks, a chemical engineer on the Bering River project, told Redinger about a very large project in the High Sierra.

"I don't know anything about hydro generation," said Redinger.

"You got any better prospects for a job right now?" asked Banks.

"No, but what could I do at Big Creek?"

"David, I'm a chemist and they sent me to Alaska to do survey work along with some lab testing. Don't you think there's got to be something at that project for both of us?"

"Dunno. You've got more experience but if you're going, I'll tag along."

"Never been to California and I've always wanted to."

Their conversation was many miles distant and happened two weeks ago. Now Banks was in charge of the cement-testing laboratory at Big Creek and Redinger was a transit man on a survey crew. The chemist would leave the project after a few years, but Redinger planted deep roots. Although he did not know it at the time he would buy into Eastwood's dream, forever connecting them both to Big Creek.

* * * * * * * * * *

From the terrace of Sinclair's house on Nob Hill, Eastwood estimated he could see no less than twenty miles inland, past his new house in the hills above Oakland. The day was unusually clear with the usual fog hanging back from shore which gave an extraordinary blue-sky view north, south and east. While he missed the constant presence of the Sierra in Fresno, seeing the bay on one side and the ocean on the other was more exhilarating than he might have imagined.

Sinclair handed him a seaman's glass and pointed north. "Right there. The federal prison on Alcatraz. You can see the sun glint off the soldiers' insignias on their uniforms."

Eastwood laughed. "I can almost read the expression on their faces!"

"Now take a look at the pier. That's my schooner the Lurline toward the left...at least it was mine until I sold her last year. Clarence Macfarlane got it finally. He wanted it was because I beat him in it when we had our first Transpacific Race."

Taking the glass from his eye, Eastwood smiled broadly masking his sadness at seeing Sinclair's deeply lined face and red-rimmed eyes. "That was 1906 and you won it again two years later."

"That I did, but it was the first one that got Macfarlane's dander up. He couldn't get anyone interested in a race against the wind coming back from Hawaii. They all wanted it to be one way, so he set out to prove it could be done. Pulled into Megg's Wharf with King Kalakua's flag on one mast and the Hawaii Yacht Club on another."

"Very impressive..."

"…except he picked April 6th to make harbor, and when there was no hoopla at the pier he was really hot under the collar. After thirty-six hours on watch, all he wanted was a bath, the biggest porterhouse steak available and some acclaim like the county band playing as they slipped in next to the pier. His crew furled the sails and had breakfast in the galley while Macfarlane waited for someone to come.

"Finally, a doctor made it aboard and cleared them to debark. When he griped about no reception, the doctor asked him if he'd noticed anything unusual and he said 'yes, where's everybody?' He got shoved topside and was told to look around. No buildings and no people except for a long line at a tent encampment."

"Was the fire out by that time?"

"Mostly but there were some that burned for the next three days. The doctor realized Macfarlane had no way of knowing the city'd had a terrible earthquake earlier in the day."

Eastwood traced the pier area with the glass. "That why you sailed out of Los Angeles port instead?"

Sinclair nodded, then sat in a lawn chair at the edge of the terrace. "Yes, but that's history. Now take a look downtown. There's the new Mills Tower and the Hammersmith building. That one to the south is the Italian American Bank. Got that one rebuilt by the year after the quake. Started getting it cleaned up even while aftershocks were still scaring the begeebers out of folks."

Eastwood lingered with the glass on a horse-drawn trolley. "Mr. Huntington would be smug about you still using horses for your trolleys. He appears to have an abiding dislike for this city."

With a shrug Sinclair said, "No doubt. But I need to discuss something else with you now that your plan for Big Meadows has been approved and verified by two outside engineers. Both of them suggested changes but otherwise they feel the Multiple Arch dam is the right choice for the site. Is that going to interfere with your plans if the Big Creek board takes Rollins up on his suggestion they use your design for that project?"

The subject was sobering for Eastwood. "No. Even if they choose to use it, they already have a construction company in charge of the work. They're already doing the foundation work for the impoundment to be done. All three dams at one time, too."

Sinclair motioned Eastwood to sit beside him. "I have no concerns about your professional exactitude. It's Freeman that bothers me."

"But he's out of the picture now…"

"…only from a construction point of view. He's still an investor and he's carrying a grudge for having been dismissed from planning and building the small hydro plant. I doubt he has any quarrel with you but since I pushed for your plans, he's after me. Expect trouble because it's a vendetta with him. He can be dangerous."

"But he won't do anything with you having the new president of the board on your side. If nothing else Freeman appears to be respectful of authority."

"Only as far as he can use it. He's still upset that I got the plans to be done in the west. It made no sense to have the work going on in New York when they have no experience out here." Sinclair sagged deeply into his chair. What little color was in his face vanished.

Alarmed, Eastwood looked toward the house just as the valet came onto the terrace with a wheelchair. The sound of the wheels on the flagstones alerted Sinclair and he motioned with his hand for the man to wait. Eastwood was torn between wanting comfort for Sinclair and wanting his counsel. He wondered if a stellar career of ramrodding electricity from novelty to necessity was over as Sinclair appeared to be aging right before his eyes.

"I had Ed Hawley on my side because we worked together before Big Meadows. When he died last winter, the new president continued what Ed had started. Now I don't have the same kind of connection with him." He stopped and seemed to search for strength before continuing. "I brought you here to warn you about Freeman…and to tell you that I have taken a leave of absence from my job."

The valet moved quickly toward Sinclair who made no protest when he was lifted into the wheel chair. As he was wheeled toward the house, Sinclair reached out for Eastwood's hand.

"John…watch your back!"

* * * * * * * * * * *

The late May air at Shaver Lake was warm and pine scented. A doe and two fawns stood within the thick understory of a grove of pines watching John and Ella Eastwood load the last of their provisions onto a pack mule. That the deer did not run at the sight of humans told Ella they were very hungry. She lifted the flap of a saddlebag and took out a double handful of rolled oats and piled it on the ground for the animals.

The Eastwood's annual quiet time together hiking in the mountains was more than pleasure. It was necessity for their spirit. The stagecoach ride from Fresno had been long, interrupted by endless stops to let freight wagons heading for the Big Creek construction pass. Courtesy required that workingmen had the right of way. By the time they reached the general store near the lake the day had begun to lengthen. Anxious to be on their way, the Eastwoods decided to make camp the first night under the giant trees within shouting distance of the lumber mill. They would make Balsam Meadow the next day.

The move to Oakland had been difficult. With construction scheduled to begin at Big Meadow when they returned home, this annual campout was more eagerly anticipated than any other. Worry about Sinclair's health abated with the news he was recovering, but Eastwood would be comfortable at Big Meadows only after his friend and mentor returned. His experience with Big Creek and the financial hierarchy left him wary but still enthusiastic about the project.

The mountains welcomed them with a carpet of wildflowers in small open areas—gentian, monkey flowers, columbine, cowslip and paintbrush. It was as though the two of them were alone in the world with only the flutter of bird wings, rustlings in the underbrush and an occasional treetop windsong. In the lead, Eastwood raised his hand to stop Ella. He pointed to a nurse log covered with seedling trees, moss and ferns.

Ella smiled, then drew her hand slowly upward in the same direction and pointed to a small cottonwood tree nearby where two branches held a woven basket nest. "Vireos. I saw the mother taking them a meal, but she flew off as we came close."

"You want to stop here? I could put the tent by that flat rock."

Ella laughed and shook her head. "No. It's the meadowsong I need."

Above all others they loved Balsam Meadow, their special spot. Quiet and serene, it was a place of regeneration and strength and to find it already occupied was disconcerting.

"Hallo the camp," shouted Eastwood when he saw three men in the clearing.

"Hallo to you. We're passing through," David Redinger replied. "Just stopped to eat." The other men in the survey crew waved a greeting.

Eastwood tied their pack mule to a tree and shook Redinger's outstretched hand. Realizing how close they were to Big Creek and remembering the reaction of the Stone and Webster man at Morgan's, he hesitated. "I'm...John and this is my wife Ella. This is a special spot for us, but there's more than enough room to share it."

"Can't think of anything I'd rather do, but we're working seven days a week. Gotta get a lot done before the snow flies. Heard anything about the Big Creek Project?"

"Umm...yes, I have."

"Well, if you come again next year, look us up. I'll give you a tour. Just stop at Powerhouse #1 in Cascada. They'll find me." The two survey crewmen began to walk away as Redinger picked up the transit with one arm and waved goodbye with the other. At the edge of the meadow he turned and looked back, Eastwood still watching his departure. The same thought descended on both of them in a moment of precognition: *I don't know why but we'll meet at Big Creek and again in this hallowed place.*

"That which does not kill me, makes me stronger."

Nietzsche

Chapter 18

THE FREEMAN FIASCO

As work was about to begin on the foundation of the Big Meadows Dam, surveyors found that the site chosen for it was not entirely within the company owned property. They selected an area several hundred feet upstream, requiring Eastwood to add two additional arches to his original plans to cross the canyon at that point. In any other mountainous place it would have made little difference, so he made no addenda to the original plans other than adding to the distance to be crossed. However, he still needed to get a feel for the project at the new location.

Hiking up a hill that he chose as the southern anchor of the Big Meadows Dam, Eastwood was startled to find someone already there. A young man who looked much like himself twenty years previously stood at the edge of the ridge, one hand shielding his eyes against the rising sun, the other holding the reins of a horse. Eastwood tramped loudly to announce himself since the man appeared to be engrossed in the view.

"Good morning," he called out.

"Yes, indeed," came the reply. "Can't beat the view. I'm Everell Collins, sir, just getting to know the area from this perspective."

"John Eastwood," he said offering his hand. "Got to be a rancher or logger for this country."

"The latter, sir. My family bought some acres east of here in the Quincy region and I need to know the differences between the soft-woods in the High Sierra and the hardwoods hereabouts."

"You must be a new breed of cat in logging. The only ones I ever knew were more interested in harvesting everything there and finding a market for all of it."

Collins laughed. "My father's one of those, sir, but he sent me to be educated and now he's not sure he should have."

"Never knew an education had any drawbacks, son."

"We don't disagree about everything, but cutting down every tree just to get to the more valuable ones isn't good. I look to harvest the softwoods for basic construction. Birches and other hardwoods like ash for interior work. I'd much rather thin a forest than level it."

With an inward sigh, Eastwood looked out across the expanse of foothills where scattered oaks cast long morning shadows on the grassy hillsides. The financial end of building dams took so much energy, he had little left to appreciate the bounty of the mountains. The two of them stood in an area of immense beauty where the northern end of the Sierra Nevada sloped down to a vast high plateau to meet the southern end of the Cascade Range in the watershed of Mount Lassen.

Marked by a network of rivers, creeks and streams, the region was not covered with deeply forested pine tracts but rather clusters of birch and maples mixed with conifers. Where the highlands remained dark green all year, the foothills wore a riot of color each fall as leaves turned to signal the onset of autumn. For months leafless branches traced sun-lit line drawings against snow and then against green grasses before new leaves covered them again in summer. Surrounded by splendor, Eastwood resolved to make an effort to keep business from clouding his vision or tempering his creativity. "I applaud your approach to forestry," he said to Collins. "I hope the next generation will continue in your path."

Collins mounted his horse, and reached down to shake Eastwood's hand. "That, sir, is a given. My son Truman built stilts onto the legs of his bed so he could better see the trees outside his room."

*　*　*　*　*　*　*　*　*　*　*

The new site proved to be far more difficult than anticipated. With slower moving waters, the canyon had filled with far more soil overbur-den than Eastwood estimated and to reach bedrock required crews to dig deeper and deeper into the soil. Added to the unexpected cost for much more concrete, when the bedrock was finally uncovered, a slow steady stream of water oozed from below. By itself the problem could be handled, but combined with the depth of the trenches, the worry that the seepage could uplift the foundation was on everyone's mind.

To ensure a solid connection of the base with the concrete, Eastwood made certain the rock surface at the bottom was rough and jagged. He inspected the full length of the open trench one afternoon in mid-July. Scrambling up the embankment, he looked up to see Sinclair motioning to him from the end of the cableway atop the construction area. A laborer offered Eastwood a hand up the steep slope, but before leaving the construction area he signaled the concrete man to begin pouring, then met his friend at the road alongside the work.

"I heard you were back on the job, but didn't expect to see you here," he said, "and what's more this surprise doesn't look like good news."

Sinclair motioned for Eastwood to get in the automobile. "It's not my choice," he said as he shifted gears and continued down the hill. "I heard from Seymour in Fresno...about something...um...that concerns you."

Eastwood pointed to a clearing next to the road. "Stop over there and just tell me."

As the engine came to a stop Sinclair turned to face Eastwood. "It's Huntington. Seymour said he talked to the editor of the newspaper and he's holding off putting the story out, at least until I tell you about it."

"HH can't do anything more because he's already shut me out of Big Creek. I've already accepted that so what's left for him to do to me?"

"Unfortunately a great deal. He's called for a stock assessment to raise more capital. You have to pay $5 a share by the first of September."

Eastwood paled. "...and if I don't come up with the money?"

Struggling to answer, Sinclair paused, brushed at his moustache, picked an imaginary piece of lint from his sleeve, then murmured, "You lose it completely."

The silence between them was suffocating. Eastwood felt his anger overcoming reason. He leapt from the automobile and let out a pitiful yell as if asking the gods to rain fire and brimstone on his nemesis. He picked up a thick branch and chopped at a boulder until there was nothing left of it but a stub and splinters. Sinclair came around and grabbed for Eastwood's shoulder.

"If you need the money I'll gladly see you get it."

The battle resumed between Eastwood's reason and anger. This time reason won. He flung the last of the branch as far as he could hitting a small tree and scattering two scrub jays from its top. They squawked their surprise, the sound of their anger like his bouncing through the forest from stone to stone until it vanished.

With a sigh of resignation, Eastwood shook his head. "Can't do that, my friend. If HH did it once, he can do it again. That's like gambling in my book and you mean much more to me than money."

Eastwood stood with hands on hips staring at the mountains to the south. "He may have won the day and he may be in charge of the project, but he'll never own it. Big Creek is *mine*...it'll *always* be."

* * * * * * * * * * *

Despite the need for far more excavation than originally estimated, the first concrete for Big Meadows Dam was poured within a month after work began. By the end of August two of twenty-six arches were completed. While he said little to Sinclair and Eastwood when he inspected the construction early in August, Freeman began talking about his misgivings abut the Multiple Arch Dam to everyone else. In a letter to the board of GWPC he questioned the safety of the dam. In further discussions with individual members, he made the presence of water seepage a major problem.

Word began to filter back to Eastwood that Freeman also expressed his displeasure and concern to many other engineers. That did not bode well because if he heard about it from other professionals, it was a certainty that the board would know about it as well. Reluctant to pressure Sinclair, but feeling the need to state his case, he wrote a letter to him about it. Sinclair telephoned to say he would be defending the construction at an emergency meeting of the board of directors the following week in San Francisco.

By the time the meeting was gaveled open, every member knew about the trouble stirred by Freeman. President Mortimer Fleishacker opened discussion without preamble.

"It's come to my attention that the construction of our dam is of questionable integrity," he began. "I've been getting calls from people everywhere, including the California Railroad Commission that the seepage spells certain disaster for us if we do not switch to a traditional design rather than the Multiple Arch."

All eyes turned to Sinclair. He leaned back in his chair and fixed a steely look on Fleishacker. "As you know I have never had a failure in all my years in the electricity and dam business and I do not believe this one will be the first. There is an abundance of opinion coming from respected engineers that the design is excellent and based on irrefutable science."

"Are you saying that Freeman is not respected as an engineering professional?" asked Fleishacker.

"Are you forgetting this is the same man we fired when his calculations for the small hydro plant proved to be tenuous at best? That was when you called on me to clean up the mess he made of it, and I'm of the opinion that he is still miffed about that. He's the one whose calculations so vastly underestimated the need for concrete that the final structure cost twice his original estimate."

One member stirred uncomfortably in his chair. "He has a sterling reputation back east, and don't forget he had a hand in some of the biggest installations in that part of the country…like Boston's Wauchusett Dam and New York City's Catskill Aqueduct," he defended.

"No, I've not forgotten, but one could question why he moved west when he was held in such high esteem in his home area," replied Sinclair. "He also has a reputation for ignoring costs which may not faze a municipality, but certainly is important for us as a private company. We have no tax rolls to tap when our costs bloat out of sight."

Fleishacker gaveled gently on the table. "Gentlemen, we have to consider both cost and safety which is certainly a cost. However, we have another concern. The Railroad Commission said they have doubts about the untried spillway and the siphon gates. If we continue with Eastwood's dam we will have to deal with a bureaucrat breathing down our necks."

"They weren't interested in us before," said Earl, "and they knew about the design. They even approved it."

Support for Eastwood's dam was eroding and Sinclair elected to act decisively. "I move we drop the new spillway design in favor of a traditional arrangement. That way we can get the Railroad Commission to back off and we can look into Freeman's complaint more thoroughly."

Earl raised a hand. "I second the motion." The vote was unanimously in favor.

The rapid drop of confidence in Eastwood's design was slowed until Sinclair could work privately to build it back again.

"A man that does not know how to be angry does not know how to be good."

Henry Ward Beecher

Chapter 19

FALL 1912 – THE ENEMY WITHIN

Private and Personal
Mr. Arthur P. Davis
US Reclamation Service
San Francisco, California   *September 26, 1912*

Dear Mr. Davis,

Thank you for your support of my belief that the Eastwood Multiple Arch Dam is not one for the Big Meadows project. It will be judged by a more or less ignorant public, not so much from a technical point of view but rather by comparison to the familiar solid gravity dam of masonry or earth. The psychology of those airy arches and lace curtain effect of his stiffening props is not well suited to inspire public confidence.

Mr. Eastwood is an honest, intelligent, conscientious, hardworking engineer of good inventive capacity, but I fear he has become so impressed with the beauties of the design that I presume he will build his house shingled with semi-cylindrical tiles and ultimately have his hair trimmed in scallops. But have we a right to build these

*thin structures, under heavy unit loads, where failure would have such
a terrible effect?*

> *Yours truly,*
> *John R. Freeman*

* * * * * * * * * * *

The touring car came to a halt just a few feet from the construction
office before Eastwood recognized who it was. He waited inside as the
driver helped Sinclair out of the back seat. Eastwood's heart sank as he
saw his friend slowly steady himself and then deliberately assume a posture of strength, giving his brimmed cap a rakish angle and lightly using
a golf club for a cane.

The board of GWP Company had met privately after having heard
from Eastwood and then Freeman, each giving their reasons for continuing construction as planned or taking an entirely new approach to
building the dam and hydroelectric plant. Having presented his material and argument first, Eastwood felt at a distinct disadvantage but he
continued to hope that he was going to hear good news because both
science and logic were on his side.

He chose his own way of posing by appearing entirely intent on
drawings until the door to the office flung open and banged against the
outside wall. "Sinclair!" he called out. "I saw a strange automobile
coming up the road and thought it was lost. What happened to the
Olds?"

The driver stepped back toward the car as Sinclair pumped
Eastwood's hand vigorously. "Got a deal I couldn't refuse from Audiwerke
in Germany. The company plans to ship them through the Panama
Canal next year when it's supposed to open. Said I was the right man to
drive it around The City to drum up business."

"I swear, Sinclair, you could fall into a privy hole and come up
smelling like a rose! Come sit by the stove and tell me what brings you
here." Eastwood picked a log from a pile on the floor, stuffed it into the
pot bellied stove, then pulled another chair next to the one he had
offered. The driver returned to the automobile after Sinclair was seated.

"It's awfully quiet here," said Sinclair. "Everyone gone?"

"Not yet. There's a small crew above readying equipment for winter storage. Just can't understand why we need to button things up here.

It's only a tad over 4,000 feet and at Big Creek they're going to work through the winter at about 7,000 feet."

"Ah yes, Big Creek. Seems strange that we've been a part of several sites with similar names…you with that one, then Big Bear Lake and Big Meadows…myself with Big Bend. We've seen a lot of changes you and I…"

Impatient to hear the board's decision, Eastwood tried to get the conversation back to the subject. "This one's going well, and we've got five arches complete…"

"Changes. Haven't we seen them in the last fifteen years! Who'd have thought putting small barbs on wire for fences would cause a range war in cattle country."

"Well, Texas took care of that when Frying Pan Ranch decided fencing was the right thing to do. Now they all do it. A cowboy in the Shaver Lake area told me cutting a wire fence is a major crime now…something like stealing a horse, but tell me about the board… "

"I heard from a man in the Mack Truck Company office that Henry Ford's putting in something he calls an assembly line. Imagine! One man putting the same part of an automobile into a certain place, one after the other all day long. Some say he'll be making a Model T every minute of the work day. Takes a man two days to put one together now. Where will he sell all those…"

"Sinclair," Eastwood said softly. "You came with news and I'm thinking it's not good if Henry Ford is more on your mind than what the board decided about this dam." He stood up and poked the fire in the stove, trying to make room for another log. The silence between them was uncomfortable. In the distance the only sound heard was the call of migration. From a distance the autumn music increased as an enormous flock of Canada geese came closer and closer until the air was filled with a cacophony of honking birds. Both men watched through the office window as the sky darkened with thousands of wings beating the air then gradually vanished as their symphony sank silently into the hollows of the mountain nooks and crannies. Finally, Sinclair spoke.

"The board said to shut down for winter but I get the distinct feeling they will not resume the Multiple Arch Dam in the spring."

Eastwood sat stoically staring at the fire in the stove without acknowledging he heard. He sighed deeply and said quietly, "I gave them the best dam for far less money and they are going to choose one that will likely be as wide and deep as it is tall." He turned to Sinclair. "They must have money to burn with a million dollars already spent."

"There's a different kind of mindset and I don't understand it. I had letters from both the Hume Lumber and Big Bear water people attesting to their dams reliability but somehow it's more important to worry about the Railroad Commission and the US Reclamation folks. Both your dams are working perfectly and there's not one leak anywhere."

Frustration consumed Eastwood. He leapt up and began pacing the office. "I told them the uplift that Freeman made sound so worrisome is more of a problem with his kind of gravity dam. Hell, Pennsylvania's Austin dam was just that kind of construction and uplift was what destroyed it! My dam can resist the pressure much better because it's distributed! What kind of idiots are they that they can't see the difference?!"

"John, it didn't help when you called him a blithering idiot for saying reinforced concrete was not safe for this dam but he recently recommended it for construction at MIT."

"It happens to be true! I also told them Freeman's recommendations are more annoying than real and will cost them money. They'll cause enormous regret as well."

Eastwood angrily slapped his forehead and stopped his pacing. "Freeman said that my understanding of stress and concrete was 'imperfect.' My dam is not a curiosity, a freak or accidental discovery, but the result of hard work!"

"I know that," Sinclair said soothingly. "I'm told he sold San Francisco on the Hetch Hetchy reservoir dam on the basis of bulk. He said it was imprudent to put up anything less than a massive structure because the ignorant public would look at a lesser dam with fears of it failing."

"The board fired Freeman because of his so-called expertise and now they accepted that?!"

"Took it hook, line and sinker because it was already sold to the Railroad Commission and the Reclamation people. In all fairness, the board is worried that the Pacific Gas & Electric Company will step in and take over our share of the market."

"And the board accepted that?!" repeated Eastwood.

"Freeman sold them on the idea that your dam looks fragile and the public is complaining about it."

"*And the board accepted that, too?!*"

Sinclair nodded, then leaned forward to grasp a log from the pile next to the stove. He handed it to Eastwood. "You want to bang this around?" he said with a small smile.

Slowly Eastwood walked toward his friend, took the log from his hand and stared at it. Then he turned and hurled it through the window. The two men stared at each other as the sound of shattered glass and the log tumbling outside echoed then vanished like the honking geese. "Let's go home," he said gathering his plans from the table.

"Yes, but there's one more thing you should know. That new automobile out there was made by August Horch. He started up a company and then went into shares, something like you were forced to do with Huntington. Within a few years, he had a disagreement with the management of the board of directors. He lost everything, even his ability to use his own name on any other automobiles he might build."

"Sinclair, what do automobiles have to do with dam construction?"

"Not the dams. The man. Horch started up another company to build an even better model of automobile. His name in German means *listen*, so he calls the new model by his name as it's said in Latin— *Audi*. As sure as we are standing here, I predict few people will know about or drive a Horch in the days to come, but the Audi will be around for a long, long time."

"When old words die out on the tongue, new melodies break forth from the heart; and where the old tracks are lost, new country is revealed with its wonders."

Rabindranath Tagore

Chapter 20

VOYAGE OF THE AMERICAN KINGS – 1913

Early July in New York was stifling even at four in the afternoon with a stiff onshore breeze at the water's edge. Cunard's *Aquitania* rode less than gently at anchor as hundreds of passengers boarded up the broad gangway, each holding fast to the handrail to steady themselves against the ship's roll. Crewmen stood waiting to assist ladies by offering an arm, and most accepted the offer.

Always exciting, this departure held more than its share for Henry and Arabella Huntington. It was a trip postponed from the previous year when they were in New York. HH had planned to surprise Arabella by taking her to France and marrying her there. However, his plan to sail on the Titanic was abruptly cancelled when the ship hit an iceberg and sank on its maiden voyage to the US. He had to talk her into the idea of getting back on an ocean liner but had the grace to wait until she mourned the loss of her friends John Astor and Martin Rothschild.

"Belle, the *Aquitania* is a much stronger ship than the Titanic ever was," he told her. "I've made arrangements with the Captain to show you the new route it will take, well out of the way of any floating ice."

With Arabella still reluctant to take the trip, he played his trump card and gave up on any surprise. He proposed to her and she said yes, but still hesitated to board the ship until he read to her from the information he had about it.

"It's called *The Ship Beautiful* because it looks as if Sir Christopher Wren designed it…like a living museum with tapestries, old panels and coats of arms. It has Elizabethan needlework and the Gainsborough Suite where we will stay has a Sitting Room done in 18th century style with antique mezzotints of famous artists." Arabella stood at the mantle of a fireplace with her back to HH. He looked for a sign she was weakening and then droned on. "The decor is Louis XVI and on another deck there's even a swimming…"

"Alright! I'll go, but if that ship gets into any trouble whatsoever, I will never forgive you!"

HH was not certain she would follow through until they boarded and the band played *Aloha 'Oe*. Impatient to be aweigh, he concentrated on the group as it played a stirring rendition of *Stars and Stripes Forever*. Staring at the bandleader, he leaned forward to get a clearer look.

"Yes. It's Sousa," said a man to his right.

"You sure?"

"Very. I'm responsible for them being here. The name's Hearst. William Hearst."

He offered his hand and HH shook it. "We've met, Mr. Hearst, in San Francisco some time ago. The name's Huntington. Henry Huntington and this is…"

"Mrs. Arabella Huntington," Hearst finished. "Madame, I remember your husband Collis very well." She offered her hand fingers down and Hearst drew it to himself and kissed it.

At the sound of her name, the captain of the ship who had been greeting passengers stepped up and cleared his throat, waiting for permission to speak. "Captain," said HH, "Mrs. Huntington is anxious to see what we discussed in correspondence."

"Of course, sir. This way to the chart cabin, please madam."

"I'll be around here or in the suite," HH said as she folded her parasol and took the captain's arm.

"Or in the Garden Lounge," said Hearst. "Will you join me for a drink, Mr. Huntington?"

"If you'll tell me why you're responsible for them," he replied pointing to the band.

"They're going to tour in Europe. I convinced Cunard to let them sail in exchange for a concert each evening."

* * * * * * * * * * *

Hearst pointed to a table with wicker chairs in the outer area of the lounge on the starboard side of the ship. Glass panels protected them from wind and spray. Large planters scattered around mixed smells of wet earth and greenery with salt air. One could easily imagine they were sitting in an old garden in the south of France overlooking the Mediterranean.

"Thought we'd be taking the *Lusitania*," said HH, "but it's in dry dock. From the looks of this ship I'd say we got the better end of that deal."

Hearst smiled knowingly. "She's getting outfitted with big guns. German subs are getting rather good at sinking ships and the British are preparing for the worst."

"You with the royals on this?"

Hearst laughed. "Not by a long shot! I make it my business to know because that's how newspapers should be run." He signaled a waiter and then ordered two empty glasses. "Got something you've never tasted before, I'll wager," he said to HH, then pulled a silver flask from his pocket and laid it on the table. "It's Drambuie."

"You're right. Never heard of it, let alone tried it."

The waiter returned with a tray holding two glasses, then placed them in front of Hearst who poured a small amount from the flask into each of them.

"I guarantee you'll like it and the story behind it."

HH took a small, tentative sip, then smiled. "Right so far."

Hearst tasted his drink, then let it linger on the tongue before swallowing slowly. "It's from Bonnie Prince Charlie—King Charles Edward Stuart of Scotland. Unfortunately he challenged the reigning Hanovers in England and they went to war. His army was undone at Culloden.

"He fled to the heather, as they say in those parts, with a price on his head that would be the equal of a couple million dollars today. Captain John MacKinnon hid the king on the Isle of Skye. Before leaving for France the king gave the secret recipe for his personal liqueur as a token of appreciation.

"The MacKinnons made the drink for themselves for generations and called it *An Dram Buidheach* which is *drink that satisfies* in Gaelic.

Four years ago, the current MacKinnon moved to Edinburgh and got into the whiskey trade. Made a batch of what he calls Drambuie and sold a dozen cases." Hearst tipped his glass to HH. "One of them to me."

"That's all news to me, but tell me how you knew the *Lusitania* was being fitted for war."

"I'd like to say it was because I'm in the business of news, but Cunard had that ship and this one built in Scotland. Got the Drambuie there and met the owner of the John Brown Company in Clydebank at the same time. Cunard sent the *Lusitania* back to Brown for the refitting and, well you know how it is…the ladies leave the room after dinner and gentlemen talk. What brings you to Europe?"

"I'm a collector…mainly rare books, but paintings as well."

"I collect antiquities but I'm interested in more than the written word. It's buildings that appeal to me."

HH laughed. "You coming to visit the ones you bought?"

Hearst shook his head and took a languid sip from his glass. "Not by a longshot. I ship them home stone by stone. Got doors, ceilings, panels, arches—you name it. This trip I'm going to get an entire stone building from the 14th century. The village people call it a barn, but it's more like a cathedral with arched windows and craftsmanship that would make some people weep and run their fingers over the bas relief carved on the walls."

HH was stunned. He had already spent millions on books, art work and statuary, but it never occurred to him to buy an entire building and have it shipped home, especially one that was five hundred years old. While HH lived in San Francisco, Hearst's reputation was a subject for discussion everywhere and even though he was still angry over his rebuff at the board meeting more than a decade previously, HH grudgingly admired the man who single-handedly started the Spanish-American War.

The two men shared a common trait in demanding control of those around them. However, while HH confined his activities to business, Hearst was actively manipulating public policy and opinion. He appeared to be intent on controlling the opinion of millions of people. The idea was staggering.

HH drained the last of his Drambuie. "And what will you do with that building when it gets to San Francisco?"

"Not sure. I started building a place in the Pleasanton area but lost interest in it. After my father died, mother moved back from Washington DC. She wanted to restart construction so I turned it over to her. It's just as well. I like the family ranch at San Simeon much better. My father loved to camp out there when I was a kid, but a tent's not my idea of fun."

"But a barn is?"

"Huntington, you need to take a trip to the south of France. What's a barn there is nothing like what you have in mind, and a book to them is not just a book. Some of the monasteries in that area are loaded with hand-lettered and ornamented books more than a thousand years old. A lot of those religious orders are dying off for lack of money. It's not just the aristocracy looking for investor dollars."

* * * * * * * * * * *

Despite the fact that at the same time Freeman extolled the virtues of reinforced concrete at MIT's new construction, he condemned it at Big Meadow, saying that "it has imperfect theories of stress and shrinkage may be irregular." He was hired by the board of directors to work with Julius Howells to design and build the new gravity dam several hundred feet upstream from the five arches of the incomplete Eastwood structure. Freeman lasted only through preliminary plan completion before leaving on an extended vacation in Europe. Sinclair shook his head in disbelief at the brazen destruction of Eastwood's reputation.

It was clear to him that rather than wanting credit for the dam, all Freeman wanted was to discredit Eastwood. Thoroughly dispirited and again declining in health, Sinclair resigned from the company in the spring of 1913. Before he left, he made sure Eastwood was properly paid for the work he did in good faith.

On the day Eastwood came to Sinclair's Nob Hill home to pick up the check, the Bay Area was thickly cloaked in a marine layer down to ground level. He inched along the road steering with one hand and moving the windshield wiper with the other. His two kerosene lantern lights on the front of his Ford gave a golden glow to the pea soup all around, and a mournful fog horn at water's edge marked each minute that passed as he motored up the hill.

He parked in the circular driveway and then reached for a small box on the passenger seat and hurried to the house. Before he reached the door, the valet was waiting. "Mr. Sinclair is expecting you, Mr. Eastwood... in the library." He pointed toward the rear of the house beyond a sweeping staircase, and then vanished with Eastwood's damp coat and hat.

Eastwood hesitated, not wanting to see his friend failing. It was difficult to watch him slow in the last two months and having to stop to catch his breath. An inner voice said this was goodbye and it was impossible to ignore. Eastwood sighed deeply and then proceeded to the library.

Books lined the walls on three sides with the remaining one open to the world by way of floor to ceiling windows separated in the center by a great stone hearth. Sinclair sat by the fire with his back to Eastwood. Deep carpeting muffled his footsteps, and it was startling to hear his friend speak in a strong voice.

"About time you got here, Eastwood. You let a little fog slow you down?"

"No, not the fog. Ella insisted that I bring you a package of treats and she spent an hour picking the best ones just for you," he lied.

"You better not have dipped into my box of dried apricots, Eastwood, or you'll have to go back for more!"

"I already got that warning from Ella because these are different. She melted some Hershey chocolate bars and dipped them in it. I told her it was a waste of good apricots until I tasted them. Our friendship never had a stronger test than that the box get here still full." He placed the box on Sinclair's lap and then pulled up a chair to sit beside him.

"Looks like she left the pits in them but they're white. Some kind of game?"

"No joke. She stuffed them with almonds when I reminded her they were your favorite kind of nut."

"John, that's a lie. You've always been my favorite kind of nut." Eastwood leaned back and laughed hard, partly from the joy of hearing Sinclair as his old self and partly out of relief that his spirit was strong despite his infirmity.

"Maybe that's why I keep engineering…just for entertainment. My grandfather would have loved that. He was a Royal Dutch Engineer who supervised construction of the dikes in Holland over a hundred years ago."

Sinclair bit into an apricot and leaned back in his wheelchair. "What a century of change it's been! A lot of good things happened along with the bad. I saw an advertisement in the newspaper the other day that made me think. It was a huge eye in the middle of a Pinkerton pitch for customers. The idea was that they're private eyes for others. Not a bad idea, but their picture book of criminals has made a big difference in law enforcement. Now people can recognize criminals by their mugs and report it far from the scene of the crime."

"That was why Butch Cassidy tried to change his face with surgery. How about the telegraph? Now there's an invention that changed a lot of things, but I think it's the telephone that made a bigger difference."

"Maybe so in the east but out here there's something better. Smokeless gunpowder. Local sheriff told me once they got to use that, a posse couldn't tell where the shots came from in the badlands. They got picked off like cherries from a tree."

"Too bad there isn't a posse for criminals in corporations," observed Eastwood ruefully.

"You've had more than your share, but it's a matter of control and that's not new. The Boston Tea Party happened because the British East India Company got the tax put on tea, and look what happened next. I think that when a corporation was deemed to be a 'natural person' by the court a decade ago, business got a free pass into exalted status. Nothing moves without business, least of all the government."

Eastwood stood and stirred the fire, then added a new log. He remained by the heat as if to warm himself against the chill of bad memories. "I have come to realize this electrical industry will best serve the people by standardizing the transmission of power and regulating it by government as a necessary monopoly."

Sinclair took a bite of another apricot. "You won't find a lot of support for that view, John, but it's never stopped you before. How're you able to keep from being bitter about how you've been treated?"

Eastwood laughed and faced his friend. "I have some successes, money in the bank and two people who believe in me as much as I do myself...Ella and you. I don't know how much more time either of us has, but I'm damned certain that whichever of us goes first, the other will remain behind in spirit...and the heart."

In summer of 1917, three dams arose to form Huntington Lake. Steam locomotives pull three-yard capacity dump cars from the batch plant nearby. Cement was dumped into chutes that directed it into place for the dam face.
From the Edison Collection

"What can give us surer knowledge than our senses? With what else can we better distinguish the true from the false?"

Lucretius

Chapter 21

THE EARTH MOVES AT BIG CREEK —1913

David Redinger placed the telephone receiver back onto the hook. Getting a raise and promotion came with added burdens and this one would require two long days hiking. The crew at Tunnel 2 needed the "prezacts" checked and he was the only engineer available to do it. A combination of *precision* and *exact*, the work required him to use spring balances on steel tape lines and make computations with a transit to determine the direction for digging.

Even with constant assessments by the men in the crew, the possibility of error was always on their minds. The digging for each tunnel had a number of adits (entries) and exits into the main line done at the same time. The practice decreased the time necessary to get the job done but only with accurate computations. The tension as one crew came close to the one on the opposite side of the dig was always high, but the men were confident in the skill of engineers. They considered them one of their own, meaning they felt free to play pranks. Sometimes when the breakthrough was done, the man holding the plumb would deliberately hold it a foot off the mark until the young engineer would blanch and swallow hard. It was a moment to treasure and worked more than once. It was Redinger's turn to face that possibility at Tunnel 2.

January was brutal with more than five feet of snow falling within a short time. One of the engines on the railroad was blizzard-bound for nineteen days while a crew of a hundred and fifty men strained with wooden shovels to dig out several miles of track by hand.

The emergency was Redinger's first experience as a boss and the men got the best of him very quickly. When one broke his shovel, Redinger sent him to oversee another crew further down the track. That brought on a flurry of broken shovels until he finally caught on and sent two of the men back to the shop to get a new supply. It was a long trek on foot and the men wouldn't get back until the next day. It was a lesson well remembered by all.

For two weeks no one moved except by foot, struggling through deep snow on snowshoes. Even now with all the whiteness gone a month later Redinger knew it could happen again without warning. A snow-less February was strange. However, on the heels of the January storm, it made the weather worrisome. Work on the dams continued all winter long with the help of large canvases stretched over the concrete processing plant and each of the areas where they poured. Fires stoked steam engines to keep temperatures above freezing under cover and insure the concrete cured properly. The construction was worked twenty-four hours a day.

The heavy storm revealed how quickly construction had become dependent on telephones. Only when lines went down in the blizzard did they feel cut off from camp to camp where work proceeded in a dozen different areas. Tunnel diggers were not affected by the storm once the crew got far enough underground, but everyone else was.

When the stationmaster at Big Creek realized he had no way of warning the trains not to come, he hiked five miles in the deep snow to use the telephone at the next station. For five days he stayed there as contact between the crews digging the tracks out and the waiting trains in the Valley. One of the construction families came to his rescue and made sure he was fed and kept warm in the station.

"When they invited me to supper," Walker told Redinger, "there was somethin' different about them dishes. They was kind o' see through, so when the lady had her back turned I checked the underside. I was eatin' off Haviland china!"

In a rag house with a wooden floor, canvas sides and roof, Redinger chuckled to himself at the time. Now he was headed up the mountain in a rigorous climb. He thought about taking a railroad pump handcar but it was even harder to pump up the steep inclines. In addition there was always the danger of the train coming around a bend and having to dump the handcar quickly to get out of the way.

Stationed at Camp #1, the first camp down mountain, Redinger faced an all-day climb to get to where the dams were closing in the Basin for water storage at the far opposite end of construction. With a sigh of resignation, he put on a warm coat, strapped on a pack with a slide rule, change of clothes, fistful of beef jerky and a canteen of water. Then he picked up the heavy Berger transit and stepped out into a crisp early afternoon.

He headed toward the railroad line hoping to get a ride at least to Big Creek from the next station, West Portal. He'd learned a lot in a short time and was a long way from his first week when he found that an upper bunk was the best choice. For months he was relegated to the lower one and endured night after night being showered with chaff, dirt and pieces of a straw mattress as the man above turned in sleep. He never complained but also never lost sight of how to get along in a work environment that had no precedent for any of them. Myriad challenges that faced them nearly every day sharpened their wits and honed a resolve to get the job done well.

Redinger faced a hike of seven miles in a rise of 4000 feet packing a sixty-pound load. Unless he was able to get a ride with a wagon, beyond that point he had another 4,500 feet rise in the next 6 miles.

He reached West Portal in good time and listened for the familiar squeal of steel railroad wheels grinding against twists and turns in the route. The forest was quiet. Even when he bent down to put his ear to the rail, he heard nothing. No train would rescue him this trip.

At Big Creek he stopped to eat and inquired about any wagons due to make the trip to the Basin. Again disappointed, he packed up and moved resolutely toward the road. Not only was he pushing himself to get to the job site, he was wary of meeting a grizzly on the way.

It was only recently that he found the meaning of certain rock cairns along the road. It was not unusual to see them marking a trail. Indians had used the route for hundreds of years and it was common sense to cut a road following that same way up into the mountains. Hunters and trappers often raised rock markers for retracing their way back, but these were different. Each of the ones placed by Miwoks marked the spot where someone had been killed by a grizzly. The tribe honored that person's courage in meeting so great an animal. Redinger had seen the memorial cairns from a wagon seat but now he would be at ground level and feeling vulnerable. While the time was right for hibernation, the weather made him uneasy, thinking it could coax the bears out of a den early.

For all his concerns, he made it to the Basin in one piece and right at suppertime. Wearily he entered the cookhouse, dropped his load at the door and went directly to a table. He knew that smell—a hunk of beef had been cooking all day long and the aroma was intoxicating. He set to eating like it was his last meal—hot coffee, beans, meat, mashed potatoes, biscuits, honey, carrots and two huge slabs of apple pie laced with heavy cream.

Jory Morgan laughed as Redinger finished the last of his pie. "Ain't seen a man eat like that since we was shoveling snow off the tracks, Mr. Redinger!"

"Well, Morgan, if this is how you eat every day, maybe I should put in for a transfer to work here."

"Don't know if we could afford you, sir…'sides, we jist got this cook after we run the last one out with a rope!"

Redinger smiled broadly. "So I heard. The noose party came in the front door and the cook went out the back. Understand he's not been seen nor heard from since."

"You got that right, and we ain't had no trouble with this one…at least not yet. Pays to get a little blood in the eye now and again."

Stretching back in his chair, Redinger nodded in agreement. "Thought I'd be heading for the sack but the food was good enough to make me right again."

"You sayin' you trucked on up here from Camp 1 in one day?"

"One hellova day."

"You lookin' fer a bunk?

"Thought I was but I'm ready to go again. You working tonight?"

"Yes, sir. You heard we got a problem."

"Nothing we can't handle, Morgan. Sure was quiet on the way up here, without you blasting rock. Gotta do something about that."

Morgan grew quiet. He studied his hands for a moment before continuing. "It jist didn't feel right…I mean I got no education, but you work a tunnel for a while and you get to know it inside out. Something was feelin' kind of *off* but I cain't tell why." He turned to Redinger and grinned. "Got Cornish miner blood in me. That makes me half hound and half a digger...well mebby not half 'cause a real miner from the Old Country sings, too."

It was a sweet memory. Sing they did at Christmas time in the tradition from the land they left, making exquisite harmony deep in the tunnel where the music surrounded them all. Electric lights throughout the tunnel were turned off and lighted candles turned the event into a bit of the Old Sod. Even those who knew nothing of the land from which Morgan came, were one with the songs that night.

First outside and then deep into the tunnel Redinger worked all night, finally finishing just as the breakfast call rang out. Morgan was right. The digging was well off the mark.

Redinger stumbled into the cookhouse, and again ate until he could hold no more, then tramped to the bunkhouse and took the first top bunk he found. Even if he had to take a lower, no amount of straw dust and chaff could waken him for hours.

*   *   *   *   *   *   *   *   *   *   *

Delayed by the furor at Big Meadows and concerns for Sinclair's health, it was August before the Eastwoods took their annual camping trip to the High Sierra. For the first time they took the Big Creek train, the San Joaquin and Eastern Railroad, and rode from the Valley to Camp 1 station in a mere five hours. The train ride was 56 miles and although the stagecoach road was shorter, they had previously made the trip in a very long sixteen-hour day with station stops to rest horses and passengers.

The train ride was nearly half over before Eastwood began to relax. Only when he smelled the sweet pines and felt the forest deepen around the train did he sigh deeply and stretch his legs under the bench seat in front. A workingman across the aisle from the Eastwoods tipped his soft hat and offered a scone from his lunch pail.

"The wife's a good cook," he said.

Eastwood nodded, "Thank you," and passed two of Ella's nut stuffed dried apricots to the man. "I'm John Eastwood and this is my wife, Ella. She's the one who puts up the fruit," he said as he reached to shake the man's hand.

"Tully. Jethro Tully from County Cork."

"Well, Tully, if you're going back home, you got on the wrong train."

"Aye, that would be the case, but I'm on the way back to work."

"Big Creek?"

"That's the place. I'm a hammer man on a drilling crew. Got the best record for slinging the hammer and that got me a raise. Ain't never hit a man turning the drill yet and I make good money now. Not like injuneers. They get the best pay and the woods is full of them sivil injuneers."

Eastwood smiled. "I'm one of them, too. Does that mean I have to give you the scone back?"

Tully laughed. "No, sir. The givin's for good. You workin' the Big Creek, too?"

Eastwood swallowed hard before answering. "There was a time when I thought I might be, but..."

Tully shifted uncomfortably at Eastwood's discomfort. "I c'n understand that," he said quietly. "Everybody wants to work up there, even in the dead of winter. Don't like time away from the wife and kids, but I never found a better crew. The bosses are kindly, too. Maybe you could try again next year."

"I'm designing a dam somewhere else, but I always had a soft spot in my heart for this area. That's why we vacation here every summer."

Ella leaned forward to see past her husband. "I'm curious about what's in your pocket. I've seen you drop pieces of scone in there. You smuggling somebody into camp?"

Tully's sun baked cheeks reddened. "No, ma'am. I'm takin' Critter back home." He reached into the pocket and pulled out a small chipmunk. "This little fella helps make time away from home a tad bearable. I took him home thinkin' he'd make a good pet for m' kids. Stopped at the big department store in Fresno to get Lovey...that's my wife...a new coat. Had this little fella and his two sisters in a cage but when this fat lady—excuse me, ma'am—buxom lady tried on a coat next to me she knocked the cage clean off the counter whilst she stuffed her arm in a sleeve. Them little chipmunks turned that fancy store into a hoot and holler!

"Ladies was screamin' and standin' on counters and beatin' at me with coat hangers and such. I found this little feller because he hopped into the pocket of Lovey's coat I was holdin'. He likes my pocket where he can stay warm. Never did find the other two and with that store an uproar, I hightailed it out of there fast. Good thing I already paid for the coat."

"And you couldn't bear leaving the chipmunk at home?"

"No, ma'am. Critter's a keeper but the wife said he weren't a fittin' pet for the kids and I had to take him back. Guess things look different for a lonely man deep in the wildlands."

Ella tried to stifle her smile behind her hand but the harder she tried to be primly sympathetic, the more she was unable to restrain her glee. She erupted into laughter, infecting her husband, the owner of the chipmunk and passengers in the entire railcar.

"Mr. Tully," she said when she was able to speak again. "I would be happy to take Critter back to the woods for you. We'll be camping tonight not far from the construction."

"Thankee, ma'am, but if it's all the same to you, I'll jist keep 'im at the bunkhouse. He comes and goes by knothole near my bunk. The men roomin' there 'pear to take a shine to 'im, too, 'specially Mr. Redinger."

Ella looked quickly at her husband. "John, is he the…"

Eastwood smiled and squeezed her hand. "Yes, I'm sure of it. Good to know he's still here."

"Spider" tripods were designed and built for use on steep slopes to keep survey equipment level. High pressure compressed air jack hammers were used to carve out a level path for penstock lines leading to Powerhouse #1 from Huntington Lake.

Stone & Webster Photo from the Edison Collection

Namaste: *The belief that there is a Divine spark within each of us that is located in the heart,* chakra. *The gesture is an acknowledgment of the soul in one by the soul in another.*

Chapter 22

CONNECTION AND TIMELESSNESS

Before any work could be done on the Big Creek Project itself several small communities within the construction area had to be built. Thousands of men hand-cut tens of thousands of logs to create millions of board feet of lumber—enough to send a line of 2 by 12's end to end from California's border at Mexico to Grant's Pass, Oregon. The project was spread over an area fifteen by twenty miles within some of the wildest country in the west. By the standards of the times, it was instant settlement of mountainous regions just south of where the Donner Party was stranded sixty-five years earlier.

Each area needed water tanks, cookhouses, bunkhouses, offices, barns for horses and mules, blacksmith shops, a doctor's office, small homes for managers' families, and forms for dams, as well as enormous warehouses to store equipment and supplies. Construction began at a number of strategically placed camps heading from both directions to meet crews doing the same.

The decision to move the project into high gear was made to capture the winter runoff in spring of 1913. With electricity coming from the company's San Joaquin Light & Power Company, work went on without letup, two shifts doubling the expected number of workmen needed. That meant the need for butchers, cooks and servers doubled as did equipment and supplies. Some buildings, mainly cookhouses had to be enlarged as they were being built.

The Basin was a natural location for water storage. Two thousand feet above Powerhouse #1, it needed three small dams to enclose the watershed of eighty square miles of runoff. As trees in the Basin were harvested, crews laid thirteen miles of train tracks within it to gather the logs for lumbering as well as to harvest granite for fill, ballast and reinforcement in the dams.

Mules and the newly improved fresno scrapers created roads in the wilderness. The men were amazed at how fast a fresno with a scoop could fill with leveling earth and then deposit it where it was needed instead of having men and shovels do the work. In areas where roads went along mountainsides, survey crews devised an entirely new tripod from ordinary plumbing parts for transits to work on steep rock slopes. Trains made the trip to and from the Valley several times a day, bringing equipment, concrete, tools, men looking for jobs, food, oil fuel and tons of nails.

Two tunnels would be cut through solid granite creating a fifteen by fifteen foot corridor through the mountains. The tube would be large enough to accommodate a railroad line simply for temporary use bringing in men and tools, then removing all the debris created in the void. Number 1 was planned to run water from the lake in the Basin to large steel pipes leading to Powerhouse 1 for the necessary consistent water flow. Tunnel Number 2 would direct water to Powerhouse 2 to make electricity again from the same run of water.

Hard rock boring was done by hand with pistol drills. Each adit and exit required a blacksmith at the entrance to sharpen bits constantly. Once holes were drilled they were filled with dynamite and exploded. The ensuing blasts rocked the mountains constantly. With each explosion, men entered the tunnel to hand clear all the rock debris, loading it into trams pulled by mules. On call day and night, engineers ran to check the headings in the tunnels after each blast was set off.

The ambitious drive to get the dams, tunnels and powerhouses built in eighteen months was a brilliant move, but it came with a huge cost and dire consequences. The investment pool of money was drying up.

In Los Angeles Henry Huntington came home from France with his new wife and a new attitude toward his investments. In the months following his personal banishment of John Eastwood, HH had few contacts with Kerckhoff and Balch but early in spring it came as a pleasant surprise to find that the two of them wanted to cut their ties to Big Creek. With little discussion, they came to a quick agreement. The two men surrendered their investment in the Pacific Light & Power Corporation in return for total control of all the gas subsidiaries in the company. The partnership was dissolved and HH went his separate way with 96.8% of all stock in PL&P. Balch privately called the break a very welcome divorce.

Abruptly HH found himself close to complete control of the Big Creek project. He had hungered after it and connived to make it happen, but strangely it came at a time when the drive to go it alone in business was beginning to pall. Arabella made a big difference in his life and although the two of them had been together for several years, marrying made an enormous difference in their relationship—especially for HH.

He was sixty-three years old and finding personal contentment that had never before been a priority in his life. Free-spirited Arabella had wakened new perspectives to him. The collection of antiquities drew him to a new worldview. However, that newly minted mind-set had to take a back seat to a looming crisis at Big Creek.

The decision to accelerate the construction schedule was half the problem. Stone & Webster's insistence that traditional gravity dams were the only design to consider for the sites nearly destroyed the project. Eastwood's complete computations for the entire system were incredibly accurate in the field, but the construction firm forgot to account for the far greater cost of gravity dams as compared to the multiple arch design in the plans. A major increase in manpower and construction plus the vastly more expensive traditional dams put Big Creek at a crossroads.

All construction was shut down just before the Huntingtons set foot back in California as man and wife. HH came home to a hornet's nest of confusion, consternation and near calamity. No other shred of business could be considered until the Big Creek question was settled—to abandon the project or somehow regroup.

Despite the early hour, E.H. Rollins was waiting for HH when he arrived at his office. The two men wasted little time getting down to business.

"What's happening up there now?" asked HH with a scowl.

"Nothing. Stone & Webster can't pay the men beyond the next two weeks, so they have all been told to go home and wait to be called. They're still feeding them so nobody's left so far."

"You mean they're not working and still feeding off me?"

Rollins frowned. "The men are working free to pay for their keep. They stack lumber and get some of the maintenance done there's no time for otherwise—like sharpening tools and cleaning out the warehouses. The mules are free riding in pastures. You want to get rid of them until they can earn their keep?"

HH ignored the sarcasm. "And what alternatives do you see for the problem? We can't expect any income from the project until it's finished and we're still about three months away from that."

"Am I to understand there won't be a complete shut-down?"

HH stood from his chair and poured two cups of coffee from a carafe. He offered one to Rollins and then took a sip of his own before answering. He sat down again and appeared to be wrestling with his response.

"Big Creek's been in the planning for more than a decade. I wasn't sold on it from the start but didn't want Mulholland to get his paws into it. Thought I was just tying it up until it finally got to the point I had to fish or cut bait. Decided to drop a line and see what it could do. Never thought I'd get caught up in it like I have...even when the fire at Powerhouse 2 destroyed the upper floor and set construction back. I've never been up there but in my mind I could see those rafters coming down and bringing the fresh poured concrete with them."

Rollins sat motionless, stunned by something he was seeing for the first time—a caring side that HH had heretofore kept hidden. He took a long, slow sip of coffee to gather his thoughts, but before he could begin, HH spoke sharply.

"There will be no shut down. I'll use other investments as collateral for the money to finish. This is the last chance for any of us to sew up a project of this kind. By the time Mullholland gets his way with the rest of Los Angeles, the last electric supplier left to compete with government will be Big Creek and I want my name on it."

This was the HH that everyone knew, even though he seemed somewhat different. Rollins put his cup on the desk and stood up.

"Agreed. We tell Stone & Webster to get back to work, but we do it together. I have my private railcar at the downtown depot and we can leave in the morning for Big Creek."

* * * * * * * * * * *

The sun was still well above the mountain horizon when the San Joaquin and Eastern Railroad pulled into Big Creek Station. The Eastwoods bade farewell to their seatmate and his pocket pet, then headed for a young man standing next to a saddled horse and two pack mules. The young man scanned the people getting off the train, as he held a sign to his chest: *Mr. Eastwood, here, please.*

Ella walked straight toward him while her husband went to unload their camping gear and supplies from the next car. "You been waiting long?" she asked the man.

He tipped his cap and smiled. "No, ma'am. West Portal calls the storeowner when the train leaves that station, so we figured you'd be here right about now. Can I help you get the mules loaded?"

Ella shook her head. "Thanks, but my husband's a mad planner. He knows exactly where he wants to put things so I just hand him what he calls for. Please thank the owner for the service. Thanks to his offer to have you meet us, we can make Balsam Meadow before dark."

* * * * * * * * * * *

In his private railcar parked on the siding at Big Creek, E.H. Rollins was feeling expansive. Not only did he convince HH to come to the project, the man actually seemed pleased to have made the trip. It was the first time the majority stockholder in Big Creek had ever seen anything of the construction work and he appeared to be impressed. A substantial amount of water had already reached the impoundment at the Basin even as construction of the dams continued.

Standing atop one of the dams, HH remarked that it was much larger than he had imagined. "Doesn't seem right to call such a grand lake the Basin," he said more to himself than an observation to share with Rollins.

"On that we agree, but it looks like it already has a new name. When the men heard you're putting your own property on the line to save the project, they started saying it should be *Huntington Lake*. Have to agree with them."

HH said nothing but looked out over the immense tree-cleared Basin. Men in boats were continuing to cut trees as water inched up closer and closer to the edges of the confinement. He stared a long while as if to save the picture, then moved silently toward the company automobile.

Back at the railroad depot in the private car, a valet mixed drinks at the bar. He served one to HH. As he approached Rollins the man's eyes drifted out the window, then widened slightly. Rollins picked up on the message and casually looked out the window himself. Ella Eastwood was approaching a man holding a sign at his chest, *Mr. Eastwood, here, please.* A distance behind, her husband John was pushing a railcart loaded with baggage.

Everyone knew of HH and his directive that Eastwood would not set foot on the project and any worker deliberately speaking to him was subject to immediate dismissal. It was too early to test the newly minted HH who seemed to have taken the place of the old one. Rollins stood, stretched his legs and wandered casually toward the window. He stood before it to prevent HH from seeing the man outside who represented so large a presence at Big Creek. Rollins felt a strange irony that he and HH were at the project to rescue it and the reason it needed to be saved was because dams that should have been built by the visionary who planned the entire system were replaced by a much more expensive design. The antagonism HH held toward Eastwood had cost several million dollars. It felt entirely appropriate that it was coming out of the pocket of the man who had personally earned the debt.

"If you like the Sierra, HH, you should come to see the Rockies where I live in Colorado."

HH swirled his drink. "I'm impressed with Big Creek, but what makes you think one mountain is different from another?"

"It's a matter of inspiration. Sierra Nevada and Big Creek. The Rockies and the light bulb. There's a big connection there."

Looking at his drink, then at Rollins, HH laughed. "You must be drinking a different kind of Scotch than I am!"

Rollins stood with his arms akimbo. "In an electric kind of way, both ranges have loomed large in our business. You know about what we have here, but at Battle Lake just a few miles north of Denver, Edison found the inspiration for his incandescent light bulb."

"Now I'm certain you're drinking something different!"

"The lake's in south central Wyoming and Edison went there to fish some years ago. He got fish, plus the idea for the filament in the bulb. Seems the end of his bamboo pole fell into the campfire and when he blew it out, the end continued to glow. Took that to the lab and began to experiment. The rest is history."

"Alright. I'll grant you that, but my wife has other ideas for travel." HH looked out the window on the opposite side of the car. "This depot looks a lot like the ones my uncle Collis put up years ago…brings back a lot of memories. I'd like to sit out on your observation platform to soak it all in again."

Rollins glanced sidelong at the Eastwoods. They continued to pack the mules and the man with the sign stood as he had, apparently unable to help and unwilling to abandon them before they were ready to travel.

"Good idea, but let's wait a few minutes for the train exhaust to disperse. You know how it is when they come into the station. Tell me, did you hear about US Mail being delivered by aeroplane?"

"Now there's a joke if I ever heard one!"

"No joke. The army used a bi-plane and now they're claiming a plan to take passengers from place to place."

"You can't be serious! Who the hell would want to risk life and limb leaving the ground by questionable means, and then staying up there for a while? It's not something I'd do and then hope for a soft landing. It's a novelty and makes no sense."

"Trains were a novelty at one time, but not now. Likely wouldn't be a Los Angeles city without them, at least in our lifetimes, and I really like getting fresh fruit and newspapers from a long ways off in a short time."

He stole a quick look out the window and sighed inwardly with relief. The Eastwoods were headed up the road and sign man was astride his horse. Rollins motioned to the valet to put chairs on the platform. The man pointed to the door where he had anticipated the request.

"Another round, sir?" he asked.

"A jug of wine, a loaf of bread—and thou
Beside me singing in the Wilderness."

Robert Burns

Chapter 23

DAWN AT BALSAM MEADOW

A pair of Blue Jays woke John Eastwood before daybreak could conquer the dark. From the high reaches of a Lodgepole pine, they squawked over cone seeds as if it were their last meal. Although he put up the tent the night before, he and Ella chose to sleep in the open. Without a moon, the sky was a dazzling canopy of sparkling lights, occasionally streaked by shooting stars.

Eastwood was startled to find that he woke in the same position he had assumed the night before to watch the Sierra sky show. He turned to Ella expecting to see the slow rise and fall of her chest as she slept. Instead, he looked directly into her open eyes.

"'Bout time you made it back to the living," she chided. "I was afraid the fire was going to be my job but there're still a few coals you can coax." He leaned over and kissed her lightly.

"Coffee," he replied, pleading like a boy asking for permission to skip school.

She pushed him away. "First the fire unless you like it iced."

Sunrise at the edge of the meadow was their most looked-for time in the Sierra and they hurried to be ready for it. While low in the stone surround, the fire was still hot and quickly ignited the small twigs Eastwood used to stoke it. As flames grew he threw on larger pieces bathing the campsite in soft light.

By the time Ella put hard cooked eggs, crusty rolls, a slab of cheese, an apple and several stuffed dried apricots onto each of their tin camp plates, the coffee water was steaming. She threw the grounds directly into the pot, cowboy style, then removed it from the edge of the fire to steep.

Suddenly ravenous, Eastwood took each of the eggs and peeled shells, stopping to take a large bite of the first one before completing the task. "Never thought thinkin' and desk work could give me such an appetite," he said with an apologetic shrug. "That coffee ready?"

"Grounds aren't settled yet, but I can strain it."

Ella stretched a kitchen towel over each mug and then poured the coffee through it. "Feels like I got bit by the same hunger bug," she laughed.

Eastwood grabbed both plates in one hand. "Get your coffee and let's go," he said reaching for his mug. "We're months overdue from our usual May or June trip."

The sky grew to half-light, erasing all but the largest stars and leaving the solitary thin cloud above them rimmed in pink. They reached a log in the center of the meadow where years ago he had notched a seat for each of them. To the left of each indentation in the fallen tree he also carved a flat space for their mugs and plates. The round meadow was a huge earthen bowl in the woods still marking the outline of the lake it once was, surrounded by a tall green belt of pines and hardwoods. Red dawn deepened on the eastern side of the meadow until it filled the entire mountain glen in shimmering color.

The Eastwoods, their clothing, and their breakfast—all were bathed in an astonishing glow. In five minutes it was nearly gone and from a break in the pine tree curtain, a lone figure strode toward them through the remains of the magic. Even without seeing the face, Eastwood knew who it was. He stood and walked toward him.

"Jory Morgan, my favorite Cornish tinner!"

"Aye, but me tinnin' days are long done. It's hard rock mining now and that only for space. Ain't no saving what's dug out for a smelter – all goes into dams and such. Got you to thank for that." He tipped his cap to Ella. "Miz Eastwood."

"I swear Jory, you never age a day. How do you manage it?"

"Wal, ma'am, some say it's the water. We get to wash up in it and it's always between cold and damn near zero."

"Then you won't mind if I make you some coffee."

Ella stood, gathered the tin plates and started for the camp. "Here, ma'am, let me take those. You shouldn't oughta wait on me but I could really use that coffee."

She handed him the plates and continued toward the fire. "We took the train this time," said Eastwood. "Have you tried it?"

"You mean the San Joaquin & Eastern? I hear folks in Fresno calls it the Slow, Jerky and Expensive. I still likes a horse. Last time I took the train it stopped in the middle of the forest for the conductor to deliver a baby. The lady's husband thought she just had a bellyache 'cause there's eleven hundred twists and turns through the steep parts. He figured they was makin' her seasick."

"I know that way like the back of my hand," said Eastwood. "It's a beautiful place to have a baby, but I wonder if they had to pay another fare to get back to the Valley!"

Morgan's laugh bounced off the mountains surrounding the meadow. "For a man who took his first ride on that train, you shore got the right idee about it! Ain't your Erie Lackwanna and I heard a guy from back east call it a bunch of junk, but the station at Big Creek's open twenny-four hours a day like the big city ones."

"Too bad they can't afford steps off the cars," Eastwood observed.

Morgan shrugged. "It's the price of passage. In the tight slope cuts, rocks shift and shaves 'em off. You come up in a bleacher?"

"Guess not. What's a bleacher?"

"Flatcar with foldin' chairs. Sometimes they put on a canvas roof if it looks like rain. Not bad where they go 'bout five miles an hour, but the ladies have to hold onto their hats when they hit 25. Got no steps at all on that one. People climb up and down a small ladder. How was the box lunch?"

"Not bad, but Ella's cooking spoils me. Nobody's chicken can compare to hers. Afraid the dogs that follow the train from that point got more than I did. Bet it didn't take them long to figure out that Stevenson Creek was the place those lunches get loaded onto the train."

Eastwood sobered and put his hand on Morgan's arm. "How did you know I was here and that this was my first ride on the Big Creek train?"

Morgan accepted a mug of coffee from Ella and tipped his cap in thanks. "It's Mr. Redinger. Told the general store owner and the stationmaster to let him know when you got here. Woulda been here himself but work stopped because they run outta money, at least until Mr. Huntington came to visit. He took a look around then pledged more of his own money, so there's ketch up to do. Appears Mr. Huntington wants real bad to get Big Creek power to Los Angeles before Mulholland brings his water to the city from the other side of the mountains."

Eastwood felt both elation and hesitation. "That didn't look like Huntington's rail car on the siding."

"It's Rollins. Redinger told me he's the one talked the big man into comin' up here."

The hesitation vanished and bravado took over. "And the reason the money dried up?"

"The dams, but you know that."

Coffee from his mug splashed out in all directions as Eastwood elatedly threw up his arms. "Actually I didn't, but suspected it. How will you make up the time?"

"Dunno, but every time we get stuck, somebody comes up with answers to anything...like drilling stands. Some places we slide on the granite half way to straight up. Couldn't take good measurements from the transit, so some guy came up with the idea of making three legs out of two pipes each, one smaller to slide inside the other...connected 'em with a tee coupling a little larger than the pipe. Then he put a threaded plug in the tee at the top of the coupling and now we c'n adjust each leg by itself and level the transit."

"So who gets credit?"

"Don't matter. We're family—all of us from boss to ditch digger. Found that out when the company asked me to work the Mulholland project as a spy. I stuck it out for a month and had to come back early. Missed the "family" too much but got a good look at why Big Creek is different. They ain't like us. I c'n work a survey crew and engineers know they can trust me to handle the tape, level rod and paint bucket. Never saw that anywhere's for a workin' man. Where else would you find a man like Mr. Redinger who looks out for the likes of us!"

"Well, I don't know about Mr. Redinger," said Ella, "but I do know about my husband. He wants to see as much of Big Creek from a distance as he possibly can, Jory, and so do I. We have two pair of strong binoculars here..."

"Won't need 'em, ma'am. Mr. Huntington left in the wee hours. Problems out of sight, are out of mind, we say here in Big Creek."

April 1914. The Stone & Webster designed rail car.
Pacific Light & Power Photo, from the Edis

"We cannot command Nature except by obeying her."

Francis Bacon

Chapter 24

THE WHEELS TURN — FALL OF 1913

Fall came early with a deep cold snap that quickly yielded to sunny days at Big Creek. Hardwood trees turned crimson and gold overnight heralding an Indian summer with record heat. David Redinger paced alongside the railroad siding, looking anxiously for the infamous S.L. Shuffleton auto-railcar devised by Stone & Webster's head of construction for the western region.

Shuffleton had told engineers to refit a Ford automobile with railroad wheels so the company would have transportation to and from the Valley to Big Creek without depending on the railroad schedule. The invention was an impressive improvement over the older hand-crank cars used by maintenance crews of other railroads and without having to rely on the strong backs of workers to pump up the mountains the Ford fairly flew up and down the rails. Shuffleton became so adept at driving the route he took great delight in giving his passengers an exciting ride to the mountain station taking the more than a thousand quick turns and "S" curves with abandon. No one ever made the trip without automatically stomping the floor beneath, searching helplessly for an auxiliary brake pedal. Men at all the workstations and camps throughout the Sierra took bets on when the floorboards on the Ford would give out.

Redinger did not want the job he had been given—meeting a man from the San Francisco Hearst newspaper and taking him for a tour of the project. Today was a momentous one when the turbines would be tested for the first time to actually produce electricity. He wanted badly to see it happen but with construction winding down chances were good he would be out of a job soon. It would be foolhardy to whine about wanting to do something other than engineering.

The rail-car could be heard a long time before it made the last turn into the station siding. Steel wheels strained against the rails sounding like a banshee in mortal agony as it swerved around the last turns. Redinger expected to see the passenger thoroughly traumatized and sweating through his hat brim. Instead the middle-aged man appeared to be completely at ease. He jumped out even before the car came to a complete stop, thanking the driver as he removed his bag from the back seat.

"Mr. London," called out Redinger.

London gave a smart salute, but it was clear to Redinger his active manner was a sham. Deep circles underscored London's eyes. He stumbled with the bag, then willingly yielded it to Redinger's offer of help. It was early afternoon but it was clear that the man needed to rest.

"Let's go to the dining hall. They're making apple pies and I've been smelling it all day, Mr. London. Big Creek covers a lot of territory so I'll tell you what to expect, and you can tell me what you want to see."

"Lead the way, and the name's Jack."

"Yes…ah…sir."

The dining hall was empty except for three cooks at the table nearest to the kitchen. "Mr. Redinger, this is early even for you!" said one of them.

"I'm here to inspect the kitchen, so keep a civil tongue in your head," he laughed. "How about a meal for my guest here and I could use some grub myself."

"Meaning pie?"

"And coffee."

Without a word, one of the cooks went into the kitchen and reappeared quickly with a plate piled high with meat, potatoes and beans. "We always keep some food warm on the back of the stove for latecomers, or in the case of Mr. Redinger, earlycomers," he said as he put the plate in front of London. Behind him another cook placed two large plates of steaming apple pie, a small pitcher of thick cream and two mugs of coffee on the table.

Abruptly electric lights flickered, then died. A collective groan arose from the dining hall. All the Big Creekers were transfixed, as if waiting for a signal to breathe before the lights suddenly came on with startling brilliance. The room erupted in exuberant shouts that were echoed all over the camp. London sat open-mouthed, not understanding the reason for the show of lights and the reaction of the men.

"It's the first time the turbines are working!" shouted Redinger over the din. "They've been tested before but this means the power is going out to all the camps for miles around! We had electricity before from the PL&P plant down-mountain, but it was low voltage. Look at those lamps now!"

"Looks like I picked the right day to come," said London watching the cooks dance a jig.

Redinger laughed, then sobered. "We thought the right day was three and a half months ago, but things happen."

"Meaning what?"

"Meaning a fire in the carpentry shop that spread to the concrete forms for the powerhouse. The whole damn roof collapsed and we had to start over again after we cleaned it all up."

"I heard about it. My boss went to France on the same ship yours did."

"Shuffleton?"

"No, Huntington."

"Oh. The *big* boss. Almost met the man when he came out here in August, but I was up at the Basin when he was down here, and down here when he was up there. We were shut down, you know…ran out of money…but he put up more and we should be finished in a month or so. I'm surprised the two of them even talked. You know…there's a lot of competition between LA and San Francisco."

As the words came out, Redinger realized why London was there. The reporter had to be looking for a way to ridicule the project in print. HH's old grudge against The City still made newspaper headlines in both San Francisco and Los Angeles. The cosmopolitan against the rough-cut upstart. The establishment against the outsiders. In the northern part of the state, it was not going down well that HH was putting up the biggest power plant with the longest transmission lines in the world.

HH's business competition extended to self proclaimed engineer Mulholland of the newly established Los Angeles Department of Water. Word was that HH wanted Big Creek on line before Mulholland brought water to the city. It appeared that he would win the race until the fire. Now it was impossible to know if construction could be completed before water arrived from the Owens Valley. Redinger surmised that HH was caught between the devil and the deep blue sea, but he would not be the one to push the man's reputation one way or the other. He would not lie to London, but he also would not even hint there were other problems at Big Creek.

"You know, Jack," he began, "the world's largest Pelton wheels are here, and when the transmission lines are done, they'll be the longest anywhere as well."

"Kinda hard to believe when that Toonerville Trolley railroad is a pile of junk, according to the railroad men I've heard tell."

Redinger stifled a strong protest. "That pile of junk brought tens of thousands of tons—and I mean *tons* not pounds—of freight up a mountain more than a mile high with two grades that are nearly straight up for thousands of feet."

"So what's so special about hydroelectricity? Niagara's been doing it for years."

"It's not the machinery, it's putting it in places where you can use the water. In New York you have a large river and great waterfall that's easy to get to and easy to tap. Here in the west water's in the mountains and people live in the flatlands. Not only that, getting to the water when it's on the other side of the mountains is another problem. We solved that by digging two tunnels through solid granite for miles."

London nodded and smiled. "I can see there's a lot to learn up here. Tell me about something you had to do that was different from Niagara."

Redinger forked a large piece into his mouth and rolled his eyes with pleasure. "Still warm! Bet you can't get that at the St. Francis Hotel."

"I won't argue that, but are you avoiding the question?"

"Hell no! That's easy. Putting in the penstocks."

"Like corrals and animals?"

"Like high pressure pipes made in Germany and shipped over here around the Horn. Our water comes from the impoundment and runs through a large pipe or tunnel. When it gets close to where it drops into the powerhouse, the pressure increases and pipes can burst. The company got specially made penstocks from the Krupp factory because they know how to make cannon barrels to take high pressure."

"All well and good, but I don't understand how you can make electricity from water running into a wheel."

"Simple. The water goes into a fast fall through two huge penstocks. That increases the pressure and when it goes through nozzles to concentrate the flow, shoots through a few inches of space, and hits the Pelton wheel at 350 feet per second. That means when that water hits the wheel buckets, it's at 900-1000 pounds per square inch, more than enough to turn the huge turbines and create electricity."

"Okay, so you lay a pipe, and…"

"No, We didn't just install a pipe. Things that are easy in the flatlands are major problems up here. We laid the first lengths of penstock and then found with the temperature here going from 30 at night to 75 during the day, the pipes were expanding and contracting in the trenches. They moved like giant snakes in the trench and for every bend in the line, some of that pressure could be lost. We had to figure out how to deal with it and some of the men came up with the solution."

"Some of the men?"

"That's right. The bosses listen to us when we have suggestions because we're out there day after day and see what's going on."

"Sounds like you could teach the Germans something about their pipes."

"Doesn't keep us from learning."

"How's that?"

"Krupp sent two men here to help us work with the penstocks. I figured the two of them were partners, but when I happened to say that to the guy in the tall boots, he got mad."

"So what's so bad about being partners?"

"Dunno. He said to me, 'He iss *not* my partner…he iss my man" and I figured that "man" would never be heard by the boss."

London sighed deeply. "I worked the Klondike and know what you mean. Mountains make partners out of anyone who wants to tap into the riches, at least those who want to survive. So how'd you keep the penstock from kinking?"

"Started from the bottom at the powerhouse and filled the pipes with water to keep the temperature even, then backfilled the trench immediately instead of waiting until it was all connected."

* * * * * * * * * * *

On 5 November 1913 the Los Angeles Aqueduct was dedicated. William Mulholland stood before an audience of thousands and proclaimed that the rude platform on which he stood was an altar. He signaled for the sluice gate to open and as Owens Valley water gushed three hundred miles from its source he announced, "There it is. Take it."

"A people without history is like wind on the buffalo grass."

Sioux Proverb

Chapter 25

THE BOUNTY OF BIG CREEK – NOVEMBER 8, 1913

The air was unusually warm for November with a strong east wind bringing the last of the Mohave Desert's summer heat to the coast. On the terrace of his San Marino Ranch, Henry Huntington sipped coffee and watched a lone horse and rider coming toward him through rows of orange trees. Even from a distance the silhouette of George Patton Sr. was unmistakable.

He rode with the grace of a man born to the saddle and when he arrived at the edge of the gardens, he dismounted, walked through the roses and tied his horse to a tree by the terrace. He walked a few steps before retracing them to retrieve a packet from the saddlebag.

"You got the information?" asked HH.

Patton waved the envelope and sat down across the table. "Right here. I hope it's what you want."

HH shook his head. "Don't know what I'm looking for so how can you be wrong?" He reached for it but resisted the temptation to open it immediately. Nothing so inanimate ever captured him before, but the 1495-dated pristine copy of Higdon's *Polychronicon* he purchased was rapidly assuming a monumental presence in his life. The broker told him all about its provenance, but that was not enough. HH demanded to know why it was so important to history, a question he had never raised for prior purchases.

All other sources gave the same information he already had in hand. It was not until he complained to Patton about it that another source emerged. The Patton family knew a long-time professor of history and antiquities at a small college in New England. George Senior offered to ask him about it. The result was in a packet of papers where HH now rested his hand. As it was a personal quest he was unwilling to share with anyone as yet. He would read it privately.

"What do you hear from Second Lieutenant George the Second?" he asked.

Patton reached over to shake hands and Huntington was relieved for the opportunity to let go of the envelope.

"He sends his best but still wishes he had done better at the Stockholm Olympics."

"Fifth place in the world's first Pentathalon and not enough," he chuckled. "Never could settle for anything less than first. Did he talk about what's happening in Europe?"

Patton nodded. "Yes. Everyone he talked with is certain there will be war. Of course with the Kaiser in control that's a certainty. It's a good thing they're a long way off so we won't be affected."

"Too late. We already are. I can't get any more of the steel pipe for Big Creek from the Krupp Works in Germany because the company's being forced to make cannons. Not sure our steel is good enough to take the pressures in the Sierra and..."

The Huntington butler hurried to his employer. "Mr. Huntington, sir, there is an urgent telephone call for you."

"Important enough to interrupt?" barked HH.

"Mr. Shufflton says it is, sir."

"Not another damn fire!"

"He didn't say, sir, but he repeated to me that it was urgent."

* * * * * * * * * *

In Los Angeles a thousand trolleys and rail cars were used every workday to meet the demands of public transportation. Mornings saw every car filled to capacity with some standees hanging onto posts while balanced on the outside edges of the cars. No one could have guessed that the trip to their jobs on this particular day would depend on the strength of a single pipeline.

The city's Redondo Station plant of Huntington's Pacific Light and

Power Company was engineered with boilers to produce electricity. As a technology of the times, it was reliable and was the mainstay power of the region, in particular for the use of trolleys and street railcars. At the height of the early commuter rush hour, a pipe burst in the plant and before the water could be turned off, the flood extinguished fires in both boilers.

Steam pressure dropped and the generators stopped. The plant was dead in the water as were thousands of commuters who sat waiting for power to return to the cars.

At first engineers felt they could get the plant back in operation within twenty minutes. They continued to be hopeful when the delay extended to an hour but the Redondo plant manager was not. Police demanded that something be done and the manager did. He called Shuffleton at Big Creek and asked if he were able to send power.

Transmission lines were complete and all necessary installations were workable. The problem was the entire system had never been fully tested. Electricity had to travel a world record of nearly three hundred miles, then enter the substation where it would be stepped down from previously unheard of high voltage pressure in long distance lines from the source. Tens of thousands of connections would spring into action and work in concert with hundreds of newly invented transformers.

The room-sized transformers had to receive the generated power at 6,600 volts and increase it to unprecedented 150,000 volts to send the electricity to Los Angeles. At the Eagle Rock substation, the power would slam into another set of transformers and be stepped down to a range between 18-72,000 volts before moving through the lines to homes and businesses. It was akin to sending water through new pipes at astronomical pounds per square inch without testing it gradually for leaks and flaws. It would take the collective engineering genius of an army of men and require them to perform the drama of a lifetime without a rehearsal. They would have to prove they really trusted themselves, their technology and their dependence on one another.

* * * * * * * * * * *

"Well, Shuffleton, don't tell me there's another fire up there," growled HH.

"No, sir. No fire. However, there is a really big problem with the trolleys."

"And what the hell does that have to do with you at Big Creek?"

"Everything, sir. The Redondo plant is completely shut down and

*Engineers are dwarfed by water-cooled transformers at Powerhouse # 3.
This kind of technology was untested but worked perfectly when power was
first sent to Los Angeles in November of 1913. Note the informal "uniform"
of the day—high top boots and brimmed caps.*

From the Edison Collection

has been for an hour. They don't expect to be able to fix it for two days and have asked if we could begin sending power."

"If you can do it, what are you asking me?"

"Sir, we haven't fully tested the system and can't be 100% sure it will work without adjustments."

"And how many trolleys and cars are stopped?"

"All of them."

"All of them?!"

"Yes, sir. There's not enough power to keep anything going without Redondo. The entire system is down. Police are keeping order but it's been over an hour now and tempers are flaring."

"What other choices do I have?"

"None, sir."

"Then do it."

* * * * * * * * * * *

At Big Creek, water was diverted to the wheels and a turbine began to turn.

In less than a second power moved seamlessly through the step up transformers and then the step down to fill the lines to the city. Drivers tooted to warn riders the trolleys were about to move, and a great cheer rose from the crowded cars. Business returned to normal.

The Los Angeles Times reported that "Electrical energy from the far-off Sierras stretched a hand robed with lightning across the gulf of valleys and mountains to the doors of this city yesterday morning to kick the clogs from the wheels of a thousand trolley cars. It was the debut of Big Creek power into the Southland, the first employment of an undertaking on which over $12 million has been expended and which has required thousands of laborers for over two years."

For days the news of Big Creek filled the pages of the newspapers speaking of 20,000 horsepower bursting from turbines, rushing toward the city, from only one unit. At San Marino HH read it with amusement.

"Three days after you beat me to Los Angeles and I save your bacon. Top that, Mulholland!" said HH.

Nearby, a startled Arabella dropped her needlework. "Where'd that come from?" she asked bending to retrieve it. "You've been awfully quiet since we got back from Paris. Must have been because you got married," she teased.

HH was silent long enough that Arabella returned to her embroidery. The measured ticks from a large grandfather clock were the only sound in the room until he rose from his chair and strode purposefully to the desk, picking up the envelope Patton had given him.

"Will you light the fire?" she asked without looking up. "There's a bit of a chill here by the window where I need the light."

He did as she asked, then pulled a chair closer to hers. "I want to discuss something with you and I trust you won't make light of it."

She laid aside her needlework and looked directly at him. "I know something's been bothering you, but it worries me when you're so serious."

He took her hand and struggled to begin. "Belle, I'm sixty-three years old and my entire *life* is changed thanks to you. What concerns me is that it's changed to the point I don't have much interest in the work I've done all my life. If I don't go to the office I lose my footing." He looked away and she waited for him to continue. "Since last spring," he continued, "I've been thinking about...retiring...to do something else. Problem is I have no idea of what something else could be."

"And this *worries* you?" she asked incredulously.

"For fifty years I've been doing the same thing day after day so, yes, it worries me to want something different from what I know so well. Since I was a boy I've worked and if I don't go to an office, I'd feel like a stranger to myself...probably rot in a chair."

"Henry. My first thirty years were nothing like the last thirty and I wouldn't exchange them for anything in the world. What makes you think changing what you do won't be for the better?"

"I think my mother said it well...something like trading the work of the devil you know for the one you don't know."

"And what is it you think you want to do that's so different?"

He opened the packet. "I'm tired of government with constant new regulations and I've done enough development that it holds no excitement, but this..."   He opened the packet and handed her the papers from it.

As Arabella scanned the papers HH walked to the library, pulled on museum gloves and took the *Polychronican* from its glass covered pedestal.

"I don't know this man," said Arabella as he returned, "but he's writing about the book you bought last spring."

"Yes. This one." He laid the book on his lap. "Ever since I laid eyes on it, this book's been on my mind."

"But you've got many more in the…"

"Not like this. I need to find out why something over 400 years old has such power over me."

"You have the *Gutenberg*…"

"Yes, and I think that one started it all. When this one was added to the collection, I couldn't ignore what I was feeling. I remember it got my full attention when the broker used the word *incunabula*."

"One word?"

"One word, and it means a place of birth, or cradle. Even though I know the book was published at the beginning of moveable print, it had to mean much more to nag at me like it does." He ran his gloved fingers over the name Wynkyn de Worde on the spine of the book. "I think the answer's in the writer."

Arabella shook her head. "All he did was publish the book Trevisa translated from the original Latin. Ranulf Higden was the one who actually wrote it—a really flawed bit of world history up to that time. My understanding is that the value's in the fact it was the result of a very early printing press. Even Higden's book was based on the work of others. Why would you think de Worde is so important?"

HH shrugged. "All I know so far is that the value for me is because it puts business in an entirely new light. I always thought I worked for myself and to demonstrate to my father I could do it successfully…even better than he or Uncle Collis did."

"De Worde was a Dominican monk. Why would you feel his work is so important?"

"He was a printer and while his work was mostly for religious use, he was much more. The professor says in these papers that he worked in the Vatican and made two trips a year to Nuremberg. No one knows why, and that bothered me. I'm a businessman and I travel, so I think he went there to do business."

Arabella sorted through the papers, "Here's something…says Nuremberg was the 'crossroad of two major long distance trading routes and was a cultural mecca for two hundred years. Measures and weights were the standard there and all others copied prices in the city. Materials came from all over the known world at the time, and were used there in manufacturing.' Sounds very worldly for a monk."

"The professor also calls it the secret capital of the Holy Roman

Empire and suggests de Worde could have been a kind of papal legate. Think of it...twice a year he lived in an area that had the finest engineering instruments of the times for astrologers and physicists. It was where business and trade flourished during the late Middle Ages. I think it was a key reason for the birth of the Renaissance."

"And how does de Worde and Nuremberg connect with Henry Huntington in 1913?"

He straightened the papers and returned them to the envelope, then stood holding the *Polychronicon* so she could not fully see his face. While he trusted her, he did not afford the same for himself.

"I'm holding hands with the cradle of modern business and like Patton says, there are no accidents in life, only opportunity and challenge. Maybe...just maybe...this book has come into my hands for a reason I don't understand."

"This communicating of a man's self to his friend works two contrary effects, for it redoubleth joys and cutteth griefs in half.

Francis Bacon

Chapter 26

COMPETITION AND CONSOLIDATION

By 1910 the Los Angeles Edison Company was the only real competition to Henry Huntington's utility in the region. With every merger or purchase of other small companies, Edison's President John Barnes Miller not only extended their territory but also plowed money back into improving the technology. Miller was in charge of the company for so many mergers and buyouts, fellow managers called him the Great Amalgamator.

In 1902 Edison Company was a $10 million business and with public transportation still eating up most of the available power, the two growing electricity giants existed in relatively comfortable proximity. Edison engineers searched for new sources to generate electricity and the lure of hydropower drew it to the Southern Sierra Nevada on the Kern River. The area was incredibly wild and nearly inaccessible to people making the trek. Getting machinery and supplies to the site was an entirely new challenge.

Where it took Big Creek a mere two years to get the first phase complete and on line, unusual circumstances at Edison's three plants at the Kern River required five. Miles of roads had to be blasted out of rocky prominences before any timber could begin to be harvested. Where Big Creek built its own railroad and got supplies right up to the sites, teams of horses and early Mack trucks carried all Edison supplies from the railroad depot up twenty miles of nearly impassible road.

In Los Angeles electricity and water continued to drive politics riding on the coat tails of newly elected Governor Hiram Johnson. A reform candidate, Johnson responded to public demand to push for state regulation of all utilities partly because of a lack of standardization, and certainly because the industry's growth was untamed and unwieldy at best.

At the behest of several city councilmen of the same socialist persuasion as the governor, the city boldly entered into negotiations with the private electric companies to take over transmission of all power within its jurisdiction. After a year of fruitless discussion, the city quit talking and again turned to the people. City fathers asked for a $6.5 million bond issue to run their own set of competing power lines—an idea that appalled the management of Edison Company.

This time the company did not stand back while the city attempted to invade its established consumer base and then let the election unfold. It went to the people in a series of advertisements describing the situation and outlining what the city planned to do. Then it offered four better alternatives to adding a new set of poles and wires to march alongside those already crowding city streets.

While HH ran his PL&P as an autocracy, Edison was more of a democracy, offering reliable service and responding quickly to customer complaints. Management showed impressive willingness to adopt new technologies in all areas of their business, and that extended to recognizing that the astounding rise in use of electrical power coincided with the growth of mass communication.

Employees had adapted to use both print and radio in unexpected ways such as spreading news from across the country. Few radios were in use when the 1912 presidential election results were sent to the west coast. Edison operators pre-arranged a signal of flashing lights to pass the word. Two blinks meant a Woodrow Wilson win. From there the human grapevine and telephone took over.

The ad campaign concerning the bond issue for a new Los Angeles transmission system was successful for Edison. The bond failed and the city returned to negotiations with the private electric companies. At the same time Los Angeles used the last of the previous bond money for Mulholland to begin construction on the new Saint Francis dam in Francisquito Canyon.

Into this maelstrom of politics, Eastwood's Big Creek was born and by the spring of 1914, Los Angeles negotiators again came up empty in taking over the Edison transmission lines. The City Council felt confident enough to bring up the bond issue for another vote. This time it passed because of two events: confidence in the availability of electricity from the Sierra and the owners of kitchen appliances got to vote for the first time in California. Women.

* * * * * * * * * *

Eastwood rattled his newspaper. "Look at this! Not one word about Big Creek!"

"Maybe San Francisco's not interested in news from so far away," said Ella.

"So far!" he sputtered. "Pages of information about the Panama Canal and even more about Washington DC!"

"John. Both of those stories are about the City. The Raker Act was passed by Congress so they could dam Hetch Hetchy Canyon in Yosemite...plus they won the bid to hold the Panama Pacific World Exposition to celebrate the Canal."

Eastwood scowled. "It's only been five years since the quake and there they are, spending money they don't have."

"But people are afraid to come to San Francisco. They need something so the rest of the country can see beyond the fires and wrecked buildings."

Eastwood discarded the newspaper and they sat silent in their lawn chairs facing a calm Kings River. They watched the dark shapes of steelhead trout meandering upstream seeking a place to spawn. The early run was beginning and soon the water would roil in a frenzy of reproduction by fish which had left five years previously and returned to create the next generation before dying at the place of their birth.

Ella broke the stillness. "So what's bothering you that has nothing to do with newspapers and recognition?"

A woodpecker high in an oak tapped at a crevice searching for stored acorns. It ate the nut and was gone before Eastwood spoke.

"I've come to terms with losing Big Creek to Huntington and I'm thrilled that the first phase is done and running." He took a last gulp of coffee from a mug on the table between them.

"All I want to do is design fine dams and be done with the construction part of it. I'm tired of turning the other cheek so some dimwit can take another swipe at me."

"Are you saying you want to retire?"

He shook his head. "No, but I fear I can't do better for you."

Ella smiled and patted his shoulder, then laughed, startling the woodpecker into abandoning a search for more acorns. He flew off leaving behind an angry chatter to echo off the canyon walls.

"As I recall," she began again, "the only meal I missed in the years we've been married was that one vacation in the Sierra when that mama bear chased us up a tree, then played with her twin cubs right underneath for hours waiting for us to come down. I not only have a house in Oakland, but another right here in God's Country. Now tell me why you think changing what you do for a living will be for the worse."

"You mean it won't be a come-down?"

"If you mean will I think less of you, or would I lose position in the eyes of others, the answer's no."

"But..."

"But nothing. Now go talk with Sinclair and see what he thinks. I'll stay here so I can visit friends. You can come for me on your way back after seeing the Kennedy mining people about their dam in the Sierra."

* * * * * * * * * *

After making a date for lunch by telephone, Eastwood left for the Bay Area where he would meet Sinclair at the wharf where his yacht had been berthed before it was sold.

It had taken little effort for Eastwood to find the new owner of the yacht the *Lurline* and get permission to meet his friend there for lunch. Sinclair was well known in marine circles especially his connection to the annual TransPacific Yacht Race.

The St. Francis Hotel chef came on board with a picnic hamper filled with Duck L'Orange, an array of cheeses, crisp sourdough bread, a thermos of hot salmon bisque, apples from Seattle and cognac from Paris. As he put the finishing touches on the table set on the aft deck, Sinclair was on the gangway, his wheelchair pushed by a burly nurse.

Half way to the deck Sinclair motioned to stop. The nurse set the brake on the chair and helped him to rise, then followed close behind as he laboriously made it to the boat under his own power. Holding onto both rails for support, Sinclair hailed the officer of the deck in time-honored fashion, "Permission to come aboard, sir!"

"Permission granted, sir."

The piper's whistle sang out, honoring Sinclair as though he were an admiral of the US Navy. His eyes glistened as he surveyed his old haunt. A smiling Eastwood took his arm as the nurse moved the chair to gently touch the back of Sinclair's legs. He sank into it.

"Must be my birthday!" he laughed.

Eastwood released support for his arm and then shook his hand warmly. "I just wish I had the keys to the city."

"Never mind the ceremony. Where's Ella and my chocolate nut stuffed apricots?"

Eastwood pointed to the table. "Right there and this time they're special. She dipped them in caramel *and* chocolate. Said she remembered you loved them together and figured they mated well with the fruit. Have to admit she was right and she's had to smack my hand more than once when I get greedy about them."

"Hah! That wife of yours never smacked you for anything. You may get knocked around in business but your home's still your castle. How did the Los Verjels dam up by Sacramento go?"

"Done. It's small...350 feet long. The good news is that I found another benefactor in V.T. McGillicuddy. He wasn't eager at first but after all the bills were paid, said he thought my figures were off because he saved so much money."

"So how did he get to be on your bandwagon?"

"It was heaven-sent. The rains came early and the dam filled to capacity three months after we finished. It even over-topped without a sign of stress, so now he's telling everyone the multiple arch dam is the best design there is."

"So how'd you get it past the Bureau of Reclamation after the mess at Big Meadows?"

The nurse pushed the wheelchair close to the table and then left the two of them alone to eat. Eastwood sat to Sinclair's left and pulled the dishes within easy reach.

"That was the biggest surprise. There's a new engineering inspector there...name's Hawley and he supports my design, too."

"A relative of our late chairman of the board at Great Western Power Company?"

"Don't know and I'm hesitant to ask. I think he's not or he would have mentioned it after what went on there with Freeman.

The problem got a lot of attention in the newspapers, but all I know is that he liked what he saw in the plans and said the overtopping proved he was right."

"So what was the reaction at the Bureau of Reclamation?"

"Now they recommend my design."

"The one they said was *not* safe last year?"

"The same, but there is one qualification. They only recommend it for smaller dams and they'll never use it because they're looking at bigger and bigger ones. Mark my words. One of these days they're going to try and dam the Colorado River."

Eastwood poured the salmon bisque into two bowls and passed one to Sinclair. Both fell silent as they ate slowly. A flock of gulls landed on the aft railing, eyeing the table. The nurse appeared, waving his arms to chase them.

"Not here you don't," said Sinclair to the birds as he covered the apricots with both hands. "These are mine and I share with no one!"

He pushed his bowl away and sat back to eat them. "Now tell me what you have in mind. What is it you can't tell me on the telephone?"

Eastwood took a last spoonful and sat up straight. "Have to confess I felt a bit self-righteous when I heard the Big Creek project nearly went broke because they didn't use my dam. At the same time I realized that the Los Verjels dam was quick, easy and didn't require much oversight from any agency—state or federal."

"And you aren't anxious to tilt at any more windmills?"

"Forgive me if I say my legacy in engineering is Big Creek and you know that doesn't come from a name over the door. When that finally dawned on me even though I had nothing to do with the actual construction, it gave me some peace with the way it was taken from me. Also made me realize that design is king and construction is a terrible task master."

Sinclair chewed an apricot in the silence and Eastwood sent a long look toward the Sierra Nevada. From a ring of gulls circling the boat, one bird broke ranks and came in for a landing again. The nurse responded with a volley of oranges and the angry gull dropped away.

"And you want to know if it'll be enough to just design?" asked Sinclair softly.

Eastwood nodded. "I've never run from a fight but if I toted up all the time spent in construction conflict, it would surely be far more hours spent doing what I do best."

"And the problem is?"

Both men laughed. "I guess the problem is that Ella didn't send me with enough apricots!" said Eastwood.

"You never conquer a mountain. You stand on the summit a few moments, then the wind blows your footprints away."

Arlene Blum

Chapter 27

A WATERSHED YEAR — 1914

The year 1914 was memorable for all of southern California, but especially for engineering progress and water itself. The times birthed the endowment of three legacies for the public good—from Henry Huntington, Big Creek and William Mulholland.

In the Sierra Nevada, Stone & Webster prepared to depart after completing the initial phase of Big Creek. Company engineers left behind a jerry-built snowplow consisting of a huge twelve bladed box fan attached to the front of an engine. The little railroad called the Millionaire's Limited going to the Valley and the Hobo Express coming back would never be stranded by blizzards again. The invention came just in time as winter storms raked the area again and again leaving deeply drifted snow.

In the Los Angeles area, those snows were continuous rains, which wreaked havoc at the port causing $10 million in damage. The US Corps of Engineers began to look at ways to control floods. With an over abundance of water, some people began to question if the massive Owens Valley Project was really needed. Their carping was ignored by the general public which hailed Mulholland as a city father with a lasting legacy. It was a heady time for invention.

In the east, the US Signal Corps flew mail between Washington

DC and various locations surrounding the capital. The Signal Corps had subsidized the Wright brothers' invention, but the use of aircraft was still considered by most to be a novelty.

However, there was a vast difference in how the east coast viewed invention compared to the still-wild west. While in the eastern US a ten-year-old Charles Lindbergh became fascinated with airplanes, Glenn Curtiss in southern California was already building and selling them to military officials around the world. For three years he had been teaching US Naval personnel to fly his aircraft. Japan purchased three of his "flying boats," an amphibious craft with both wheels and floats.

The Glenn L. Martin Aircraft Company had already been in business for more than a year and from its ranks of engineers much of the industry would develop: William Boeing, Donald Douglas, Lawrence Bell and James McDonnell. The baby aircraft industry was growing up fast in California and needed electricity to run its factories. For the first time the demand for electricity vastly increased for homes and factories instead of Huntington's public rail transportation.

After the momentous week when Mulholland gave water to a thirsty Los Angeles, and Big Creek rescued the city with power from the mountains, Henry Huntington came to the realization that his personal legacy up to that point was not in the development of railroads and property. It was Big Creek.

He reasoned that without power and water there would be far fewer people living in cities. Stores and factories would be shops in homes. New appliances such as electric kitchen stoves, indoor water heaters, toasters, irons and incandescent lights demanded power. Without it life would be hand water pumps, privies, wood-fed stoves and oil lamps. Primed with great water and power wealth, Los Angeles was poised for a giant leap forward. At the same time HH searched for comfort within his radically changed mindset.

In the Sierra Nevada with Stone & Webster's crews gone, Big Creek settled into a routine power production. It took less than a month for the Sierra to shake it up and for engineers to realize the need for expansion joints. During the wee hours of December first, a flanged portion of penstock on Line Number 2 pulled apart in single digit cold, abruptly rupturing the pipe. The powerhouse flooded not only with water but mud, sand and debris as well. The damage put both generators out of commission. Worse, water sprayed over a transmission tower, and the rapidly forming ice collapsed it.

The damage was quickly repaired but David Redinger missed all the excitement. He was laid off in late November along with hundreds of others. The builders were gone but they left a legacy—the Big Creek family. No one who ever worked there did it without being changed and forever joined to a mountain connection that crossed culture, gender and age. Each was branded with a bond no matter how far they traveled.

Redinger felt the loss keenly even after the excitement of opening an office in Los Angeles with fellow engineer Harry Banks. He would give everything he owned and go into debt to get back to Big Creek. Few customers came to the fledgling entrepreneurs and they felt increasing pressure to pay rent with little income. Just before they had to find work another way, the two men were startled to hear their all too-quiet office phone ring. Redinger nearly fell out of his chair reaching for the receiver.

"Banks & Redinger," he said struggling to sound professional.

"Rex Starr here," said the caller. "You interested in working for PL&P?"

Redinger gulped silently. It wasn't Big Creek but it was part of the same company. Maybe it was the back door to making it back. "Could be, although we have a number of interested parties coming to us of late. What'd you have in mind?"

There was a fraction of a second pause. "Can't compete with business, but I need somebody like you at the Redondo plant. Pipelines are taking a terrible beating in these rains. Need somebody to look at reinforcing them and you did a lot of that at Big Creek. You interested?"

Redinger's heart sank. Redondo. Not far away, but the reality of his dwindling savings could not be ignored. "Well, I might, but I'd be leaving Banks without help to deal with the customers." He bit his tongue hoping he had not ruined his chances of gainful employment.

"I could be interested in the both of you," said Starr, "but I can't help you with the customers."

Resisting the urge to shout *yes* Redinger picked his words carefully. "I'd like to talk with him about it, if that's okay with you."

"You need much time to, ah, talk with the customers, too?"

He knows, thought Redinger, *but I can't change my tune now.* "I'll present it to him and call you back as soon as possible. Will that suit you?"

"Fine. Just let me know today."

It was an eternity before Redinger heard the click to signal Starr had hung up. He slammed the receiver down and bounded into the adjoining office to tell Banks the news. Elated, both men wasted no time in packing up equipment and papers. The firm of Banks & Redinger dissolved without fanfare.

"Don't you think you should call him back with the news we're comin'?" asked Banks.

"Can't just yet. Gotta tell all our 'customers' to find another engineer first."

"To hell with imaginary customers! I want the job."

* * * * * * * * * * *

War continued to heat up in Europe and while the US government proclaimed neutrality, American business did not. United States Steel's Charles Schwab clandestinely made arrangements with the United Kingdom to produce armaments in defiance of official government policy. The company was not the only one to strike it rich in the field. Demand for power from the Big Creek system rose with each report from Europe as yet another country mobilized for war and ordered armaments from wherever they could be made. In the west, the door to Big Creek opened within a month for Redinger after he accepted a job with the Pacific Light & Power.

For a few weeks the schedule was light but with Central Valley businesses growing rapidly, Huntington made the decision to put in another powerhouse. Hoping to cash in on the war bonanza, the board decided to build Powerhouse #8. The location was out of sequence from the plans but more easily done at a lower elevation. Construction started in early July and with less strenuous weather extremes and a longer construction year, it was expected to be finished in nine months.

Redinger was put in charge of a reconnaissance party to find the best way to get water from the South Fork of the San Joaquin River on the eastern side of the Kaiser Ridge into the Big Creek system. Eastwood's original plans were highly detailed, but still needed specific coordinates for the lengthy tunnels. Redinger planned to leave on July 5th in the wee hours to hike up to Huntington Lake. Supplies, equipment, mules and the rest of the group awaited him there, and the party expected to set out by dawn from there.

A trainload of fifty young women from Fresno State Normal School put a serious crimp into Redinger's plans and introduced a major change in his future. Harry Banks broke the news.

"They're planning a big dance to celebrate the Fourth! Even brought up a band to play!"

"But we gotta leave for the Basin by 3 AM."

"I got it all figured out. We go to the dance and then leave at midnight, then take off as planned. You gotta meet Miss Edith."

Redinger grinned. "And what's the rest of her name?"

"Dunno, but she likes to be called Dee. What more'd ya want, an engraved invitation?"

The change in plans went well except that Redinger never worked up the nerve to introduce himself to Dee and stayed until 2 AM trying to overcome his shyness. He did learn that Dee was an administrator in the Home Economics Department and that the school hoped to establish a mountain campus to hold summer classes. With construction crews gone many of the buildings at Big Creek were empty. The PL&P was eager to realize some income from them and college officials were pleased for the opportunity to oblige them.

Elated at having spent time in the company of young ladies regardless of the cost to sleep, the two men set out hiking to Huntington Lake. They arrived an hour before breakfast and headed for the engineer bunkhouse to get some sleep. All beds were taken with additional men spread out all over the floor as well. Redinger decided to try to "sleep soft" and see if the one bedroom upstairs was occupied.

He tiptoed around the sleeping men and headed upstairs to the room reserved for "brass hats." The door was unlatched, the sign it was normally unoccupied. He moved quietly toward the bed in the dark, then sat on the edge of it and removed his boots. His heart stopped when he heard a feminine voice ask, "What's going on here?" The chief engineer had brought his wife to the camp!

Redinger grabbed his boots and bedroll, running headlong down the stairs. The only spot remaining for him was a pile of tarps in one corner. The shock left him no sleep and the call to breakfast couldn't come fast enough.

* * * * * * * * * *

The hike to Blaney Meadows took three days of carrying the survey equipment with them. They stopped often to verify the rise in elevation and to calculate continuous gravity fall. At Pavilion Dome the crew could see the camp at Huntington Lake some two thousand feet below. Getting there was extremely difficult with the men having to hack their way through thick brush and maneuver around steep inclines.

The only way Redinger could take an important measurement was to inch his way along a ledge, using precarious right hand holds as he held the survey leader's rod. At the necessary point he made his calculations but then realized he could not make his way back without exchanging the rod to his other hand. He was stuck on the face of granite with a sheer drop of a thousand feet.

"Banks! I can't get back!"

"Use the skyhook!"

"I'm serious. Can't make it without dropping the rod."

"Drop the damn rod!"

Six feet long, the rod was the team leader's responsibility, a necessary tool in surveying the route. Redinger struggled with the decision, tried again to move back and found he could not. Reluctantly he dropped the rod and inched his way back.

Survey equipment was essential and while they could work without the rod, what they lost next was essential. In another steep rock area, a crewman moved carefully to set the Berger transit at a point beyond the trail. The steep scarp held a narrow ledge for several yards before widening out into the perfect location for the next measurement.

The crew watched carefully as one man struggled with the Berger transit inching his way along the sheer face of the mountain with the instrument in one hand and grasping handholds in the rock with the other. His step was careful, but the granite was a mass of winter exfoliation. Each year water seeped into tiny cracks, then froze at night, causing the rock to splinter into a mass of fine slab shavings off the sides. The crewman placed his weight on one foot and felt the rock move.

Instinctively he dropped the transit and grabbed a small pine tree growing out of a crack in the granite. The crew gasped as the equipment glanced again and again on the mountainside before landing in a small clump of trees hundreds of feet below.

"Get back here!" barked Redinger.

"I'm sorry Mr. Redinger, I…"

"Forget the damn transit, just get yourself back here!"

From the trail above a rope dropped down toward him.

"Grab that rope and knot it to your overalls. We'll pray it holds."

The crewman snagged the rope and then laid his head against the rock face in relief. It was an eternity before helping hands reached out to drag him the last few feet.

"That's the end of this trek," said Redinger. "We got all of a hundred yards covered today and I say it's time to head for home. Should have taken the hint when the squirrels ate our plumb bob strings."

The trip back to Big Creek was nearly forty miles, and the men were determined to make it in one day. They were up before dawn and headed down the mountain like hungry horses heading for the barn. They ate on the run and rest stops were on your own, then catch up.

The trip back took half the time of climbing up. When the crew was within sight of the camp they turned off the trail and headed straight as an arrow home, sliding down the great granite rocks on their seats. Once there, they ducked around watching for women, embarrassed that the seats of their pants were shredded clear through to bare skin.

Construction of the Million Dollar Mile Road from Powerhouse #8 to new construction of Powerhouse #3. Workers cut across granite walls of the San Joaquin River canyon.

G. Haven Bishop Photo, from the Edison Collection

"Memories may escape the action of the will, may sleep a long time, but when stirred by the right influence…flash into full stature and life with everything in place."

John Muir

Chapter 28

MEMORIES AND APPRECIATION – 1914

The Redinger survey party was surprised that the Fresno State women were not yet finished with their summer studies. Disappointment in the failed assignment vanished with the fact they would get another chance to dance. Redinger thought he had muffed his chance with Dee. He was a very competent professional, but a school-boy when he spoke to her.

The students and teachers left for the Valley in an atmosphere of other tensions. Events in Europe heated up following the assassination of Archduke Franz Ferdinand in Austria. The German ambassador in Paris was summoned by French authorities to explain why one of their pilots flew over Nuremberg, leaned out of the open cockpit and lobbed several bombs.

The Ambassador ignored the question and demanded to know why a French soldier killed a German soldier. He left the meeting in a huff only to return a few minutes later to add that he forgot to mention his government had declared war on France. He stalked out again and left the country. American President Woodrow Wilson announced that the United States would remain neutral and the war in European trenches began.

By September PL&P decided the world situation was too uncertain to continue with the expansion. Worried about starting construction only to have it stymied because of a lack of penstock, the company decided to wait out global political machinations. Redinger was laid off again. He was hired by the Bureau of Reclamation to work on the Salt River Project in Arizona.

It was strange to spend winter in the warm sun after battling deep snows and freezing temperatures at Big Creek. The men had to share their large tent with mules and horses. The one tent of some luxury was reserved for visiting VIPs who didn't have to sleep with animals and were kept warm by a kerosene stove. Any time the tent was empty, Redinger and his buddies took it over.

"I knew we were tying on the feedbag here, but I didn't expect to have to live with the mules," he said to fellow Big Creeker Ollie Scheiber.

"Could be worse," replied Scheiber. "At least they're friendly. I haven't been kicked yet."

The work of creating the huge Roosevelt Dam was exciting, but short-lived. Redinger worked a succession of projects from Alaska to San Francisco, and San Luis Obispo to Phoenix, but never failed to keep PL&P informed of his whereabouts. He also wrote regularly to Dee. There was no doubt in his mind that he had left his heart with her and his home at Big Creek.

* * * * * * * * * *

John Eastwood dove headlong into promoting his multiple arch dam. He issued the *Eastwood Bulletin* newsletter and wrote to the editors of engineering magazines. A number of his letters were published including one in *Engineering News* of New York when he criticized the gravity dam and its weakness for uplift. Knowing the readership would put him in the public eye from coast to coast, he chose his words carefully in comparing the traditional construction to his own design. He called it the Ultimate Dam and while there was widespread coverage in the magazine, it did not result in the kind of response he sought.

"I just don't understand why people prefer to spend so much more money and get a structure that is inferior to the multiple arch," he groused to Sinclair on the phone.

"I don't understand professional engineers," agreed Sinclair, " but I wonder if talking at length about the money aspect is the wrong emphasis."

"It works in the market. I know Ella will buy at a store that has beef roast for nineteen cents a pound rather than twenty. Who would have thought putting a price of ninety nine cents would sell something that cost a dollar across the street?"

"That's just what I mean. It's the psychology of it, something like Freeman promoted about your design."

"But it saves a lot of money!"

"Yes, but sometimes people don't feel they're getting the best if they don't have to pay for it."

"That's crazy!"

"I know. It's also human nature. I think you should stress safety."

Eastwood retained his doubts, but yielded to his friend's expertise. He never mentioned the cost savings again in his advertisements. He also never got to speak with Sinclair again. His friend and mentor died a few days later.

At first he called himself the Eastwood Construction Company to impress people as more than a one-man operation. Unwilling to let go of the construction supervision entirely, he advertised his services in three ways: a fixed amount for completed work, cost plus a fee for engineering and project supervision, or simply a fixed amount for design and specifications only. His first customer following the Los Verjels project was for the Kennedy Mining and Milling Company in the Sierra foothills near Jackson.

"It's a dam to collect mining debris and tailings," he told Ella. "It won't take long and it's less than a hundred miles east of us."

"Why would they need a dam to collect that? Can't they just pile it out of the way?" asked Ella.

"Not that easy. The tailings are what's left after the ore is leached with cyanide to get to the gold. They use the river to wash it away and the rocks go with it after the valuable metal is harvested."

"So you're saying the cyanide goes downstream, but surely it's washed away and can't cause problems."

"Wish that were so, but there's enough left to poison cattle and the ranchers downstream have gotten the state to create a new set of building permits. We now have a Debris Commission, and they say the mine can't let any of the waste get into the stream."

Construction began in June, and the 455 foot long dam was complete by December. It was the last dam construction Eastwood personally supervised.

* * * * * * * * * * *

On a cold, wet December day Henry Huntington walked the vine-covered ramada that connected his estate with the Patton's. The rain had stopped and thick honeysuckle leaves glistened despite the dark skies. The small privacy bell the two families had installed announced a visitor and he walked quickly to meet George Senior.

"Nice day for ducks," said HH. "You here to check out the rose garden for the parade float?"

"The ladies sent me with their thanks. Last New Year's Day their entry in the parade got the biggest round of applause and they intend to do it again."

"I liked when they had the football game that one year. You suppose they'll ever bring it back?"

"Not sure if Stanford wants to come back, losing 49-0 to Michigan and the game over in the third quarter. I do like watching the other games even if I don't play polo or bust broncos."

"Last year there were a lot more automobiles and fewer carriages. I think the roses look so much better on a horse-drawn vehicle and as far as I'm concerned they can get rid of the Roman chariot race."

"I remember the time they had an elephant race a camel, but I don't think you came out on this kind of day to talk about the Tournament of Roses. What's on your mind, Henry?"

HH sat down on a bench. "I've been thinking a lot about Oneonta lately. Anytime Belle and I are in New York we take time to visit upstate where I was born and raised. New York and Albany are growing like weeds, but I doubt that will happen so far out in the sticks where Oneonta is."

Patton sat next to him and was silent for a time. He rested his forearms on his knees and spoke without looking at HH. "I get the feeling this has something to do with the *Polychronicon* and that you already have something in mind."

HH nodded. "Got a letter from a cousin who still lives there. Says the town is trying to build a public library...they have for years, but not making much headway on it. I get so much pleasure out of reading and collecting books I thought it would be a way to give back for today and the future as well."

"What about a place to put it?"

"I still own the house where I grew up and it's in a good spot for a library, but don't want to kick out relatives living there." He rubbed his chin and smiled. "You think it's the right thing to do?"

"What about your collections? You've got one at the ranch and another in New York…plus putting up the new building at the ranch to hold what you already have and what's sure to come from future acquisitions. Would you be able to handle it all?"

"Are you saying I'm going off the deep end here?"

Patton shook his head, then reached over to shake Huntington's hand. "Not by a long shot. If you're willing to take that large a leap I'd be more than willing to take it with you."

"Does that extend to going with me to Oneonta to find out what I can do to make it happen?"

"I'm ready anytime you are as long as the snow is melted back there, and we can visit young George at the same time."

"The interval between the decay of the old and the formation and the establishment of the new, constitutes a period of transition, which must necessarily be one of uncertainty, confusion, error..."

John C. Calhoun

Chapter 29

THE WAY WE WERE — 1915 - 1917

The Edison Company continued to seek a legal compromise with the city of Los Angeles. Three-quarters of the company's business rested in the city and without it, the specter of bankruptcy loomed large. Optimistic despite the risks, company management continued to develop the Kern River Project.

Stories of the trek up to the powerhouses were legend. On a trip to the Central Valley, David Redinger met a crew at a hotel in Bakersfield.

"I remember a time when I had to leave my luggage here when I was headed for Big Creek. Came back a month later and the suitcase was right where I left it, just a lot dustier," he told his tablemates at dinner.

"Hah!" scoffed Ed Carew. "You're lucky you got a fancy railroad at Big Creek and I got a story to top that. Last year I went with a bunch of high hats to Kern River. Two automobiles, engineers, supervisors, a photographer and mechanic. Was supposed to take two days for the hundred fifty miles.

"Weren't two hours on the road before one of the cars broke the suspension on those damn rocks in the road."

"Was that the end of it?"

"Hell no! We sent two guys back to the closest company substation to get help and we got settled in. I went hunting for rabbits for supper and another guy built a fire. One of them engineers had a cribbage board in his pack and a couple of them played for hours until the sun was low. The guys got back with the part and we fixed the automobile in about an hour.

"Got too dark when the fog rolled in so we had to stop at a hostel the Southern Pacific keeps for their crews. Stayed there the night and ate pretty good, then got started at dawn. Got as far as Palmdale for gasoline and found a stud holding the universal shaft was broke clean off. Fixed that with a piece of gas pipe and a length of baling wire."

"Did it hold up long enough to get you to the Kern?"

"You don't know the half of it. Dust on the way got so thick we had to take turns walking ahead of the automobile so we didn't drive off the edge. Damned near choked to death doin' it. Got to here for water and the bunch in the other car said they had enough. They headed back to Los Angeles.

"The rest of us got to the powerhouse about noon, but had to park two miles away. There was another company car there and we figured it was safe ground. I was damned mad about it at the time after how long it took us to get there, but turned out to be a good idea. Rains came that night and the Kern was so high the next day it washed out the road."

"I bet you were glad to get back home."

"Hah! That took some more doing. Couple of the men at the powerhouse wanted to get to Los Angeles so we set out in two cars again. Tried to ford Cotton Creek and the differential broke. Had to leave it right there stuck in the middle of the water.

"That meant we all crammed into the one car to get here to Bakersfield. The ones who were with us decided they had enough and took the train to the city. Was four weeks before that automobile got drug out and fixed."

"You're right. I can't top that except for the time I wore the seat of my pants out getting back to camp."

"Oh hell, t'weren't all that bad. We found some grapevines with dried fruit that night at the hostel. Tasted pretty damn good, and after that we call the road The Grapevine."

* * * * * * * * * *

The Fresno students were not the only Valley people to discover Big Creek. A steady stream of people came to enjoy the deep woods, sail on Huntington Lake and camp out. The tiny settlement of Big

A group of ladies aboard the excursion car await the beginning of a tour of the Basin behind Huntington Dam.
Pacific Light & Power Photo, from the Edison Collection

Creek boasted of several new stores, including a barbershop, grocery, movie house and even an art shop. The PL&P elected to build a lodge to make a little money on budding tourism with the company-owned SJ&E Railroad providing transportation.

The *Fresno Republican* reported to readers that:

The San Joaquin and Eastern,
It has a winding track…
The train goes up on Monday;
On Tuesday it skids back.

At 7000 feet the company built the Huntington Lake Lodge on the south shore within easy access to the road. Henry Huntington took such particular interest in the Lodge that he personally found a new manager when the original one became disabled. During the summer months a boat towed a barge on the lake for the pleasure of dancers. In August, moonrise over the lake was spectacular. The hotel was booked solid and the boat ride to watch the event on the water sold out as well.

Life at Big Creek was serene but the world was heading for chaos. On May 7th a German U-Boat torpedoed the *Lusitania* taking the lives of 1,201 passengers and crew, including over a hundred Americans. President Wilson's warning to the Germans not to endanger American lives died with them.

The young George Patton watched global events unfold while serving at Fort Bliss. His military life was a series of routine cavalry patrols until serving as aide to General Pershing when he killed Pancho Villa's head of security, General Cardenas, and a bodyguard. Patton carved two notches in the handle of the single-action Colt he would carry into battle the rest of his life.

* * * * * * * * * *

At a board meeting of PL&P in early 1916, Henry Huntington announced the decision to continue construction of Powerhouse 8 at Big Creek.

"With the Krupps Works unable to furnish us the necessary penstock, I think we should raise the dams at the lake instead and double the capacity of the present powerhouses by adding more generators," he said. "Work will begin immediately to stockpile materials and construction as soon as the snow pack allows it."

The vote was unanimous in favor of the action and David Redinger found himself back home in Big Creek. Rex Starr, his benefactor from previous employment with PL&P was named to manage the job.

Redinger and Starr stood on the walk atop the smallest dam at Huntington Lake to review what needed to be done first.

"Get the sawmill reconditioned, and we'll need a new rock crusher in that same area. I'll have power lines extended all around for lights and have two full shifts day and night. New railroad tracks are on the way to rebuild the Basin setup, so make sure the first things cut at the yard are ties to get it done. Storage is good but check for leaks to make sure we can put the bags of cement in there. A dozen air compressors are on the way so figure out a place they can be stored. There'll be more men working up here than down at the powerhouse, so put up another large bunkhouse and add onto the kitchen and mess hall. I figure we'll need six camps scattered around to keep the work running smoothly without a lot of traveling in between for meals and sleep. They'll need smaller bunkhouses and mess halls. Any questions?"

Redinger shook his head. "Not yet, but don't hold your breath."

In one month the smooth operation hit a snag. The hoist man running the steep incline railroad from the powerhouse to the lake fell asleep and missed shutting off the power once the car came close to the loading dock. The hoist cable continued to wind on the reel, pulling the car up until it reached the control house and crashed into it.

"Was he hurt?" asked Starr when Redinger brought him the news.

"No, sir, and he got the power turned off as the load crushed the cable house."

"Damn! Move the crane from the lumber yard to the hoist house to get it down then pay him and send him packing!"

"Sir, he's gone and didn't stop to pick up his money."

By Thanksgiving crews worked so well together the cooks decided to reward them with a special supper. In every camp mess halls were decorated with balsam, mountain holly and pine swags for an enormous holiday feast. Appreciation for the meal kept work going through the snows until Christmas Day when four feet of it buried all the camps. Everyone moved down to the Big Creek area below 5000 feet and kept busy preparing for spring.

At 4 PM on February 19, 1917 in the bunkhouse, David Redinger was startled out of the Sierra quiet by the sound of a heavy thump, followed by the ring of the telephone.

"Redinger here."

"There's a break in the penstock! Not sure where it is but I figure it's about half way up! Can't close the valve and need help. Now!"

Memory of the first break was fresh. The powerful stream of water could wash out the underpinnings of the two lines from Huntington Lake to the powerhouse. It was more than alarming. It could destroy the entire pipe system in that area. Redinger had little time to react before he swung into action.

Snow was deepening at Big Creek. That meant far deeper drifts at the top of the penstock by the lake. There was no transportation except by horse and sled. He hung up the telephone then barked at the workers anxiously listening to the one-way conversation.

"You two! Bundle up and come with me! We got a valve to close at the Basin."

The men groaned but ran to get heavy boots and jackets. By the time the three of them were ready with three horses hitched tandem to a long narrow sled snow boat carrying heavy duty jacks and necessary tools, the snow was falling heavily. They lit lanterns to help find the road to the Lodge. There was no trail broken and the horses struggled up to the Lake. The men knew the animals could die if they pushed them any further.

"You! Get three pair of snowshoes from the Lodge, and you help me reload the jacks onto this toboggan!" yelled Redinger.

The crew attached ropes to the sled and then tied them to their waists, setting out for the gatehouse. It was an enormously difficult mile walk through the blizzard and at times they foundered through waist-deep drifts. In the wee hours they reached the gatehouse and set to work jacking the valve closed. After a brief rest they made their way back to the horses and finally to Big Creek by morning.

The powerhouse logbook entered, "Gate was jacked down" without a mention of the effort it took to do it, not ignored nor unappreciated, but taken for granted. Redinger got his reward once repairs were completed—a month off to get married in June.

* * * * * * * * * *

"Nobody knows about us getting hitched except Mr. Starr," he told Dee as the train squealed its way to Big Creek. "I doubt anyone will be there to greet us but you'll get visitors once we're settled."

Dee's response was drowned out by the shrill blast of the train's whistle. One by one all whistles in the area rang out, including the standing engines at the station, the machine shop, the mess hall triangle and anything that would make a joyful noise. The small school had been dismissed so children could pound on pots to add to the celebration. Everyone in town was there to meet the newlyweds and each one had something to bang. Washbasins, tin cans, the sides of buildings, anything and everything. The din rang out through the trees, bouncing off the canyon walls and returning magnified.

As they stepped off the train, the Redingers were escorted to a huge Shaver lumber wagon driven by a crewmember in livery, complete with white gloves. The women had jury-rigged a canopy over the seat and garlands of mountain wildflowers were draped on each side. Even the horses wore flowers. Tin cans trailed the wagon as it moved adding to the clamor, and old shoes bounced in the dirt road leading to the A. O. Smith Hotel.

The driver took the long way to the hotel, slowly making his way around Big Creek several times before depositing them at the door to their reserved tent-sided rag house. The crowd milled around singing bawdy songs and banging on their "instruments."

"They'll be quiet by lights out," explained Redinger and as he predicted, forest sounds could be heard in the ensuing silence, only to be broken by the sound of rocks hitting the corrugated roof of their new home.

"They'll be gone soon," he said with some doubts.

"David, surely you know about a shivaree," replied Dee.

"Well, yes I do, but I'm not sure that's what they have in mind."

Smoke from the stove began to fill the house.

"I think they've covered the chimney."

Redinger groaned. "Maybe we should invite them in, but we don't have much food in here."

Dee laughed and opened the door. An army of friends marched in carrying food, a coffee percolator and a windup Victrola. People made themselves comfortable any place to sit, including the floor. The party, the food and the welcome lasted until dawn at which time all the men went to work.

"On all the peaks lies peace."

Goethe

Chapter 30

AN END TO HOSTILITIES – 1917

Morning at Donner Pass was brisk. Henry Huntington watched red streaked clouds line the eastern sky from the observation platform of his private car. The slow moving train snaked into a sharp u-turn putting the front of it parallel to the end. The engineer from across the neck of land between them saluted HH. He lifted his hand in response, then turned his attention back to the icy dawn. The door behind him opened noiselessly.

"So this is why you had your car shift places with the caboose at the last station," said George Patton, Sr.

HH rested his hands on the rail, then answered without turning. "It's my favorite spot in the world. I still get a chill remembering the first time."

"It's the picture you have in your library at the ranch."

HH nodded. "That's my way of trying to take it with me. On my first trip I felt something from the time the train left Nebraska. Could even feel the mountains rise beneath my feet the entire way."

"You surprise me...Eddy. I thought your little bit of heaven was Oneonta and by the way, why doesn't your family call you Henry?"

"Edward's my middle name and I have no idea how it started. It just did."

Patton stepped to the rail next to HH. He breathed deeply of pine-scented forest and wet earth mixed with wood smoke from the engine.

"You've been quiet since we left the library people," he said. "Are you having second thoughts about giving them the old homestead?"

HH shook his head. "Not at all. I'm just mulling over something else."

"You gave them the house and just as you were about to leave the meeting, I thought you'd changed your mind. Instead, you added five acres next door for a park. Is that what's bothering you?"

"No, but I have to say it surprised me at the time. I had to do it."

"Sounds like a shotgun marriage."

HH laughed but said nothing until the train was enveloped by deep forest and the sun was risen to full daylight. "I had to figure out how to place the property in the right hands and the librarian did it for me. She said she planned to bring her grandson to the back yard to read under the trees."

"It's been more than fifty years since you lived there. What're you remembering?"

"That large Silver Maple. I climbed it many a time as a kid. It's got rough bark that skinned my knees more than once, but the branches are just right for climbing. Spent a lot of time up there reading books."

"And now you collect them from all over the world."

"Well, right now I don't know if I have them or they have me. There're thousands of them at my place in New York, some at Mary Alice's in San Francisco and a hellova lot more at San Marino. I'm really glad Belle suggested we build a proper place for them at the ranch. I have the public lending library at Oneonta named to honor my parents, and soon we'll have our own private one as well."

HH turned to face Patton. "Thank you for coming with me on this trip. It's been good for a lot of reasons including that I've finally decided to retire. Edison Company's made an overture to merge with the PL&P and with my son's health failing, I think I'll accept ."

"Sorry to hear about Howard. He's done a fine job running things for you, especially with the expansion at Big Creek."

"There's more. Belle doesn't want people to know our private business, but since you're more like family, I'll confide that her sight is failing seriously. I want time to keep her busy."

It was more than he had intended to say but the visit to his boyhood home had produced a flood of old memories. The back of the house where he chopped wood for the stove. The site of his father's store where he clerked, stocked shelves and swept floors. All the connections to where he had matured and begun to show his extraordinary ability to work and run a business...almost any kind of business.

All of it was a reminder of the comfort marking his place in the world—mind pictures of his first job for Collis where he proposed to his uncle that he buy a lumber mill when the cost of railroad ties soared. HH ended up running the new business and showed his mettle when a flood on the Coal River threatened to wipe it out. For five days he labored day and night with every employee of the mill struggling to prevent the waters from destroying the buildings and stacked lumber. With only nine hours sleep the entire time HH's determination saved the business and jobs when no one gave him the slightest chance of success in the effort.

Interest in books captured him early on. As soon as he married Mary Alice the collection began in earnest. Now he had a staff in New York and another at San Marino sorting, cataloging and registering his voluminous inventory. In the beginning he read every volume. Because he was thorough, one time found the antiquities agent had not been. There was a "dummy" in one set in which the first eight pages were repeated for one-third of the entire volume. It was returned.

The manor at San Marino included a large L-shaped library of nearly three thousand square feet but that space was quickly outgrown by HH's passion for books and artwork. A new edifice was taking shape in his mind to house the collection. He would begin by opening the New York collection to scholars.

* * * * * * * * * *

In April at Big Creek, Redinger and his wife finally received word that their new home was ready for them. It didn't matter that it was buried in snow up to the top of the door. He had little time to help his wife move in once the path was cleared, as work began again at Dam #3. The expansion would require digging out the toe at the bottom of the dam where it connected to bedrock. Plans called for sheathing the entire older structure for a base. Excavation uncovered a useless concrete mixer and kegs of old nails dumped there by the original construction. The dam would be literally a dam built over a dam, so large that it would include two of the three original ones.

An army of workers swarmed over the existing structure drilling holes for steel reinforcement to keep both dams permanently bonded. At the same time a large force of carpenters built forms over all to hold the concrete. One set of workers had to hustle to stay ahead of the other.

Redinger stood atop the dam #3 within a forest of wooden forms. He surveyed the beehive of activity watching Harold Fox at work.

"There he goes again," he said to Rex Starr standing alongside. "Don't know what we'd do without him. Gets the lumber where it's needed and never forgets the nails. Even makes sure supper is..."

"Look there!" exclaimed Starr. "You see that?"

Redinger took field glasses and peered in the direction Starr pointed. "Yeah. I see her. That's the mother of one of the timekeepers."

"She's wearing *trousers!*"

"I see. Looks pretty good for a woman of her age."

Starr pointed again. "You talk with her and make sure she puts on a dress. I won't have the men ogling her!"

*   *   *   *   *   *   *   *   *   *   *

In Los Angeles talks with Southern California Edison Company broke down again. Determined to run electricity within municipal limits, the city sent workers to install power poles alongside Edison's hoping to force the issue. Although faced with the potential loss of three-quarters of its income, the company refused to retreat. In an audacious move, Edison opened negotiations with Henry Huntington's attorney for the merger of the two companies.

It could not have come at a better time for Huntington. He not only sold out to Edison, he ceded control, something insiders said would never happen. Edison management took all the top spots of responsibility as well as direct management of Big Creek. HH took only a seat on the new board for his remaining investment.

The calculated bluff exercised by Los Angeles trying to force a showdown with Edison was largely overshadowed in newspaper coverage touting the new company. It was not lost on the city that the merger created the fifth largest utility in the country. One last attempt was proposed to resolve the question of who would run electrical transmission within municipal limits.

Emboldened by its coup, Edison took leadership at the conference and moved that the entire problem of just compensation for their lines be settled by the State Railroad Commission. The city agreed with the resulting $12 million purchase price considered much too high by Los Angeles and much too low by Edison. However, weary of the years-long fight, both sides agreed to the commission compromise.

Both the merger and the sale of assets to Los Angeles set the stage for Big Creek to come to full flower.

"To win without risk is to triumph without glory."

Corneille — 1636

Chapter 31

FULFILLMENT OF PROMISE
AT JACKASS MEADOW — 1918

Edison Company management embraced Big Creek wholeheartedly. They also welcomed input from John Eastwood and encouraged his visits to the growing facility. Construction to bring water from the opposite side of Kaiser Ridge was an engineering challenge of incredible magnitude and Eastwood was eager to see it happen.

Far more than merely changing the direction of rivers in that vast watershed, it encompassed creating a new river to run thirteen and a half miles through a solid granite hole fifteen by fifteen feet—all underground. An infectious can-do feeling drove workers on the project, knowing they were about to accomplish something that had never been done before. They would be raising the engineering bar to unheard of heights.

That enthusiasm came all too close to disaster as Redinger pushed unexpectedly benign weather one day too far. He had been assigned to take a survey crew to Florence Lake at the Jackass Meadow area beyond Kaiser Ridge where the intake was planned for the new tunnel to bring water to Huntington Lake. Work went well and the weather, while cold was tolerable. By morning on November 11th that changed quickly to leaden skies and beginning snowfall.

"This is it," he told the crew. "We leave immediately."

The men ate breakfast on the run as they packed quickly, anxiously watching snow begin to cover rock outcroppings. Within the hour the trail was white and the animals were urged a little faster. Snow flakes thickened and grew larger as the crew made its way to the lake below. Sensing the urgency the pack animals speeded up even more without urging. Lunch was eaten out of saddlebags as they continued as fast as possible. The crew had hoped to stop at Mono Hot Springs for a bath on the way back, but no one complained when Redinger urged the team past the spot.

By the time they reached the crest of Kaiser Peak at well over 9,000 feet, snows reached the bellies of the animals and the men riding had to pull up the stirrups and raise their feet to keep from dragging. They slowed considerably but did not stop for fear of not being able to start again. There was no rest for the animals until they reached a sheltered spot. There they paused for a short time before starting out again. Huntington Lake was in sight when suddenly at 5 o'clock whistles rang out from all directions.

"You hear that Mr. Redinger?" one of the men shouted. "Ain't heerd nothin' like it since you got hitched."

For more than an hour the whistles continued accompanied by occasional blasts that shook the trees and showered the exhausted crew with additional snow.

"I'd like to know what's happening," said Redinger, "but we've got eight more miles to get home to Big Creek and a hot meal."

An hour later Redinger was on the telephone trying to find out if the whistles were celebration or disaster. His phone rang and rang until at long last it was answered with, "Hell's bells, we haven't time to talk— the war's over!"

* * * * * * * * * * *

Calling the way to Florence Lake a *road* was a laughable kindness. The long, harsh winter at that elevation allowed construction only six months a year. It took two years to clear a dirt and stone pathway for trucks, equipment, mules, over three hundred men, food and supplies to reach Camp 63 at Jackass Meadow. Despite the lengthy time it took, the road was still extremely difficult to traverse.

Beginning at the far end of Huntington Lake, it rose steadily up the side of Kaiser Peak, mostly at a forty-five degree angle, twisting and turning to take advantage of as much of the more gradual inclines along

Convoys of Mack "Bulldog" trucks made numerous trips to the Big Creek Project.   Sections of penstock for the construction had to be trucked well beyond the rail lines to Big Creek.   The trip bred fearless drivers once they traversed the incredible road.
Murphy's Studio Photo, from the Edison Collection

the way. Beyond the long ascent, the road leveled some, running through thickly wooded areas as it continued up to over 9,000 feet, then drifted down to the most spectacular point, an area above the tree line carved from granite.

It was just wide enough for a truck to inch across with most drivers scraping the passenger side in order to keep furthest away from a sheer drop of thousands of feet on the other. Should one misjudge the clearance, nothing could keep a truck, wagon, animal or man from dropping to the Kings River at the bottom of the mountain, a thin line of silvery water seven thousand feet straight down an eighty degree slope.

Incredibly it was not the only road of its kind in the Big Creek system. In the area of Powerhouse #2 south of Big Creek, work resumed on Powerhouse #8 with a road extension continuing southerly for another site numbered #3. The odd numbering resulted from the original Forest Service permit and sites had to retain their established number status no matter when they were built.

Again crews were drilling and dynamiting a pathway through granite in the middle of sheer cliffs. The road was called the Million Dollar Mile, an accurate title (equal to nineteen million in 2005). Although the war was over, Krupp was unable to ship penstock. Against their better judgment, management ordered it from fledgling US steel companies.

There was so little flat ground in the area that Camp 35 was established with buildings partly hanging off the cliffs, built on stilts and lashed by cables pegged into the side of the mountain. Families joined workers at the camp for the duration and mothers had to worry more about their children falling off the porch than anything else. It was a long way down.

Key to the new system at Florence Lake was the tunnel. Since the work was underground, weather above did not keep the men from proceeding all year long. It was expected to take four to five years to complete with a crew digging from each direction toward the middle. Within six months it was clear that at the rate they were going, the estimate of completion was far too conservative. A meeting was called to explore

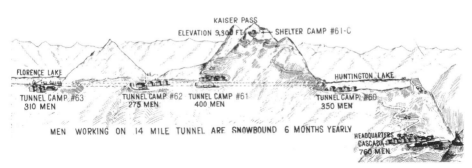

A pencil sketch of the Florence Lake section of the Big Creek Project, showing the location of the four tunnel camps used to drill the entire waterway. Note the road to near the top of Kaiser Pass.

The Edison Collection

Tunnel Camp 35 at the junction of Stevenson Creek and the San Joaquin River. Tent-cabins were built on stilts and connected to the cliff by cables. G. Haven Bishop Photo, from the Edison Collection

other possibilities to get the job done faster.

David Redinger invited John Eastwood to the gathering.

So many engineers wanted to be a part of the meeting it was held in the mess hall with a crowd standing at the back of the room and a host of workers loitering outside waiting to hear what would be decided.

Rex Starr had a large map mounted on a wall between the kitchen and the serving area. It showed the expected route under the southern flank of 10,320 foot Kaiser Peak. He wasted no time getting to the point.

"Gentlemen, we need some fresh thinking here."

"You mean like we get rid of food peelings and garbage from the camps by raising hogs and butchering them for the table?" A wave of laughter rippled through the crowd.

"Or getting cattle from the ranches up here instead of shipping meat from the Valley?" The laughs were louder this time.

"How about when you hired the card shark to get rid of the one who made his way up here to shear us sheep at poker?" The men roared at that one.

Starr banged on the table with a tin cup. "Okay, we know about the fun stuff and all that's been done. This is different. Let's hear some good ideas."

"Put more men on each end."

"Can't. There's only so much room in the tunnel."

"Use bigger charges for blasting."

"Very funny, unless you want Kaiser Peak to come down on top of you. You volunteering?"

"Better equipment?"

"There isn't any better than we have."

"How about putting in more crews drilling from the middle going both ways. Four work faces heading toward each other would cut the job almost in half."

"Also doubles problems with surveying. Gotta make sure those crews meet at the right place. Even a few feet off center could cost a lot to correct."

Eastwood spoke. "I know that area pretty well and there are two places you can cut a shaft into the tunnel route. Six faces are better than four."

Every man in the room turned to look at him. Redinger stood up

Eastwood's Multiple Arch Dam at Florence Lake
From the Edison Collection

next to Eastwood and said quietly, "Gentlemen, this is John Eastwood, the genius behind the entire Big Creek project."

All eyes were glued on the two of them at the back of the room. An electric silence fell over the hall as all those seated began to stand. From one corner of the room applause began slowly and then built to thundering momentum. Cooks and helpers came streaming from the kitchen. Those standing outside pressed to see the man and pay him honor. John Eastwood had come home.

*   *   *   *   *   *   *   *   *   *   *

In Los Angeles William Mulholland was given the go-ahead to complete the St. Francis Dam. The on-again, off-again construction had finally reached the point of put-up or shut-up. It would be his last great project and he looked forward to retiring after an illustrious career from bootstraps to public acclaim.

At the same time news of Henry Huntington's plan for a new library at the San Marino ranch made headlines across the country. The shipment of his books from New York raised an outcry from the academic community that it would put the collection out of touch for them, and sending anything of such immense value west of the Mississippi was barbaric. West coast scholars cheered the decision. HH was putting the crown on his belief in the future of California.

The donation of a public library to the town of Oneonta NY fed into his concerns about his lifework in the books and art. The disposition of it after his death was a serious concern since none of HH's children exhibited the kind of passion he felt for collecting. He had taken pains to make sure each of his children and grandchildren were taken care of in his will but the library was a separate concern.

He was not alone looking to the future. The Los Angeles Times reported that HH would donate the library to the Los Angeles Board of Supervisors. When pressed for confirmation HH said simply, "I am going to give my library to the public, but not until after I am dead."

In the quiet of their arbor meeting place between houses, he met with George Patton to discuss the way to effect the transfer.

"If I deed it to the supervisors, what can be done to protect it when they're elected out and others come in who don't support the library?"

Patton shrugged. "Not a thing. Look what's happened in the last ten to twelve years."

"Are you saying I shouldn't do it?"

"No. It's a magnificent gift to the people and deserves to have some guarantee for the future. Have you talked with your lawyer, Dunn?"

"Not yet but I have spoken to George Ellery."

"That's a start, but you need more. He can advise about how to handle the use of the library, but I'm talking about a governing body. You could look at a private foundation."

"George mentioned that, but he couldn't give me any particulars about it."

"That's why you have an attorney, Henry."

In August of 1919, a trust of indenture for the land, buildings, objects of artistic, historic and literary interest of Henry Huntington became a reality. It was written as an independent public institution, deeded to the State of California Library. HH retained the presidency with a small board of directors: His son Howard, Arabella's son Archer, astronomer Dr. George Ellery, attorney William Dunn and George Patton, Sr.

The mandate for the corporation was to set up, create and maintain a free library for the public along with a museum for his art collection, all within a park setting. The Los Angeles Times was right on the mark when it called the library "The Western Louvre."

* * * * * * * * * * *

"I wish you could have been there, Ella. Redinger said they talked with the people at Big Bear and they told him my dam bounced around at least twelve feet up and down in that 6.4 earthquake without so much as a crack. It's nearly at the epicenter."

Eastwood was still elated two weeks after his acclaim and recognition at Big Creek. They sat in lawn chairs watching salmon cavort in the Kings River at their ranch in Fresno.

"I still can't believe there's going to be a multiple arch dam at Big Creek."

"You've got dams all over the west, John. Surely one more is just one more."

He shook his head and took her hand. "All the rest combined can't hold a candle to this one. Over four hundred feet long. Most of all it's in the Big Creek project."

"That I can understand, but all the rest of your work is valuable. You sell yourself short."

She can't understand. It's my own private world. No other place holds the same magnetism for me. I don't understand it myself and I sure can't explain it to anyone else.

Ella knew much more than he thought. Without waiting for an answer, she stood and said, "I'll get us something to drink."

He waved to her in agreement, hoping she would not bring lemonade. His stomach was queasy since he came back from Big Creek and he attributed it to camp cooking. Ever since he and Redinger had taken the long drive to Florence Lake to see the location for the dam, his left arm had ached. He decided it was from holding on so tightly to the seat as they bounced along the road.

Now as August sunlight glistened on the river he thought if he bathed his arm in the cold snowmelt, it would feel better. A gust of wind lifted his hat as he walked to the water's edge, reminding him of the time he lost one to the San Joaquin on that first survey trip with Morgan. It seemed like both yesterday and forever ago.

He stepped into the water and felt pain shoot up his arm and into his chest, bending him double. River arms reached out for him as he slipped under, feeling his pain vanish in the icy cold. His hat slipped downstream as Eastwood traveled into an eternal sleep.

Lives of great men all remind us
We can make our lives sublime,
And, departing, leave behind us
Footprints on the sands of time.

Henry Wadsworth Longfellow

EPILOGUE

The death of John Eastwood signaled the end of an era. It came at a time when the new one was already blooming. Within a month of Eastwood's passing, Henry Huntington lost his beloved wife Arabella and not much later both his son Howard and dear friend attorney William Dunn. He threw himself into the work of the library at San Marino, eventually ensuring its future with a multi-million dollar endowment. The library opened to the public in March of 1927 for a few hours, one day a week. By the end of the year more than 5,000 visitors had come to see and celebrate his second legacy.

Eastwood and Huntington, along with Mulholland in a smaller role, had been the driving force in the development of Southern California in general and Los Angeles in particular. The genius who dreamed up and designed Big Creek was buried at his ranch along the Kings River. Appropriate to his life, the site was inundated by the construction of the Pine Flat dam and lake. He lies beneath the water.

Huntington worked hard for the advancement of the library despite declining health. He died in 1927 following surgery in a Philadelphia hospital and returned to his beloved California in an ebony casket, carried in his private car by the Southern Pacific Railroad. The engine was draped in black crepe and a large American flag. People lined the tracks at every town and crossing. At city hall in Los Angeles the flag flew at half-staff in his memory. All Pacific Electric and Los Angeles Railway cars paused for one minute at the time he was buried at the ranch.

Mulholland finished the St. Francis Dam after enduring a series of disquieting events resulting from his development of the Owens Valley. In May of 1924 residents of the valley, now dispossessed of much of their most precious resource, retaliated and bombed the Los Angeles Aqueduct at a critical point. Despite a $10,000 reward posted all over the area, no one ever offered information about the perpetrators.

The "Owens Valley War" escalated when armed men took over a major aqueduct gate and then turned off all water to the system. The action attracted many other residents who helped control the station. Los Angeles supervisors asked the governor to send troops to oust the squatters but he refused. The story of the takeover attracted journalists from all over the world and ended without bloodshed. When another raid blew up a different part of the system, Mulholland sent out mounted police with shoot-to-kill orders. The uprising died slowly, but surely.

While Eastwood's dams were subject to critical review by state and federal agencies, Mulholland's were not. His St. Francis Dam leaked from the day it was finished and lasted only two years. On March 12, 1928 it gave way with a thunderous roar sending fifteen billion gallons of water sweeping through the Santa Clara Valley fifty-four miles distant from Los Angeles.

The destruction was incredible but the worst loss was of lives—more than five hundred men, women and children. An inquest determined that the cause for failure was dam uplift, the same problem Eastwood had identified so many years previously in gravity dams and the same problem that was unjustly trumped up by Freeman against the multiple arch design.

Huntington and Edison Company's hesitation to use the relatively inexperienced US steel company penstock for expansion at Big Creek proved to be justified. A flaw in the penstock installed at Powerhouse # 3 caused a major accident. The pipe erupted with such force that the resulting vacuum above the break completely collapsed a major portion of the inch and a half thick penstock. When replaced, the line had additional welded steel bands for reinforcement. All sections not Krupp's steel were also banded.

Southern California Edison Company continued Big Creek

construction according to Eastwood's original plans and completed his multiple arch dam at Florence Lake in August of 1926. The problem with US steel penstock caused one more accident at Big Creek, this time with a loss of life. Two people sleeping in a cottage were in the path of the flood.

The ethos established at Big Creek continued into a multi-generational family succession of workers until preference for hiring family members of those already there was outlawed in the latter part of the 1900's. By that time a history of time and place was well established and an intimate dynasty of lives had a host of stories to be told and retold.

Aubrey Haire worked in the powerhouse and in the time-honored fashion of pitching in to help anyone, was pressed into acting as the town's sole law enforcement officer for a day. He protested at first, not knowing anything about the job, but agreed after being told nothing happened in Big Creek anyway.

He pinned on the badge expecting an uneventful day but by mid-afternoon was trying to quiet a man who was upset and threatening people with two knives. Quick-thinking Haire said to the man, "You look like an Irishman to me."

The man stopped for a moment and then said, "Me daddy was Irish."

Haire said they should talk about it over a drink and the man agreed. As they entered the bar, Haire held the door for the man, then deftly slipped the knives out of his back pocket and flung them off the porch. The two of them talked for hours until the official lawman returned to Big Creek, well past time for Haire to go to work at the 4 PM shift. Without being asked, another operator had taken his place until he was able to get to the job.

For all the thousands of men, women and children who worked Big Creek, the only instance of dishonesty anyone can remember was the card shark. The greatest memories were of work, love and fun.

Bob Day became a civil engineer because of Big Creek. "We'd go out and take readings, then go back and calculate. We used seven place tables with logarithms, and it would take us four hours to get it all figured out. Today it's done almost instantaneously on the spot."

To measure distance, engineers used what they called a chain, which was actually a steel tape measuring from 100-500 feet long. It had to be pulled tight from both ends to get rid of the drag and measure accurately.

"To see where we measured," said Day, "you had to cut down the brush with machetes. We did pretty well—accounting for up to one-

Alaskan dogsledder Jerry Dwyer with his team on the Kaiser Pass Road in March of 1922. Lead dog Babe pictured here is one of three from the team buried at the highest point of the road across from the US Forest Service Ranger Station.

From the Edison Collection

hundredth of an inch. Pretty good for prezacts. We did it like navigating by the stars where now it's done by satellite."

Day tells his students that the slide rule was the reason engineers were able to build the Empire State Building, the Boeing 707 and the Golden Gate Bridge. The little device compares well to computers of today.

Bob Enloe exemplifies the free-spirited upbringing of kids at Big Creek with a love of outdoors that sometimes defies caution. Twice Enloe was a victim of his enthusiasm for snow sport. Once on his way home from school he wondered how it would feel to leap into a new snowdrift. He took a flying leap but misjudged his distance, landing headfirst into the deep snow and becoming stuck. At first he tried to yell for help but realizing there was no one around, set about to work his way out. It took some time but he made it.

However, the lesson was forgotten another time when he skied the slope alongside the penstocks from Huntington Lake to Powerhouse #1. He climbed the hill a little farther than he ever had before, then skied down the icy hill faster than he expected. He landed in a drift at the bottom, headfirst again. This time the skis kept him from being able to extricate himself, but a schoolmate who lived nearby heard his calls for help.

Snow was a time for creative imagination. Roads were not plowed and the school bus would often skid along the steeper inclines and descents. When the boys would feel the wheels slipping they would shout, "To the back of the bus!" for more weight and traction. At the top of the hill the boys would elect to get out and ski into town on the soles of their shoes.

The hallmark of Big Creekers is strong personal independence combined with equally strong interdependence, partly by necessity but mostly by choice. Even isolated at Florence Lake for six months of the year, dam tender Ted Lofberg and his wife Lila maintained the same spirit.

The couple became experts in animal behavior by observing and reporting to other wildlife authorities, mainly by radio. She trapped and banded birds, made friends with a starving coyote who then brought his mate and pups to visit. Chipmunks would climb into their pockets and birds told them when it was time for a treat.

Edison Company established a fish hatchery in partnership with the Forest Service. The trout fingerlings were planted in streams and lakes throughout the area. The company's creative make-do extended to hiring Jerry Dwyer and his team of Alaskan sled dogs to keep the remote camps at Florence Lake in touch with civilization. Mary Clair Wonacott remembers that Dwyer would keep his dogs in top condition in the summer by putting wheels on the sled and taking Big Creek kids for rides. Three of his dogs—Babe, Whiskey and Trim—remain at Kaiser Pass in specially marked graves maintained by the Forest Service station there. The road to that point is relatively easy to traverse. Beyond it to Florence Lake it is only for the intrepid in four wheel drive.

The unique approach to digging the tunnel at Florence Lake finished the job two years ahead of schedule. In the 4.5 years it took to dig the tunnel and erect the multiple arch dam, cooks fed two million pounds of fresh meat to workers, nearly 13,000,000 pounds of ham and bacon, 11,000,000 eggs and 1,770,000 pounds of potatoes—even sending a man to Idaho to supervise the harvest. Each *month* they baked 55,000 loaves of bread, 5,000 cakes and 36,000 pies.

David and Dee Redinger remained at Big Creek for the rest of his career. In 1929 he was appointed Edison's Division Superintendent, Northern Division Hydo which meant he was in charge of Big Creek, a position he held until retiring in 1947. Although he was offered a number of promotions, he refused any that meant he would have had to leave Big Creek.

Southern California Edison grew into a major utility covering half of the state of California. It has taken a leadership role in protecting the Big Creek wilderness while offering recreation opportunity to the public. Their concerns for the continued health of the environment is evidenced in both large and small efforts—the restoration of Stevenson Meadow and the use of fallen trees to cut lumber for the construction of new buildings and picnic tables at their Shaver Lake Park for campers.

Much of the construction of Big Creek was complete by 1930, and it would do well to consider other accomplishments of the same years: air conditioners were invented in 1904 by Carrier, automatic dishwashers were developed by a woman in 1893, and the electric typewriter was available by 1902.

In the Sierra Nevada, the Gold Rush that brought California into the Union saw $2 billion worth of it dug up, while electricity generated by Big Creek has produced $6.625 billion and is still going strong. Huntington's original investors in Big Creek put up the equivalent $1 *billion* in capital at a time when the US federal government had an annual budget of $575 *million*. Hydropower throughout the country was a major source of electricity. Until the 1940's it was responsible for more than 40% of all electricity generated in the country—75% of that in the west.

Construction at Big Creek continued to follow Eastwood's plans well into the later half of the twentieth century, adding more units to the system until Edison was using the same water eight times to create clean electricity. Dam #7 built in the 1950's created Redinger Lake and Big Creek's ninth powerhouse just north of Shaver Lake was the last one, built in 1987. It is completely underground and uses new technology that allows it to create electricity, then pump the water back up to the forebay again at night when demand is low. The water is used again for times of high demand and takes a minimum of electricity for pumping to do it. While they say Big Creek is the "Hardest Working Water in the World," using the same water nine times, it is more accurate to say the water is used over and over again, endlessly.

Company management felt there was no more fitting honor than to salute the designer of the Big Creek system with the most creative generation unit. The Balsam Meadow facility is the John Eastwood Power Station.

BIBLIOGRAPHY

Basham, Charles, Project Manager, Corporate Communications, Southern California Edison, Rosemead CA 91770

Big Creekers, Bruce Black, Bob Day, Bob Enloe, Merle Glenn, C. Aubrey Haire, Ed Selleck, Russell Westermann, Mary Clair Wonacott

Central Sierra Historical Society, Shaver Lake CA 93664

Dickerson, Art, Professor Emeritus, California State Polytechnic University, San Luis Obispo CA 93401

Dickinson, Donald C., *Henry E. Huntington's Library of Libraries*, Henry E. Huntington Library and Art Gallery, 1995, San Marino CA 91108

Jackson, Donald C., *Building the Ultimate Dam*, University Press of Kansas, 1995, Lawrence KS 66049

Johnson, Hank, *The Railroad That Lighted Southern California*, Stauffer Publishing, 1997, Fish Camp CA 93623

Lewis PhD, Dan, Curator, Huntington Library, San Marino CA 91108

Mount, John, Big Creek General Manager, Southern California Edison, Retired, Shaver Lake CA 93664

Myers, William A., *Iron Men and Copper Wires*, A Centennial History of the Southern California Edison Company, Trans-Anglo Books 1984, Glendale CA 91202

Redinger, David, *The Story of Big Creek*, Revised Edition, Southern California Edison Company 1999, Rosemead, CA 91770

ABOUT THE AUTHOR

Barbara Wolcott writes for commercial technology markets and their correspondent trade publications.

Her story about off-track betting and written in a Damon Runyon parody won First Place for both the California Publishers Association Award and the National Newspapers Association. Her three-part feature about the commercial fishing crisis on the west coast was nominated for a Pulitzer in 2001. Wolcott writes about how science impacts people. Her book on the massive Avila Beach cleanup title *David, Goliath and the Beach-Cleaning Machine* was published by Capital Books International in June 2003.